Vicki Voland and the Goblins, Ghosts & Ghouls

S.P. Witchell

Jolly Good Scares

In special thanks
To
Anne Dugger
&
Jonathan
Edwards
Two very good
friends

ἥρως

For Sandra Jean.

Chapter one

"There's no wolf in there, stupid," the little girl muttered to herself.

Vicki Voland teetered at the edge of the backyard where her old outdoor easel stood. Large paw prints circled the muddied lawn just outside the woodland bordering the Voland house. The dry autumn leaves began rustling and whispering in a breeze, and a gust of wind came rushing out of the tree line, sending a chill to her knees. The gloomy day cast a shadow through the woods so dark and so worrying that it made Vicki wonder exactly how far into town a wolf might travel. She gathered her scarlet oversized hoodie around her, feeling just like Little Red Riding Hood as she ventured out to the easel.

It didn't help matters that Vicki was a dead ringer for the girl in the old fairy tale. Like Little Red Riding Hood, she too was quite small with messy blonde hair and big blue eyes. Her own mother had even commented on the likeness once long ago when reading the story to Vicki, remarking that the girl in the illustration even had the same gap in her front teeth and shared her button nose. It seemed that the backyard intruder had shared something in common with the big bad wolf as well; these paw prints were *enormous*.

They were so big in fact that her running shoe would easily fit into one and she weighed the option of simply leaving the easel to the elements for one more day. Vicki let her eyes follow the path of the huge animal tracks, cowering for a moment as those trees swayed once more in the heavy breeze. She was in the eighth grade now, hardly a little child anymore. It was time to put away childhood fears and discarded paints, time to start acting more like an adult, especially after the embarrassment of her previous summer. Even so, such a massive animal would certainly give anyone pause.

She inched forward to grab the old weather beaten easel placing her foot down into another one of the large paw prints. Glimmering mud seeped up from the last night's rain, the paw print filled with a crimson so deep and so thick that it made her pull her foot way with a gasp. An explosion of cracking branches blasted out from somewhere in the swaying trees and she snatched the easel up spilling more of her paints to the ground. She went stumbling over a brightly colored bird bath before running to the safety of the house.

The easel slipped from her hand with a great crash as she bolted through the backdoor, slamming it shut with such force that the family portrait above the fireplace fell to the floor. She stood staring out through the sliding glass door, wondering what had left those paw prints in the night, what had been pacing back and forth beneath her window. She leaned against the door resolving to let her father retrieve the easel and paints when he returned home, yet one more abandoned art station for him to stack against her closet door.

"Oh, you dummy," Vicki hissed at herself as she watched more dark red paint drain onto the lawn outside. The large pawed culprit poked his nose out from the trees; a rather well fed labrador came lumbering out of the woods just beyond the fence line. Vicki groaned as the flabby old dog crossed the yard to grab a fallen stick before running back to its owners. The man and woman waved at her from the woodland walking trail and she returned a polite smile. She turned her attention to the family portrait, inspecting its frame to make sure that nothing had broken, her heart still pounding and hands fumbling with fright.

She struggled on her tiptoes to hang the happy wintertime portrait back in its place. She took another look at the photo as she stood back from the frame. Vicki stood with her mother and father snuggling into them while her older brother Max stood at the ready with a snowball aimed at the camera. She adjusted the tilt of the portrait one more time and gave herself an approving nod.

"What was that crash?" yelled her mother from the upstairs bathroom.

"Nothing! I just dropped a few things, it's all okay!" Vicki held her breath trying to calm herself and relax.

"Don't make a mess, they're coming back with the groceries any minute," called down Mrs. Voland.

Her beloved Grandpa Eckhardt sat in his own portrait close by. Vicki found herself bubbling over with joy at the prospect of finally seeing him again after such a long time.

An entire year had passed since she had painted Mount Diablo for him. He hadn't written to her or called for the past six months at least. In just three days time he would be coming for a visit and Vicki could hardly contain her excitement. A quick knock came from the front door and she rushed over expecting to greet her brother with armfuls of groceries.

"I'll get it," she yelled up to her mother.

She steadied her nerves and opened the door to two of the very few girls left in her former scouts troop that would still talk to her. She immediately felt crushed by an enormous weight upon her chest. Rachel and Jade stood in the doorway dressed in full scouts uniforms wearing wide smiles upon their faces.

Rachel, the tallest of the three, could have been Vicki's sister only with far darker eyebrows and a slightly sharper nose. Jade was umber toned with a face full of dark freckles, wearing two buns in her head of curly brown hair. Jade's cute dimpled chin and golden brown eyes had landed her on the scouts recruitment brochure of the previous summer. Vicki often wondered if her own photo was still in the Danville spring run advertised on the back of that same little booklet.

"Vicki," sang out Rachel as the door opened. "You never made it to the park. I thought you said you were coming, is everything okay?"

Vicki leaned into the doorframe as she spoke. "I, I forgot, I'm sorry. I was getting some things ready for when my grandpa comes to visit. I guess I just got caught up with that instead."

Jade nudged Rachel in the ribs. "I told you she's busy," she whispered.

"Well, Jade and I, we were wondering if you asked your mom about us coming to read to the old folks at her nursing home yet?" Rachel gripped her hands together smiling at Vicki. "We already have the little tea cart put together and everything, we can even use our scouts cookies!" She cleared her throat and bit her lip, averting her eyes for just a moment. "We have lots of goodies for them. Unless they have diet restrictions or things like that, and Vicki you could come help us too!"

Vicki gave her an absent nod. "Oh, I still have to ask her, sorry. I bet she'll say it's okay, like is it just going to be you two though? I think it's a pretty big nursing home. You might need three or four of you to get it done."

Jade cast a worried glance to Rachel seeing that her crestfallen gaze had turned to the ground. "Vicki, weren't you helping your mom there this summer? With all the old people," she asked.

Vicki shrugged. "No, my Mom said I should wait another year especially after the cookies." The other girls grew quiet fidgeting in discomfort at the very mention of the baked goods. "Plus, I don't think I'd be any good around a whole bunch of old people anyways. I'd probably mix up their pills by accident. Everyone knows I'm an airhead," she said rolling her eyes.

Rachel straightened her posture and beamed at Vicki. "It's okay, we couldn't really take care of a bunch of old people either, we can pour them some tea and coffee and that's about it," she said as she removed her beret. "Listen, we're all going to the Iron Horse mall, do you want to come with? My dad is giving us a ride, so we're going in style," she sang her words and gave Vicki a hopeful little grin.

Vicki shook her head biting her lip. "No, no I think I better stay in, I don't feel so good. And it looks like it's gonna rain too," she said looking up into the overcast sky.

Rachel stared up into the gloom of the day, the smile fell from her face and she gave Vicki a nod. "Okay. Well, if you change your mind, maybe call me. I'm always on my phone, I promise!" With that, the two girls turned to leave. Vicki went to close the door but Rachel came scurrying back. She tugged on Vicki's oversized hoodie whispering down to her, "Vicki, I don't think you're any of that stuff, you shouldn't let it get into your head like that!" She stepped away with a sad little smile joining Jade in the driveway with one last wave goodbye.

Vicki closed the door and huffed out, turning around to come face to face with her mother. Mrs. Voland stood in the kitchen fiddling with her dewdrop shaped earrings and staring down at Vicki with a sad look in her eyes. The tall blonde woman with a sharp beak of a nose put her hands on her hips, taking in a deep breath.

"Vicki, you wanted to go with them, why didn't you go? Rachel's been calling every weekend asking for you; we hardly see her anymore." Mrs. Voland leaned back against the kitchen island crossing her arms. "And you know full well that you remembered about meeting them in the park today, I saw you getting your paints together to help them. Why are you lying to her like that?" she asked.

"I, I don't know, I'm just..." Vicki bit her lip and kicked her bright pink running shoes off from her feet. "I don't think the other girls want me there, Rachel's just being nice. Maybe. I don't know."

"*She* joined the scouts because *you* joined them first and it's been a whole year now! You need to open up again and move on. I know it's hard, but you have to try. If you keep on like this your friends are going to move on without you. You don't want to end up alone, do you?" The mobile phone rang out from within her jacket pocket and Mrs. Voland shook a finger at Vicki. "We're talking about this when I come back!" She answered her phone call and left for the upstairs.

Another series of knocks came from the front door and Vicki's heart fluttered thinking that it might be Rachel again. She reached for the door handle and paused, somewhere in the back of her mind she would have sworn that she had heard a voice whispering, *"don't."* A definitive air of foreboding swirled around her and she took her hand away from the door knob.

The silhouette on the other side of the door's large glass window loomed motionless like a tall thin statue. The person knocked again and Vicki froze in place, her eyes glued on the door handle. Cold dancing butterflies filled her stomach, and a chill went up the back of her neck.

"Hello," asked Vicki as she peeked out through the window alongside the door frame.

"Hello! I'm here on behalf of the Charles family, I have a few documents that need to be signed," said the woman from the other side of the door. "Is the representative from Hammer, Stayker, and Thumps, here yet? I need his signature as well!"

"Who? Are you looking for my grandpa? Eckhardt Charles? He doesn't live here he lives in England. He's coming here in a few days, is he supposed to meet you?" Vicki cracked the door open letting the cool September air into the house. She looked up into the woman's face.

She was a very pleasant looking woman, dressed for business and wearing a friendly smile, Vicki thought that the woman could have been on television or on the cover of a foreign magazine. The alabaster slender woman in the professional red pant suit and meticulously styled strawberry blonde hair gave a little wiggle of her fingers to the girl behind the door. The woman smiled down at her crossing her hands over the briefcase. Her green eyes darted around the kitchen area behind Vicki then settled back down to the young girl.

"Hello there, you must be... Vicki?" The woman dug into her briefcase and pulled out a sheet of paper. She checked the document in her hand then held it out for the taking. "Oh, I've been so excited to meet you, your grandfather talked about you a lot! You look so much like your mother! Go on, I won't bite."

Vicki took the large piece of paper from the woman's hand, still hiding part way behind the door. The document was full of legalese and the font looked old, very old. It reminded Vicki of an old treasure map with its faded yellow parchment and handwritten lettering

at the bottom. She could understand almost nothing on the paper save for the words:
Contract for the role of Housekeeper, penalties and stipends novation for Eckhardt C.
Charles.

"That's really for your parents to sign, are they home? Can you tell them that Miss
Charles's attorney is here to see them?" The woman brought a hand up to her mouth in
embarrassment. "Oh my goodness, how rude of me, my name is Ciara Shuck. I work for
your aunt, Ms. Charles sent me."

"Oh sure, my mom is up..." Vicki glanced down at the Shuck woman's shoes, losing
her train of thought. Ciara's tattered red pumps were covered in mud stains, one of them
being fully torn through the side as if the woman's foot had burst straight through it. The
stains were not fresh and that was what drew Vicki's attention the most. The mud was
from at least the day before but that wasn't all. Some of the mud was caked with a familiar
deep crimson.

Vicki let her eyes drift upward to the woman's shins, long tufts of black hair had been
carefully hidden away into the tops of the red pumps but a few betrayed their hiding
places. Ciara Shuck's legs were shapely, formed much like a ballet dancer's or a soccer
player's might be yet something about them seemed wrong. The woman's legs were too
skinny at the knee and too long at the heel.

"Well, if she isn't able to come to the door, I could come in and wait," said Ciara with
a broad smile. Her teeth came down sharply together, all of them being just a little too
large for that mouth. "I'm afraid that Miss Charles isn't able to join us until certain legal
requirements are met, so I'm here in her place. I'd be happy to wait with you!"

"No!" Vicki squeaked out in panic with a push of the front door. She stood behind the
door staring up at the woman's perfectly white yet abnormally long teeth. Panic filled her
body and she shivered as she spoke. "No, sorry, I'm not supposed to... I need to ask my
parents first! They, they uhm, they've both been feeling sick so maybe you should just
come back later. They might be contagious." She stood behind the door averting her eyes
from Ciara's legs trying hard to conceal her fright of the woman.

"Oh that's okay, I understand," said Ciara. She loosened the red jacket from her
shoulders draping it over her hairy arms. She continued on in an overly friendly tone,
"You can never be too careful, stranger danger right? I promise you that little paper there
will have you all feeling better in a snap!" Ciara leaned to her side staring at Vicki, she
snapped her elongated fingers together revealing her horribly distorted red nails. The

broken nails clicked together and seemed to grow longer as she put her hand back down to her briefcase.

Vicki trembled. Giving an audible gulp, she leaned into the door putting her foot firmly against it. A cold sensation crept up from her neck all the way up to the top of her head. "They're going to get better soon, there's a doctor coming. Our, our own lawyer, he's coming too- in fact a lot of people are coming any time now," she added with a nervous smile.

"Oh, really," asked Ciara as she placed her hand on the other side of the door. Her nails scraped against the paint and wood shavings began curling up underneath her fingertips as she dragged them downward. "Well that's just perfect, we have a lot of papers to go over... inside."

Ciara took a deep inhale of air, her stomach rumbled out in hunger. A second low growl emanated from the shapely lawyer's body and Vicki stepped back from the door. Her legs trembled with fear and her whole body went cold at the sight of the woman's piercing green eyes. Vicki's hand shook uncontrollably and she nearly dropped the legal contract to the floor.

"Uhm c-can you just c-come back later," Vicki asked, clutching the paper to her side. "I think I need to go check on my M-mm-mom..."

Ciara raked her nails down holding her hand lightly against the doorknob. Vicki's eyes widened as the woman loudly sniffed the air between the two of them. She let out a tiny whimper as the woman's stomach groaned out again, making her drop the contract to the floor. She brought her clumsy fingers to the door's deadbolt as Ciara stared down at her with those strange green eyes. The grumbling woman cocked her head to the side and clicked her tongue, pursing her lips at Vicki.

"My," said Ciara as her lips curled into a show of teeth. "What g-g-great big eyes you have."

Vicki struggled at the door knob trying to shut the door as hard as she possibly could, but try as hard as she might she could not budge the door an inch. It was as if the horrible woman held tightly to the door from the other side, yet Vicki could clearly see that the woman stood holding the handle without any strain at all. She was paralyzed to the spot staring up at the emerald eyes of Ciara Shuck, trembling as the woman's smile began twisting into an unnatural long crease that stretched from ear to ear.

"Hey! Get away from her!" From behind the tall woman in red came her brother's voice and his racing feet. Max came around the corner of the house and swept past the woman at the door, his wavy mop of auburn hair matted down with sweat. He glared up at Ciara and pushed Vicki back into the house, his fierce blue eyes almost matching the glow of those horrible green dots in the doorway.

The stout, pepper-haired Mr. Voland rounded the corner as well, shouting out and running at the tall woman in red. Ciara snapped around to Vicki's father and began speaking in an unsettling low voice. Max pushed Vicki further into the house with trembling hands.

Vicki stood in a daze staring at Ciara Shuck who in turn seemed to keep those green eyes fixed on her even as she traded words with Mr. Voland. Angry words were exchanged and the world became a blur around her. An entire conversation took place between her father and the woman at the door, but Vicki was unable to follow any of it. The door finally slammed shut and Max came floating over to her, he shook her violently by the shoulders until she snapped out of her weird fugue state.

"Wake up! What the heck is wrong with you, why are you just standing there like that!" Max rocked her left and right his voice reaching a panicked pitch. "Don't ever open the door for her again!"

"I couldn't close the door, I don't know why!" She raised the piece of paper up to Max and stared at her father.

"She doesn't know, Max!" Mr. Voland looked at the document in Vicki's hand. His face went as pale as she had ever seen it, as white as paper, his pug nose glowed red from a marathon of running and shouting. He wrapped Vicki in a hug and squeezed her tight. "Where were you? You said you'd be in the park with your friends!"

Vicki broke away from her father, coming out of her daze and shaking from the cold pit in her stomach. "I, I'm sorry," she said with a shiver. "I just... I decided not to go, I don't know why! I'm sorry!"

Max gripped her shoulder and gave a sigh of relief. "You're okay! We were so worried she... " Max's voice trailed off and he shook his head gripping the black wooden ring around his finger.

Mr. Voland waved his hand at Max and called to the upstairs. "Ellie! Ellie we're home!" He took his mobile phone from his pocket and cursed. "It's like they killed the network! I still don't have any bars! Even my messages are down!"

Vicki looked up between the two of them with teary eyes. "That woman was like a monster, Dad! Like a real monster! She- you should have seen her face!"

Mr. Voland squeezed her shoulder. "I know, I'm sorry... There's a lot we need to talk about."

Mrs. Voland came rushing down from the upstairs carrying a bundle of stuffed travel bags. An overstuffed duffel bag slung across her shoulder crashed into a vase by the stairwell, smashing it to pieces. Mrs. Voland paid it no mind and instead went racing over to Vicki, placing a bag into the girl's hands.

"Vicki, you're going to have to pack, right now! We all have to pack and go!" Her mother wept and squeezed Vicki with such force that the girl let out a heavy wheeze. She looked to Mr. Voland wiping a tear from her eye. "Did you get it? The call from Äther?"

"Just before we got here, we went looking for Vicki. It blew out my phone, I think it's dead." Mr. Voland rubbed the sides of his face. "That thing was already here, Zalda's little flying monkey, it was talking to her," he whispered.

"Ciara Shuck? Already?"

"What is going on! Who was that lady, *Kira Shook?*" Vicki wrestled herself away from her mother's arms. "And why did she give me this?" She held the old document up for her mother.

Mrs. Voland recoiled at the sight of the document, snagging it from Vicki's hand and immediately throwing it away into the kitchen sink. "Don't even look at it," she said with a tremble. She grabbed onto Vicki's hands. "You need to go upstairs and pack for a few days, we have to leave tonight! Max go and help her, you pack too!"

"What, why?" exclaimed Vicki. She looked around at the three of them. "Mom just tell me what's happening!"

Mrs. Voland took a deep breath smoothing down Vicki's hair as she spoke. "Vicki, you need to brace yourself, we lost Grandpa Eckhardt this morning. We all knew this day was coming, he was very old and very ill..."

Vicki whimpered and dropped her bag to the floor, her mother dragged her inward for another hug, motioning for Mr. Voland to join them. Max looked to the floor kicking his foot against the carpet trying not to tear up at the sound of Vicki's sobbing. A rumble of thunder shook the house and the quiet pitter patter of raindrops against the windows began to fill the room.

"He isn't even that old! My gym teacher is older than him and Grandpa doesn't even use a cane," she said through her heavy breaths. "He said he was gonna visit! He wasn't sick or anything!" Vicki sobbed into Mrs. Voland's sleeve and hid her face.

"He was older and more tired than he looked, I'm sorry Vicki, we should have told you. We didn't want you to worry about that too, not with all that trouble that you were having. He wanted to visit so much, he really did!" Mrs. Voland sniffled gently lifting Vicki's face to her own. "And I'm sorry, Vicki, I really am! But we have to go, right now! We don't have time to mourn yet, we need to leave home for a few days, we just have to!"

Mr. Voland sighed and rubbed Vicki's shoulders looking up into Mrs. Voland's eyes. "Ellie, we need to tell her, I think we're way past time now. That evil mutt was right on our doorstep-"

"No Stephen, don't, we'll discuss it all in Manchester," said Mrs. Voland with a sharp tone.

"Manchester! Like England? Isn't that where Grandpa's house is?" Vicki asked back at her father. Another rumble of thunder shook the house and the rain began to cascade down the window panes. "But what about school and everything else? When are we coming back home? Why do we have to go?" She sniffled and wiped the tears from her cheeks.

Max gripped the black wooden ring around his finger. "It's Aunt Zaldehyde! She's the reason why we're running, isn't it?"

"Max," hissed Mrs. Voland. "We're not running away from anyone!"

Vicki looked up to Mrs. Voland and frowned, her chest still heaving. "Well, who's Aunt Zaldehyde... is she who that woman in red works for? She said that she worked for my aunt! Her face, Mom, I know you said that it's always just my imagination but I swear for real she was a monster or something!"

Thunder crashed just above the home, the foundation shook and the windows rattled, the lights flickered on and off as a flash of green lightning blasted through the sky. Three great knocks came from the front door, each increasing in intensity. The family fell quiet and the winds outside began to toss leaves and twigs against the home.

Mr. Voland motioned for Max to join the three of them. "She's here," he whispered to Mrs. Voland. "That was witch's step if I ever saw it."

"Witch?" Vicki looked up between her parents, worried by the look of fear on their faces. "What do you mean, like a *pointy hat and broomstick* witch... Mom," she asked, pulling on Mrs. Voland's arm. "What are you guys talking about!?"

Thunder crashed again, the knocking returned. Three loud booming knocks one after the other. Leaves went flying away from the window then returned in a wet mess against the glass, as if something large and ghastly stood breathing heavy against the house. Vicki stared wide eyed at the darkening sky outside, watching as that breath caught the leaves again, sucking them inward to some unseen lurking monstrous thing before exhaling them against the glass.

Max spun the ring on his finger around and stared out the window. "Aunt Zaldehyde is a witch, a real witch, Vicki! She's evil and crazy, and now that Grandpa's gone she's not afraid to come here! That's why we have to leave!"

Vicki shrieked as the house shook once more from those thunderous knocks upon the door. "Mom! What is he talking about! Is she a witch? Is that true? Like a really real witch!? Like in The Wizard of Oz? He's lying isn't he, witches aren't real?"

"Vicki, your aunt is a very sick woman," her mother began. She brought Vicki close and spoke in a comforting tone as she began taking quick sharp breaths. "Not like your Grandpa was sick, not ill, not like that. She's very troubled."

Vicki and her mother both jumped as the booming knock at the door returned. Three more crashing knocks rattled the door hinges. Thunder rumbled and the lights in the house dimmed. Max went running over to one of the kitchen drawers to find a flashlight.

"That's a crock," Max yelled, as he pointed to the door. "You guys have to tell her the truth! You can't just pretend this stuff isn't real anymore and you can't keep hiding it from us!"

"Max we've talked about this! We're not pretending or hiding anything," said Mrs. Voland. "Just please go and take her upstairs!"

Max turned his attention to the fruit basket behind his father and gasped. The apples and oranges began rotting shriveling to black little lumps as flowers in a vase at the kitchen window began wilting to dust before their eyes. The pleasant scent of homemade potpourri disappeared replaced by the smell of rot and mold, of wet soil and the stench of spoiled meat.

"Look!" Vicki pointed to the refrigerator as it began creaking open.

Sludge came slopping out from the shelves where fresh food had once been. Green fuzzy mold began to grow up the wall from behind the appliance, becoming stringy vines of black gristly hairs, and slime began dropping down from the ceiling where the mold now took hold. The Voland family backed away into the living area their attention on the front door. Two more massive knocks hit the house. *Boom*, The first knock jostled the locks of the door. *BOOM*, the second spun the deadbolt into the open position.

CRASH, on the third and last house shaking knock the front door swung open with a gust ushering in a blast of wind and rain. Fresh late afternoon air swirled into the house driving the stench of rot from the room. The lights flickered on and off again as a shadow fell across the doorframe from outside the Voland home. Vicki let out a scream and Max fell backward in a panic. Mr. Voland moved in front of the family and Mrs. Voland hugged Vicki tightly to her hip. The door swung back and forth in the rain, seemingly opened by the wind itself until the crunch of a footstep came from the welcome mat outside.

The shadow became a thin stick of a man in a yellow rain jacket and matching hat. He stepped into the house carrying with him a soaking wet black briefcase. He paid no attention to the family as he glided his way to the kitchen island in front of them, setting the dripping briefcase down on top of it. The lights dimmed further. The strange man peered out from his hat staring directly into Vicki's eyes. She hid inside of her oversized scarlet hoodie with a squeak.

"Vicki Voland," he asked with a strained voice. "That's an odd fashion choice, what with wolves about."

Chapter two

The stickman removed his soggy hat revealing his gaunt white face and his sunken dark eyes. His bony hands unzipped his coat to reveal an unnaturally skinny body clothed in a professional black suit and tie. The man leaned to the left to get a better look at Vicki. She yelped in fear fully hiding herself behind her parents.

She trembled behind her mother, peeking around at the sickly gray man. Dry flakey skin hung from his bald mottled head and the flesh sagged terribly at his jawline. The intruding stick man's dark eyes were set so far back into his head that she wondered if he had any eyeballs at all.

Vicki shut her eyes tight as the man turned his gaze back to the parents smiling a dead man's smile. Only his mouth moved into that horrible grin, not a muscle around his face followed in the usual way that one could see someone else's expressed joy. His face creaked and cracked with the effort.

"How I must look to the young miss," said the man. "The veil is at work even now. Quite exceptional."

His strained voice carried an odd accent with it, a way of speaking from a bygone era that Vicki couldn't quite place. The man straightened his loose tie and reached into his suit jacket pocket, producing from it a shining silver business card that glowed with an unearthly pale light. He held out his abnormally long skinny arm to Vicki's father holding the card in his twig-like fingers. Mr. Voland took the card with a shaky hand reading it to himself.

"Hans Bohnberg, attorney at law. Law offices of Hammer, Stayker, and Thumps." Mr. Voland shook his head. "You could have just made a phone call!"

The thin lawyer seemed to almost glide back to his briefcase. "My apologies for the short notice, but his instructions were clear. The specified family member is to immediately read the will as soon as the whole family has gathered together. My office has taken the liberty of summoning the Charles family here," he said, opening his briefcase and rifling through the contents.

"Those relatives aren't invited into this house," said Mrs. Voland with a commanding tone. "And neither are you, there are rules to how the world works here and you need to leave!" She pointed at the open door of the house still holding Vicki tight to her waist.

"Oh yes, the blessing," said Hans, as he looked up at the mold on the ceiling and the walls around him. He shook his head snapping the briefcase shut. "I do apologize for that, our law offices will cover the damages for the intrusion and defilement. Suffice it to say your father's passing and the passing on of a certain responsibility, *supersedes* the Ätherbound conservation laws of protective creature segregation and," the bony man paused to pick up a dead black lump that had recently been an apple, examining it with his back still turned to the family. "Agriculture," he finished, dropping the charcoal fruit to the floor.

Mrs. Voland gently shook Vicki on the shoulder. "Vicki, run up stairs and pack yourself a bag for Rachel's tonight," she whispered trying to pry her away from her waist.

Vicki grimaced holding tight to her mother. The two of them struggled with each other until Mrs. Voland finally got loose from Vicki's grasp. Hans turned back around to the family holding a large ancient papyrus scroll.

"It's quite specific Mrs. Voland, the entirety of the family must attend by law. That includes the young miss." He solemnly held the scroll up with its glowing red wax seal. The seal hissed as he waved the scroll through the air. "I would have brought you to the home office, ordinarily that is the standard operating procedure, but Eckhardt was adamant with these instructions."

"Then you can take that will back to your home office and sue us, because those people aren't setting one foot into this house," shouted Mr. Voland. "And they aren't coming around our children ever! No matter what your law says!"

The skinny man frowned, or tried to at least, through his dry and tight face. "Mr. Voland, I'm afraid that simply none of that is true," Hans said, with a genuinely sympathetic tone. "The legal recourse for refusing the will could have long reaching consequences."

Vicki's mother turned around to face her with a look of grief and worry. She patted and smoothed Vicki's hair down then put her hands on her shoulders. Mr. Voland turned to look at them both. Some unspoken agreement passed between her parents before her father dragged his hands down over his face. Mr. Voland took a seat on the sofa resting his head in his hands slouched over staring at the floor.

"He's right, look what they've done already," said Mrs. Voland. She gently moved Vicki over to a small leather ottoman near a recliner in the corner of the room. Her mother took a long deep breath before speaking again. "Vicki, your Grandpa Eckhardt, and your Aunt Zaldehyde... and I... we're not from here."

Vicki gave her a nod sitting straight up on the ottoman. "I know that, you came from England, that's why Grandpa was always away," she said still confident in her knowledge of the truth.

Max sat down on the sofa. "No, Vicki. Why do you think we never visited England before? Why we never went to see Grandpa," he asked.

Vicki looked back and forth between her mother, her father, and Max. "Well... if it's not England then where is it? Is it... like, Mexico?" she asked raising her eyebrows.

Mrs. Voland lowered to her knees in front of Vicki taking the girl's hands into her own. "Vicki, do you remember the little red man? Back from when you were very little? That tiny mean man that lived in your closet?" She stroked Vicki's hands holding them together as she spoke. "Where that little man was from, that's where I'm from, and your aunt too. This won't be pleasant, I'm so sorry! I'm sorry but it's time to for you to remember."

Vicki's mouth turned dry as sand and her head began swimming with the strangeness of the unfolding situation. She looked over to her father and Max again. Mr. Voland hadn't moved, still looking down to the floor. A chill rose up from her ribs into her chest.

"That... that was the man in my closet," asked Vicki, her voice trembling as she spoke. "The little red man was real?" She shuddered at the familiarity of an angry little wrinkly face poking up over the foot of her bed. Those little bits of angry tinfoil staring at her from those dark eye sockets, and his laugh, his horrible little cartoon laugh. *That evil little red gnome.*

"Yes Vicki, he was real. But you were so little we hoped you'd forget about him and you did, and we just left it at that," her mother said. She took a sharp inhale of breath and squeezed Vicki's shoulders. "Do you remember your grandpa coming to visit us and you saw him in your room with a hammer and some nails?"

"He was gonna nail the closet shut for me..." Vicki began, trying to remember. "And Dad got mad at him..." She glanced over at her father, he lifted his gaze from the floor and gave her a little shake of his head.

"No that's not exactly what happened," said Mrs. Voland. She let go of her shoulders and motioned with her hands as she spoke. "Your grandpa came out of your closet and trapped the little red man, can you remember that? And he thwacked him with a wooden spike and a silver hammer. Then he told you to go back to sleep and forget and you did. *You did forget.* Now you have to wake up and remember. Vicki, *you have to remember.*"

Vicki sat on the ottoman staring at her mother. She let her mouth open but nothing came out. Her mother's words swam around in Vicki's head, it was as if a fog was lifting from her mind, a strange knowledge began to wash over her. It was an unwelcome feeling, like the sensation of walking past a spider's web that had a large spider in it, then turning around only to see that the spider had vanished from sight. It was that same feeling of that realization of where that spider might now be filling Vicki's heart.

A swell of panic filled her and she shifted around in her seat. Vicki remembered the night that her grandfather had come out of her little bedroom closet with such clarity now that she questioned how she could have ever forgotten. How she could have ever possibly forgotten the screaming of the little red man as her grandfather brought the hammer down upon the wooden stake.

"I can't, I don't want to! I don't want to know! He made him go away," Vicki exclaimed turning to her mother. "I wasn't supposed to see... and you, you didn't want Grandpa around any more after that... you made him go home."

Mrs. Voland frowned grabbing her by the chin. "And you were so sad, Vicki. We didn't want to keep him away but he couldn't just leave his other home behind either. You wanted to go see Äther too but he wouldn't let you. Not after that little red man came, not after how your aunt treated Max. Not after all the trouble that she's caused."

Vicki's eyes began to glaze over, her head felt hot and light. She let her attention fall upon the outlandish lawyer patiently waiting at the kitchen island. He kept his back turned to them as he went about his own business humming a familiar little tune to himself.

"Other," asked Vicki, trying to repeat her mother's words. "Where is it?"

"Äther." Mrs. Voland said back to her. "It's a whole different world, people come and go from there all the time. It's like Oz or Wonderland. It's magic and it's wonderful, I promise you that it is and we'll take you there someday if you really want. That's where your grandpa has been all this time, but he didn't want you to ever have to deal with your aunt. Not there, not here, not anywhere. When she comes here you have to promise me that you won't talk to her no matter what she does or says."

"Okay, I promise," Vicki said with a wavering voice. Those cold butterflies returned to her stomach. "And she's really a real witch? Can she really do magic things like in the movies?"

"Worse. Much worse, and we know that she helped to put that little man in your closet. She's as bad as they come, she's wicked just for the sake of being wicked," said Mrs.Voland as she stood to her feet. "We've done everything we could do to keep her away from us, especially from you and Max. I'm sorry, Vicki. I wish we would have told you before tonight but we wanted you to have a normal life. A happy life."

"Without witches," said Vicki, as she wrapped her arms around her knees. She sat with her knees pressed up against her chest as she buried the little red man's terrible face and his shrieking last breaths. "Or little red men."

"Your grandpa helped a lot of people," said Mr. Voland. He stood from the sofa to join the two of them. "And he made a lot of enemies too."

"Like the little red man," said Mrs. Voland. She let out a heavy breath and squeezed Vicki's shoulders. "I know this is a lot to take in Vicki, and I promise we'll tell you everything when this is all over. This must be so crazy already, but there's something else you need to know that really affects you in all of this and it's better to just get it out of the way now."

"What's that," asked Vicki as her mother held out a hand. Vicki held her breath looking back and forth between her two parents. "Are you and Dad witches too?"

"Not even a little bit!" Mrs. Voland said with a slight chuckle. "We're all just normal people, you and me and your father and Max. We're just like everyone else here, but the people from Äther, they can be... well they can *look* scary," she said motioning over towards the kitchen island. Vicki leaned to her side to get a better view of the skinny man.

Mr. Voland leaned down close to her. "They can even look like pretty ordinary people over here sometimes, maybe just a little bit strange. Most people can't see them clearly, it's like a great big magic veil that protects normal people from seeing things that they wouldn't want to see. Some of them were born over here and don't even know that they came from Äther," he whispered into her ear, "but now that you know and now that you can start to remember, things are going to be different for you." He moved behind Vicki wrapping his arms around her.

"Don't be scared Vicki, they look scary but not all of them are real monsters. No more than some people over here can be. Not all of them are like the little red man," said Mrs. Voland as she joined Vicki's side. She took Vicki's hand and together with Mr Voland walked her over closer to the lawyer. "They're all just people," her mother said as she ushered Vicki forward.

Vicki looked up at the skinny lawyer as Mr. Voland let go of her shoulders. Her parents both motioned for her to go up to him and she gave them a grimace as she crept forward to the skinny man. She tugged on the lawyer's sleeve to get his attention and took a step back.

He had been humming a familiar tune that Vicki often heard during the Halloween season, though she wasn't sure if it was specifically the same song or a tune that borrowed from it. The skinny man ended his humming of *Have you seen the ghost of John* and shuffled his papers into a neat pile. Hans the lawyer sighed out, closing his briefcase before turning to the little girl behind him.

The gray mottled skin of the lawyer had vanished completely along with his eyes, his nose, and any trace of flesh at all. Yellowed bone stared back at Vicki, the skull of the lawyer rattled like a maraca as it turned towards her. Vicki gasped at the sight of the skeleton man, she stared into the two dark voids that glared right back at her and she fell to the floor on her bottom. She screeched and wiggled away from Hans, kicking at him as he reached out with his skeletal fingers trying to help her back to her feet. She screamed and kicked all the way back into her mother's knees nearly knocking her over.

"It's okay Vicki, he's not going to hurt you!" Mrs. Voland grabbed Vicki under her arms, lifting her back to her feet. "Listen, all over town there are people like him. You haven't really been able to see them fully until now, but they've always been there and they haven't hurt you!"

Vicki turned away from the lawyer hiding her face in her mother's shirt. "Make him go away!"

The lawyer's bones rattled as he turned back to his briefcase. "Young lady, I'll be very glad to do just that, just as soon as we get to the reading of this will. I'd save your screaming for later. You're going to need your voice."

Mr. Voland put a hand on top of Vicki's head. "Why is that exactly?"

The lawyer turned around holding the briefcase out in front of him. "Specific instructions, I am the technical executor of the will but Eckhardt Charles had his will enchanted. Only the young miss here can read the will once all of the family members have gathered." There was a rumble of thunder and the lights in the house flickered. "I'll arrange for their arrival now."

The house shook and the well crafted brick fireplace behind the family exploded to life with green sparks. Mrs. Voland grabbed Vicki and shuffled her onto the sofa along with Max. A blazing green fire erupted in the hearth as the dimensions of the fireplace began stretching and morphing upward into the shape of a large archway. Vicki covered her eyes peeking over her fingers as the fire turned to a softer aqua color. A peal of thunder ripped through the house echoing from the newly shaped fireplace.

The bricks behind the fireplace all began stretching themselves around one another forming an open dark hallway behind the hearth. The fire died down to small green glowing embers dimly lighting the strange new hallway that would have stretched far beyond the back of the house. Vicki's father went to grab one of the fireplace pokers and the ash scoop, standing poised at the opening with his tools ready to swing.

"Mr. Voland, please! Is that really necessary," asked the skeletal lawyer, shocked at his display.

Mr. Voland spun the poker in his palm taking a well trained and effective looking stance with the poker and scoop. "Have you even met her?" he asked back with a scoff.

Mrs. Voland looked at Vicki with a face full of worry and sorrow, she turned back to Mr. Voland gently placing a hand on his shoulder taking the fire poker out of his hand. "Stephen, don't start a fight with her, the house is open to her today and that's that," she whispered to him. "We knew this day was coming."

"If she goes near either of them I swear I'll ram this right through her stupid mouth!" Mr. Voland hissed out, trembling with a rage that Vicki had never seen before. He turned around to face Max and dropped the ash scoop to the floor. "Don't let her talk to you Max. Just don't engage," he said.

Vicki stared into the fireplace, light began traveling down the dark hall coming closer to the living room. "Max," she asked. She tugged on Max's sleeve but he paid her no attention, he simply gripped the black ring around his finger and clenched his teeth. "Mom! What's going on?" she asked as she pulled on her mother's arm.

"Vicki, stay behind us," said Mrs. Voland. "Just stay there, and when they get here don't talk to any of them, you let us do the talking!" She ushered Vicki back to the sofa.

Vicki gave out a whimper and went to plop down on the seat, hiding herself behind some of the couch cushions. The fire in the hearth fizzled and popped, it smoldered before dying out. The room went quiet and the skinny lawyer turned back around to his suitcase preparing for the reading of the will. The roar of a great approaching inferno echoed out of the fireplace. Max fell back into the couch with a start as the roaring shook the bricks of the hearth.

The fire sizzled back to life, flaring up into a brilliant green flame. It popped and crackled, a single green spark fluttering up from the embers. It drifted up into the air before fading away into nothing. Vicki relaxed and let out a small sigh of relief having expected much worse. The fire flared again in vivid lime color throwing out green sparks that formed a dazzling display in front of the room. A small girl about Vicki's age but still much taller took form before their eyes appearing out of the glowing sparks of the fireplace.

The skeletal lawyer opened his legal scroll and began to read aloud. "Attending, Magra Charles, descendant." The lawyer glanced down at his pocket watch and marked off a bit of writing on the scroll.

The little witch had white curly hair with a green beret over the top of her head. She wore a green sack dress with a matching pair of dull green Mary Jane shoes. She stumbled forward out of the fire revealing her face to the family, her soft brown eyes looking up at them in slight embarrassment. She had dark tan brown skin with blushing cheeks and two striking pointed ears.

Magra looked almost normal with her sweet little face devoid of malice, picture perfect if not for the two tiny white horns protruding from her forehead. They were hardly noticeable under the girl's white hair but the horns were only half of the young witch's problems. As she scampered away from the fireplace, Vicki could see that the girl also had a barbed devil's tail hidden behind her dress.

Magra turned back and steadied a crystal shard at the base of the fireplace speaking a sharp word that sounded quite a bit like *kangaroo*. The fire made a howling noise like a distant train blowing its horn through a tunnel. The howling grew louder and louder until the entire family had to cover their ears. Max screamed and grabbed out for his father as the wind from the fireplace started blowing and tossing soot around the room. Vicki's mother and father both careened backwards into the sofa and they sat down in front of the children, protecting them from little bits of debris with their arms.

The fire made a terrible sound much like a choir of sad, distant crying voices. Darkness gathered in the place where the flames had been. All of the light in the room seemed to dim and a giant figure arose from the hearth. She was humongous, not just tall, but absolutely humongous.

"Attending, B-" The lawyer adjusted the scroll and corrected himself. "Attending, Zaldehyde Charles, first of kin."

She was bigger than any basketball superstar, taller than just about anyone that Vicki had ever seen in photos or movies. The witch continued to grow, standing up higher and higher from the exhausted ashes of the fireplace until she nearly touched the ceiling. The woman was of a strange complexion, an unhealthy pale blushed with cold blues. It was as though the natural color had been drained out of her. Her shoulder length curly hair was a bluish gray and her eyes were a most unnatural black, as if the witch only had gigantic pupils against the whites of her eyes.

The black ashes whipped around the tall but slender shape of the shadowy woman fashioning themselves into a green and red flamenco style dress. A large black broad brimmed hat adorned with long green peacock feathers and silver buckles began taking shape upon her head as she stepped out of the fireplace. The woman's face was fully revealed as the ashes flittered away into nothingness.

Vicki stared at her Aunt Zaldehyde from between the arms of her two parents. The gigantic pale blue woman looked back down to Vicki shooting her a wicked little grin from her pale purple lips. The resemblance to her mother was uncanny, with the witch sharing that exact same beak of a nose as Mrs. Voland. Vicki gasped and hugged tightly to Max, shaking with fear and shutting her eyes to the tall supernatural woman in her living room.

"Oh," said Zaldehyde with a menacing glee in her voice. "Oh this is so much better than that!" The tall woman with the prim and proper English accent raised a wand made of black polished bone towards the family portrait hanging on the opposite wall. A flash of purple and green energies went streaking out of Zaldehyde's wand into the photograph, she howled with laughter as she inspected her handiwork. The portrait had changed from the happy winter greetings to the four of them huddled together in fear on the sofa. The eight feet and nine inches tall woman cackled looking around the room for her own lawyer.

"She isn't here yet, Mama, maybe she is lost," said Magra through a thick Spanish accent. She hid her tail up into her dress and blushed at the sight of the Voland family. "Maybe we must have to wait for her?"

Zaldehyde sighed out and snapped her fingers, holding her open hand down at her side. "Oh nonsense, she was here. You must remember, Magpie, she is a weak and moronic thing. Have mercy on the pitiful beast." A fluttering of papers echoed off the brick walls from within the fireplace. Vicki opened her eyes taking in the scene and staring into the dark corridor. Zaldehyde waited impatiently at the fireplace. "She was simply too stupid and too excited like the starving little puppy that she is."

Vicki flinched as the small girl in green gave a nod shifting her eyes to the sofa. Magra chewed her lip and averted her gaze. Her long pointed ears flicked around in much the way a cat might flick its ears. She hid her face completely behind her white hair.

The gargantuan woman cleared her throat and Vicki snapped her attention back to her aunt. "Little baby Victoria," said Zaldehyde, relishing every syllable. "All *grown* up!" She stared down at Vicki with a wicked smile, her dark eyes glistened and became like two chunks of charcoal as her face contorted into that awful show of twisted joy.

From behind the tall witch came the rustling of papers and before Vicki could register what was happening a winged creature made of folded pages flew into the waiting hand of Zaldehyde. It was a bird of sorts, fashioned from the yellowed pages of a book old enough that it might have been found in a museum. The origami monstrosity squawked and cawed, fluttering its wings. Words and runes were written all over the shifting pages of the bird's body.

The bird turned its folded head to Vicki, opening its pages wide. It had rearranged the words on its wings just long enough for her to be able to read them. The strange bird hid its pages back up in a flash. The words read, Little Pig, Little Pig.

Chapter three

The tall witch towered over Vicki and her family, standing just a bit taller than the tallest basketball player and just a tad smaller than a giant. She sashayed across the room towards the skeleton lawyer, taking out a large clamshell mirror from her dress as she went. She stopped just short of crossing in front of Max and Mr. Voland, checking her reflection in the opened clamshell then snapping it shut with her pencil length fingers.

Mrs. Voland marched straight to her humongous sister. "I told you before, I don't want you talking to either of my children," she hissed out. She jabbed a finger at Zaldehyde and stood defiant in the witch's shadow. "And that includes your daughter too! You keep her away from Max and you keep her away from Vicki! And I swear, if you ever send that Shuck woman around here again!"

Zaldehyde gave out a little chuckle bending down to her sister at eye level. "You break my hurting heart my dear, and poor little Victoria must meet her new cousin! You deprive these girls of proper family. Will you never stop this ridiculous feud, Eleonora?"

"You're not a member of this family and you're certainly not welcomed here! As soon as this is over the house is going to be sanctified against you and I don't ever want to have to deal with you or your kind again!" Mrs. Voland clapped her hands at the giant witch. "And from now on you keep that stinking hairy mutt away from my children! Do you understand me? I'll have a hunter here so fast that her head will spin!"

Zaldehyde recoiled a small bit, grinning back down at her sister as she stood straight up and nearly touched the ceiling of the room with her feathered black hat. "Such are the prejudices that I've come to know you by, little sister." The gigantic woman sneered down at Mr. Voland. "You've been training them all so well, and all the better to take up the mantle of the family patriarch, your time has finally come!"

Mr. Voland shot up from the couch and stood in front of his two children. "Stuff it, Hagzilla, we're not falling into one of your diatribes!"

Hans stifled a chuckle from over in the kitchen, then froze as the tall witch slowly turned her gaze upon him. His bones rattled and he went to open his briefcase. He fumbled a document then finally held it up for Zaldehyde to see.

Zaldehyde clicked her tongue at the skeleton. "Leave it to a bonehead like you to laugh at a joke that dead in the water," she said, glaring back at Mr. Voland. She reached over and yanked the document from the skeleton's hands, giving the paper a quick glancing over before turning to address Hans. "It's beyond me why a legal matter as serious as this isn't being handled by a *reputable* law firm. Surely I'm allowed to have my own attorney look over these papers?" Zaldehyde waved her wand made of bone at the floor. A wooden seat constructed itself from the floor boards and carpet of the living room, the large witch lowered herself into the chair. She smiled, looking quite pleased with herself before continuing through the document. "I put my trust into the Company of Wolves, they handle all of my business dealings and personal finances."

Hans gave out what little sigh he could muster (having no lungs of course) and crossed his bony arms. "I'm afraid this house is still sanctified against the likes of Ms. Shuck. Hammer, Stayker, and Thumps are highly accredited, Ms. Charles, indeed if memory serves correctly it was your seventh husband that came to us for legal protection against you."

"It didn't do him much good," replied Zaldehyde with a little sing song tone of voice.

"Seven husbands," Vicki whispered in awe. She covered her mouth and hid her face from her mother who in turn shushed Vicki by holding a hand up.

"Seventh husband, dear. I've had nine husbands now, I'm a widow nine times over," answered Zaldehyde as she finished looking over the document in front of her. "Once something has outgrown its use it's best to just get rid of it. Avoid all the clutter."

"Don't listen to her, Vicki," whispered Max as he leaned into Vicki's shoulder. "We told you, she's bad news."

Zaldehyde made an uncomfortable grumbly sound glancing over the paper before lowering it to stare at Hans. "This is ludicrous! I demand that my lawyer attend this reading!" Zaldehyde hissed out as she tore the paper in half. "I'll see that will for myself before I let any of these sham proceedings take place!" She stood from her seat and grabbed at the will.

The glowing red seal flared a brilliant hue as Zaldehyde reached her large hand towards the scroll. Sparks of red energy flew out of the seal to her fingers and she recoiled from the magical barrier protecting the last will and testament of Eckhardt Charles. She gave out a small gasp of surprise and glared at the skeleton lawyer, Hans stood with the scroll in his hand unconcerned by her anger.

"The law is quite clear," said Hans, as he began to make his way over to the Voland family. "None but the assigned reader of the will may touch the seal with intent to open it." The lawyer came to a stop in front of Mrs. Voland and beckoned for her to hand the will over to Vicki.

Mrs. Voland took the scroll from the skeletal hands of Hans giving him a frown. "Can't anyone else read this? I don't want her dealing with magic, I just don't think that it's a good idea," said Mrs. Voland as she looked back to the lawyer. "Maybe it would be better if we get our own attorney too, this is all very sudden!"

"The choice is on the young miss," said Hans. "Your father had exacting stipulations."

Zaldehyde pushed the lawyer away bending down to her sister. "One of those stipulations is that every single one of us adhere to the will under penalty of curse! You knew the old bumbling fool as well as I did, don't let his final feeble attempts at salvaging his relationship with you curse your only daughter!" She brought her strange living spell book forward, its pages fluttering as it moved through the air towards them. It landed in Zaldehyde's hands and opened to a series of runes and diagrams. "It's a powerful spell but I can break it! You don't trust me, Eleonora, but you have the brains to know that you can trust our father even less!"

"He would never do anything to hurt Vicki!" Mrs. Voland said back to her. She gave a quick look back to her two children then to the scroll in her hand.

"And the rest of us," asked Zaldehyde.

A silent acknowledgment passed between the two sisters and Vicki looked on as her mother gripped the scroll between her hands. She gingerly reached out towards the scroll and her mother yanked it away from her. Mrs. Voland breathed out handing the scroll back to the lawyer.

"No, this is just too much to put on her! I don't want her to be involved with this and that's final," Mrs. Voland said to Hans.

"The choice isn't yours to make, it's the law," said Hans. "The will cannot be refused by any other."

The seal on the scroll glared brightly again and Mrs. Voland gave out a shriek, dropping the scroll to the ground. She cradled her hand as the scroll rolled towards Vicki's feet. It stopped at her toes, wobbling so that the red wax seal was turned upward facing in her direction.

Vicki reached down to the scroll, compelled to open the seal and read the will. The strangest sensation washed over her, a sort of inborn knowledge that the scroll meant no harm and that it needed to be read aloud. Vicki heard her father say something at her as his hand reach out to the scroll. The red seal answered her father with a sharp crack of electricity to his finger tips. The room seemed to swim around her, and everything became a distant echoey ringing. Her focus fixed upon the scroll and the scroll alone.

She turned the scroll over in her hand and touched the red wax seal, running her finger along the impression of the three insignias connected by a circle. A raindrop, a crescent moon, and a zig zagging lightning bolt. The seal gave a warm welcoming glow and the insignias began to melt, animating into new shapes. The raindrop splashed down and made a puddle, the moon changed from a crescent to full, and the lightning bolt transformed itself into the shape of a skull. The seal hummed out and vibrated, the wax bubbled up and melted away, dripping and vanishing into thin air. The scroll partially unfurled and Vicki marveled at the beautiful golden inked words that covered the inside. The light caught the fancy letters upon the will, a the golden sheen reflecting a prismatic array of colors at their edges.

It was magic and somehow Vicki knew that the magic was specifically reaching out to her. The warmth of the colors hit her blue eyes, lighting her face up in the golden glow of the words. More and more words began to shimmer, appearing on the will as she looked it up and down. The magic called out begging for her to read the scroll.

"**DON'T YOU DARE**," shouted Zaldehyde, breaking the scroll's spell over Vicki.

Her aunt's dark and otherworldly voice bounced around the room and shook the walls. Vicki looked around still dazzled by the magic of the scroll, her parents and Max all held their hands to their ears, covering themselves from Zaldehyde's witchcraft. The words continued to bounce booming off the walls and the floor like a never ending echo that kept its intensity as it traveled back and forth.

Vicki's eyes drifted back down to the shining words on the scroll, Zaldehyde's voice began to fade out and disperse. The scroll ebbed strange energy into Vicki's hands and she brought it closer to her face. The words shimmered, seeming to float just above the paper. They danced around in front of her like little fireflies, exuding a feeling of safety and goodwill toward her. Vicki bit her lower lip and carefully opened the scroll at both ends.

She stood up from her seat with both hands on the shining scroll. She stared into the golden ink and began reading the last will and testament of her grandfather. She found it quite strange that the will wasn't structured like those in television shows and movies, granted those wills did not involve golden magical ink. Vicki struggled with the first words as she didn't understand the language.

"I... I can't read this," began Vicki, as she furrowed her brow and tried to sound out the words. "Lesson... sigh alley, die... zoo hoe ren, dicey warty ouch mitt notch House nay men?"

The scroll burst into a bright light and for a brief moment golden rays surrounded Vicki as she held the will in her hands. She looked up as her Aunt Zaldehyde recoiled making a strange sign with her crossed fingers. The words on the scroll shifted their places on the will. The words reassembled translating themselves into english and she began reading again.

"Let all who listen also, take these words home too."

Vicki's hands gripped the scroll tightly. She found herself paralyzed to the spot. The words of the will began to pour from her mouth. Her mother reached out to grab Vicki's hand. Vicki could sense her father at her side as well, trying to offer some comfort as she read. The entire room darkened, Zaldehyde and her daughter huddled together near the fireplace and the lawyer stepped away from the center of the room. Vicki's whole body shuddered as she spoke, a buzz of electricity coursing through her head.

"Steel, my words are steel, and my blood is iron, and my breath is made of the firmament above and my will is as the stone below."

As Vicki recited the words another voice in the room began speaking along with her. She looked up to the dimly lit image of her grandfather sitting at an old writing desk in the middle of the living room. Her mother gave out a shrill cry and Max called out but Vicki herself could not react. Her words kept spilling forth along with the voice of her late Grandpa Eckhardt.

All eyes shifted to the ghostly image of the white haired man with the sharp nose. He sat at the desk with his trademark tobacco pipe, silver monocle, and perfectly curled mustache that sat over his immaculately trimmed beard. The scent of pipe tobacco filled the room and a general feeling of warmth emanated from the specter. He sat there penning the words on the scroll while speaking them aloud. His thick old english accent came from Vicki's mouth as she spoke along with him.

"Here then follows my last will and testament. I, Eckhardt C. Charles, Testator- do authorize the law offices of Hammer, Stayker, and Thumps to carry out my will and to dispatch the duties of executor upon my death. Addendum, that my granddaughter Victoria Voland dispatch all magical authority to my beneficiaries."

Vicki glanced up as the ghost stood from his desk and put his hands into the pockets of his dark red velvet smoking jacket. He stood there seeming to address all in attendance, first giving a warm smile in the general direction of the Voland family then a quick glance towards Zaldehyde and her daughter. Vicki gasped as her grandfather turned his attention to her with a sad little smile. He took his pipe in one hand and placed his monocle into his coat with the other. The quilled pen behind him continued writing as he spoke.

"Vicki, I wish I could have shown you the world that I shared with your mother and with Max." Vicki murmured the words along with Eckhardt, still enchanted by the magic of the scroll. Her eyes began misting over as she read along with Eckhardt. "I hope that in the event of my death, you'll come to know some of my life better. I hope that you'll find yourself at home with your new inheritance."

Eckhardt replaced his monocle over his eye turning away from the families. His demeanor changed and Vicki thought that the ghostly image stuttered like a movie out of sync. He motioned to someone unseen then squared his shoulders before heading back to his writing desk. He scribbled the words down on the scroll in front of him with a much more glum look on his face. His monocle glinted in the light of an unseen fireplace as he spoke along with Vicki.

"To my dearest daughter Eleonora, I bequeath onto you one half of the Charles family total wealth, including Äther gold standard and Earth mineral rights amounting to the total of Three hundred thousand dollars. 1313 Atherton street in Manchester will be in your care. To be executed immediately upon the reading of my will."

Mrs. Voland covered her mouth trembling as she stared over at her tall menacing sister in the corner of the room. Zaldehyde went unfazed by the inheritance. Vicki continued reading the scroll squinting as the letters began losing their shimmer.

"To my most cunning daughter Zaldehyde, I bequeath onto you one quarter of the Charles family total wealth, including Äther gold standard, Earth mineral rights, and magical holdings- including the shrunken head of Karkokann and the staff of the Wyrm traveler. Totaling in the amount of one hundred and fifty thousand dollars, to be executed immediately upon the reading of my will. To be exchanged for seven thousand eight hundred and ninety four gold Gorgolns at beneficiary's discretion. I urge you to change your ways, Zaldehyde. May the wisdom of the singing head be your saving grace."

Zaldehyde stifled a laugh and grinned as Vicki read on. The towering witch adjusted her hat motioning to Magra to quell her excitement over the new inheritance of a small singing head. Apparently the head was worth its weight in gold, or so Vicki mused.

"To my ever impressive grandson Maxwell, I bequeath onto you one quarter of the Charles family total wealth, including Äther gold standard, Earth mineral rights, and magical items listed herein. Item one, the Merlin emerald. Item two, Gozer maul. Item three, the Fire Cloak. Totaling in the amount of one hundred and fifty thousand dollars, to be executed immediately upon the reading of my will. Know what lies in your heart, Max."

Max remained quiet sitting expressionless while Zaldehyde let out a snicker. Vicki hadn't the slightest clue as to what the witch found so funny about the inheritance, neither did she understand why Max sat with such a look on his face. The ghostly image of Eckhardt faded fast becoming more translucent as more and more of the scroll was read. So too were the words on the scroll disappearing. Vicki held the scroll at an angle towards the light reading onward towards the end.

"To my ever knowledgeable granddaughter Magra, I bequeath onto you my estate Gryphon Helm, my library of magical seals, and collection of wands and staves. To be executed immediately upon the reading of my will. Never has there been a finer example of witchkind to grace or menace the lands. I beg you to find your own path and to use your inheritance with care. Gryphon Helm holds many powerful items and magics within its halls, but the most powerful magic you already possess."

The little witch hopped up and down with joy stifling a screech of excitement, Zaldehyde shushed her as Vicki struggled with the rest of the will. Vicki peered up over the scroll glimpsing an odd look of concern from both her mother and her aunt. Mrs. Voland reached out and placed her hand over her wrist, offering up comfort. Vicki's eyes adjusted to the fading words on the scroll now devoid of the golden luster.

"To my son-in-law, Stephen, I bequeath onto you my entire collection of journals, collection of hunting rifles, and nickel wares. Should the hunt ever call you Stephen, answer it with my blessing and aim true..."

The ghostly image of Eckhardt skipped around coming to a stop directly in front of Vicki. She looked up gasping at the sight of him. Eckhardt stood stern unflinching in his determination. His monocle gleamed and he curled the tips of his mustache with his fingers. Every letter and spot of ink on the scroll had vanished.

Vicki glanced over at the lawyer, he turned his attention to the floor. She crinkled and shook the scroll, checking to see if the magic might return. Mrs. Voland gave her a comforting pat on the arm.

"I can't read the rest of it, I think that was it," said Vicki.

"It's okay dear, you did great," her mother said to her in a low and calming tone. "Come and sit with me." She pulled Vicki towards her chair.

Vicki sat on her lap resting her head on her mother's shoulder. She held the scroll in her hand looking over at the ghostly image of her grandfather. Eckhardt stood at attention still following Vicki with his gaze. His image glimmered differently now, more translucent and glowing with a much more eerie light.

Vicki rolled up the scroll holding it to her chest. "Do you think he... did he maybe," she swallowed down her anxiety looking away from the ghost and back up to her mother. "Did he die before he could finish the will? Is that why he's stuck there, just standing like that?"

"He was a very old man," Mrs. Voland said as she gave a rub to Vicki's shoulder. "I think he would have-" The scroll lit up once more startling them both.

Vicki opened the scroll, peering at the words. They burned as bright as ever but in dazzling silver and green hues rather than the previous golden colors. The lettering looked more hastily written down, quite different to the neatness before. The letters leaned heavily to the right obviously scrawled by a different hand. She stood from her mother's lap and began reading the scroll aloud, only now the words felt pulled from her mouth in a most unpleasant way, as if someone were yanking on her breath.

"Athenaeum, the Housekeeper is here, and here is the holder of knowledge. Water vessel, and bearer both, unto this vessel pour your wealth. Steel, iron, firmament above and stone below. Let iron be wrapped in stone, let steel ignite above. Let any who deny the word crawl unclean, let any who make grievance be heard undone. Let the three unspoken decree trust in the one." Vicki's grandpa no longer spoke along with her. The letters vanished and the scroll crumbled to dust in Vicki's hands. A snap of energy traveled up from the floor all throughout her body, her hair tingled as the energy went upward and out away from her head. Eckhardt gave her one last smile with a face of abundant joy before vanishing from all sight.

Silence fell across the room save for Magra, she let out a tiny gasp glancing up to her mother. Zaldehyde made a step backward away from Vicki raising her wand above her head shielding her daughter with her other arm. Mrs. Voland put a hand over her mouth and scowled at the lawyer.

"This…" began the lawyer, "this is a mistake; no this was tampering!" The skeleton man began to rifle through his documents becoming more and more frantic as he searched. "This is outrageous! Ms. Charles, what have you done," he demanded.

"Oh I did nothing but tell the truth," Zaldehyde said with a low tone. She ushered her daughter back toward the disfigured fireplace giving an evil little wink at Vicki, then nodded at Mrs. Voland. "I warned you, and what's more you knew not to trust him! How many of the wards upon your home were to protect yourselves against him, and not just me," she asked. The tall witch shook her head in dismay and regarded the lawyer. "I'll take my inheritance in Äther, I accept the will of my father. I'll lead the exalted Housekeeper to her new charge should she feel compelled."

"You evil old hag! What do you mean, you're not taking her anywhere," shouted Mr. Voland as he and Mrs. Voland sprang up from their seats. Mr. Voland put his arms around Vicki turning her to face him. He looked around her as if checking for some kind of physical damage. "What did all of that mean? What was all that mumbo jumbo?" he yelled at the lawyer.

Hans closed his briefcase, his skull rattling as he tried to straighten the collar of his loosely fitting shirt. "M-m… Mr. Voland, I regret to inform you that by Äther law the young miss is now the principal holder of responsibilities and dutiful Housekeeper to your late father-in-law's retirement home in Everfall."

Vicki's heart began to race as the calming effect of the scroll's magic fizzled away. Her eyes widened and her breath hastened. Sweat began to form on her palms from the anxiety that came rushing back to her.

"Mom!" She reached out, grabbing for her mother's hand, then collapsed down to the sofa. Max huddled up to her and steadied her shoulders so that she wouldn't fall backwards. Vicki looked up at the concerned faces all around her. Her mother especially looked frightened. "Mom, what did he mean," Vicki asked with a slight tremble.

"Mr. Hammer or Stayker, whatever your name is, you have to tell us what that means very plainly! Right now," exclaimed Mrs. Voland. She clung on to Vicki's hand looking fiercely into the eye sockets of the skeleton lawyer. "Does that mean that she owns that property in Äther? Do we need to make some kind of arrangements to sign over that property?"

"Bohnberg..." began Hans, "... and in the simplest of terms, no. The young miss owns nothing, but is bound to carry out certain responsibilities to the Athenaeum. She must travel to Äther, post haste, or else..."

"Or else?" Mrs. Voland shook her head and glared at him. "She's not one of you, she isn't going anywhere! You have to talk to someone, anyone! Can't you talk to the people that own that facility? Explain the situation to them, this is ridiculous!"

"You tiny fool! Tell them, I dare you to try and tell them!" Zaldehyde laughed stomping her foot at the lawyer sending the skeleton rattling behind the kitchen island. "Tell them who owns the Athenaeum! Tell them who Eckhardt Charles bows to! Tell them what the Three Lords have done!"

"The point is moot," said Hans, as he turned back towards the Voland family. He collected his briefcase in front of him and stood in front of Mrs. Voland. "This is an obvious farce, someone has tampered with the will and placed your daughter in an inheritance that was intended for someone else, I'm sure. I will contact the owners, but until that time I must insist that the *Housekeeper* be on her way, this is all under penalty of curse! For everyone present!"

"Well who owns it, the retirement home," asked Max. He glanced over at Zaldehyde and Magra as they began to step back into the fireplace. "And who was it supposed to go to?"

"And what curse," asked Vicki. She frowned as the skeleton rattled and shifted the contents of his briefcase around. "Mom, I don't want to go work in some weirdo retirement home! I don't even know how to change a baby diaper, I can't change a monster! I don't want to go to the witch world! Don't let them take me!"

"Vicki, we'll get this all cleared up, don't you worry," her mother said with a pat on Vicki's shoulder. "It's nothing that we can't fix! You're not going anywhere! We're not letting you go, no matter what that will says."

No sooner had her mother said this than she let out a pained squeal.

Chapter four

Vicki recoiled screaming as her mother twisted in a most unnatural way. Her mother's shoulders bent backward cracking out of place her knees buckling inward. The popping of joints and bones filled the air around Mrs. Voland, she screamed as her body contorted and elongated.

"Mom!" Vicki shrieked as she fell back from her writhing mother. Mrs. Voland looked back at her with inhuman eyes, they had become dark black and wild. "Mom what's happening," Vicki cried out.

Mrs. Voland screeched reaching out towards her husband just as he too began to squeal and jerk around. She stumbled forward as the muscles in her leg began to shift and bulge, reshaping themselves into a hindquarter. Her face jutted forward with a loud pop, her nose stretched out into a wet snout.

Mr. Voland laid a cloven hand on Vicki's shoulder, his fingernails fused together and bristly hairs springing up from his lumpy arm. "Vicki," he snorted out, "Don't go with…" Mr. Voland tried to form his words but his teeth popped out of place forming tusks at the front of his mouth. He held his hands to his new tusks oinking and convulsing as his back cracked into a new painful shape.

Max yanked Vicki away from their squealing parents, screaming along with her as they both watched Mrs. Voland's hair melt away to the floor and her ears stretch far above her head. Mr. Voland fell to his side oinking uncontrollably as his legs snapped and kicked wildly out from behind him.

Zaldehyde shook her head in dismay as Mrs. Voland dropped to all fours stretching out of her dress. Where there had once been a woman there now wallowed a pig snorting and squealing with wild panicked eyes. Mrs. Voland oinked and went running to Vicki.

"Mom?" Vicki wept and shook at the sight of her mother, recoiling and covering her ears from the horrible squealing.

"Oh Eleonora, even now I see the resemblance," Zaldehyde laughed through her hand looking down at the pig with contempt.

Mr. Voland let out a howl wriggling around on the floor, his arms flailed about as his lower body twisted into hooves and a curly tail. His back raised and bubbled into a hairy mess of bumps and warts. The large hog fell to all fours grunting and whining fully changed at last, giving a sympathetic oink to his wife. The two pigs squealed running circles around Vicki and Max.

"Pigs! You turned them into pigs," Max yelled spinning around to the skeleton lawyer. "Change them back! You have to change them back!"

"The curse is beyond my measure, it's legally binding to my office to obey it. It's very clear, anyone who tries to stop this contract of Housekeeper will be cursed forthwith, it must be honored!" Hans shuddered and his skull rattled. "In order for this curse to be lifted the young miss must travel to the Athenaeum and be accepted as the Housekeeper. I can lobby for the owners to reconsider the appointment of the Housekeeper but that will take a few days at least. The will must be carried out immediately lest the curse worsen, and I simply cannot involve myself beyond this. You young Mr. Voland must now be the one to make the arrangements for her departure."

Max winced as he spoke. "Oh god, Vicki, you have to go with them. You have to, there's no other way! You have to go with Aunt Zaldehyde!"

Vicki gave a whine turning back towards her looming aunt, the huge woman smiled down at the two children her wicked eyes gleaming with a sick delight. "What! With her, with them! No way!" Vicki shrank away from the gigantic witch and clung to Max. "You said she's evil! You said not to trust her!"

Max pushed her away and spoke sternly. "She is! But you have to! For Mom and Dad, look at them!" The two pigs had taken to rummaging through the kitchen garbage. He motioned over to the witches standing at the fireplace. "It's the only way, I know this is crazy and it's all at once and I'd go instead if I could," he said laying a hand on her shoulder, pulling it away with a loud gasp.

Max held out his cloven hand, his fingers had come together into a lumpy hoof of fingernails and twisting knuckles. He felt at his face turning his hand round and round visibly shaken by the new grotesque appendage. He stared down at Vicki's back with wide eyed horror.

"What is it?" Vicki reached down behind her feeling at the thing that now hung freely just at her waistline. She touched the velvety, curly thing tracing its corkscrew shape between her fingers with a whimper and a tremble.

"Let's take a breath," began Max.

"It's a pig tail," Vicki screamed as she hid her face into her hands. She sobbed into her palms heaving out heavy breaths. "What do you mean, *take a breath?*"

Zaldehyde hissed and the house shook violently around them. "You'll be a piglet by six tonight! Your brother will be a ham by five!" She grinned down at Vicki, folding her arms. "I hope you like the mud little one! Perhaps my Magra will have you for a pet!"

Max oinked and covered his mouth, he regained his composure then reluctantly turned to Zaldehyde. "Aunt Zaldehyde, will you please take Vicki with you?"

"No!" Vicki glanced over at her bizarre cousin. Magra gave a sympathetic look back at her and Vicki hid her face against Max's shoulder. She teared up when he pushed her away again.

"Vicki, there's no other way!"

"But not with them, I can't! I can't!" She fled from the tall witch and the pigs scurrying to the stairwell.

Vicki ran up the stairs to her room slamming the door shut behind her ignoring Max's plea. She pressed herself up against the door and began bawling, wishing that life would just return to normal. Maybe this had all been a bad dream. Maybe she would wake up and life would make perfect sense again.

The cheerfully decorated room with its rainbow colored curtains and pink fluffy bed offered little comfort now that the squealing of her parents echoed throughout the house. Her eyes fell upon the hand-painted birds and pink flowers of her closet door. It had been a father daughter project some time ago, the two of them had painted it together when she was around eight or nine, just at the time when she had joined the scouts. That crushing weight returned, pressing down her as she turned her eyes to the dresser near the bed.

A colorful little picture frame sat face down on the dresser top, toppled over long ago and never rescued. Somewhere in that closet was an old vest with badges and patches sewn into it with pride. Vicki's heart pounded in her chest, her ears throbbed with pressure and her hands went ice cold. She felt down at her new tail and winced.

"I can't!" Vicki sobbed into her hands. "I can't do it! I can't do anything!" She slid down against her bedroom door taking great care to not pinch the curly new appendage.

Then from the window through the rain and over the sobbing there came a song. A tiny blue bird hopped along the outside window sill, singing and chortling as it dodged the raindrops from the sky. It held its wings open singing at her as she stood and edged closer. The stormy wind blew through its feathers, tossing the little bird left and right.

Vicki climbed over her bed, hurrying to the window. She pulled the frame upward to let the poor thing in, not even thinking on how to care for a wet bird. She scooted away from the window waiting for the bird to enter. She sniffled and gathered her hoodie around her, shivering in the chilly rainstorm.

The bird hopped forward staring at her with its deep black eye. It tilted its head a few times, chirping a merry tune at her, hopping around the window sill one more time before spreading its wings wide. The little blue bird sang out one last song then took off into the winds and rain, climbing high up into the storm clouds.

Vicki stared after the bird wondering if she too shouldn't make an escape out through the window. Cold guilt filled her stomach and something much worse slithered through her heart. Rain came blowing in through the window, tossing the silk curtains around her like dancing ghosts. She bit her lip and shut her eyes tight.

A light knock came from her bedroom door and Max poked his head in. "Vicki?" He stayed on the other side of the door and swept his palm over his hair. "Look I know this is really crazy. Monsters and magic and everything, I can't even imagine what this is like for you," he began.

Vicki closed the window and ran to her dresser, pulling her backpack over to her feet. "I-I'm going," she stammered. "I have to, you're right!"

"You are?" Max gave her a smile. "I mean, good! That was kind of a full 180, are you sure you're okay?"

"Just don't talk about the monsters," said Vicki as she struggled to open the dresser. "I'm scared and I don't want to, but if I don't go Mom and Dad will never get better!" She threw her backpack across her shoulders and huffed out, straining against the drawer. "And you too! So I have to go or else!"

Vicki's face grew hot and she dropped the bag from her shoulders. It landed with a thunk on the floor behind her as she went to yank open the drawer with her every ounce of strength. She failed to get the dresser open and fell into quiet despair. The drawer always stuck but today it seemed impossible to budge. Vicki let her head drop onto the top of the dresser and sobbed out.

"It's okay, Vicki," said Max as he came into her room and opened the drawer with ease, both hands now transformed into cloven hooves.

"No it's not okay!" Vicki cried out. "I can't even open my own stupid dresser! How am I gonna do anything ever?" She kicked her backpack over fuming and grabbed some clothes from the dresser drawer. "I don't know how I'm going to do this," she said as she hugged a sweater against herself.

Vicki folded the sweater up as hastily as she could placing it safely away into the holographic unicorn and sloth covered backpack near her vanity. She began cramming other items into the backpack, a few outfits and her favorite toiletries, stifling her tears as she worked. She was just finished stuffing the pack full when Max put a hand on her shoulder.

"You can, you can do this. Remember what Mom and Dad told you, the people from over there are just like people over here. I met a ton of them when I was little, none of them ever did anything to hurt me, you're going to be okay! I promise!" Max leaned in close to her and whispered. "And she can't hurt you, she's just going to get you to that nursing home and leave. Otherwise she'll start turning into a pig too, or worse!"

Vicki sniffled trying to steady herself against the weight of the backpack. "But I can't ever do anything right, what if I mess everything up? Mom and Dad could be piggies forever because of me!"

"You won't screw it up, Vic, you can't keep thinking like that," said Max as he ushered Vicki forward. "You go with them and we'll all come get you once Mom and Dad turn back to normal."

The two of them left the room, Vicki turned looking around one last time taking in the painted birds and rainbow curtains. She gulped down her fear and followed Max down the stairs where the witches waited. The oinking of their parents quickened as Vicki came down the last step.

Vicki shivered and gave Max a frown. "I wish you could come with me."

"Well I wish I could too, but I have to take care of Mom and Dad."

Vicki stared down at the two pigs, her mind racing with visions of monsters and frightening images of places that she had only seen in horror movies. Her mother raised a snout upwards and oinked, her big black eyes wet with tears. Even now her mother protested on Vicki's behalf and Vicki would have gladly stayed to let her parents deal with the monsters instead.

Zaldehyde stepped forward demanding that Vicki follow. "Where we go is time sensitive. Come now child, you're trying my patience and I have other matters to attend to!" She flicked her wand and Vicki's bright pink running shoes came sliding to the girl's feet with a screech against the linoleum floor.

"I'll go," said Vicki as she stepped into the shoes. She tried averting her eyes from the gaze her menacing aunt. "I'm coming."

Max squeezed Vicki's shoulder and pushed her forward. "You can call me on the phone over there, it kind of works just like it does here. You heard the lawyer, he said it will only be a day or two before they fix everything. All those people over there know Grandpa, everyone in that place was his friend! You can do this."

Hans spoke up from the kitchen island as he began to collect his belongings. "And I shall meet with the owners as soon as they are available for review. The new Housekeeper must arrive safely of course, Ms. Charles, or all who attended this reading will share the fate of your sister." The skeletal man turned his gaze to Zaldehyde. "The curse should begin to reverse upon her arrival in Äther, I expect you'll already have her there in Everfall safe and sound by tonight."

"Of course, my daughter will see to it." Zaldehyde sighed and thrust her wand into the air. The fireplace roared to life once more, pink flames lit the hall of brickwork casting shadows far off into the darkness. "Shall we," she asked without much sympathy as she shoved Max away from Vicki.

"Wait," exclaimed Max, digging into his pocket with his clumsy cloven hoof. He produced his lucky wooden ring and held it out to Vicki placing it in her hand. "Grandpa said that this ring would keep you in the right direction, so you wear it. Just for good luck."

"I'll call, I'll call a bunch," said Vicki through a sniffle. She gave Max a quick hug looking at the two pigs as they fought over a banana peel and frowned. She put on a brave face for Max as she placed the ring on her thumb and turned towards the fireplace. Vicki clasped her hands together, trembling as she made her way over to Zaldehyde.

"And now, my poor deprived child, you'll finally see the other half of the world." Zaldehyde ushered Vicki forward with a heavy nudge. "To Wytch Elm." She waved the gnarled black bone wand into the air over Vicki's head.

Vicki looked back to Max one last time, and he returned her look with concern. A bright pink flare surrounded her, hot sparks hit her skin and she yelped as she covered her face with her hands. Fizzling carbonated soda noises filled the air around Vicki and she stumbled in place as the floor around her lurched left and right.

She peeked through her fingers as white and pink swirls of fire spun around them. Her cousin stood unfazed by the fireworks standing perfectly at ease even as the bricks under her feet shifted and rolled forward like waves on an ocean. Vicki lowered her hands watching as the bricks in the long fireplace hallway began turning to gray cobblestone. The floor jerked forward and she nearly catapulted down to the ground.

"I think I'm gonna be sick," Vicki mumbled through her hands.

Magra smiled tapping on her lower lip with her crystal wand giving a nod. "It's okay if you do, everyone does the first time!"

Vicki reeled and shut her eyes tight. "I'm going to fall," she yelled out. The floor stopped moving and the pink fire around them dissipated with a loud pop. She stumbled forward past her cousin and held her stomach as the room spun around her.

Magra steadied her by the shoulder. "It's okay, it's okay prima, let it out!"

Vicki looked up into the bustling brick alleyway area around her and placed her hands over her mouth, stifling the scream that welled up within her throat.

Chapter five

The green sun poked over the wayward leaning small buildings made of brick and stone, the acrid scent of woodsmoke and burning hair hung in the air around the alleyway. Puddles of gray and pink oily water splashed and oozed as other witches came out of the great blackened metal furnace behind them, all of them looking down at Vicki with a hearty laugh at her expense. Some of their faces were twisted into inhuman features; one woman walked past with dark empty eye sockets giving Vicki a menacing grin. Vicki jumped to her feet screaming as a man with one huge singular eyeball in the middle of his head went pushing past her, annoyed at the sound that she was making.

She went stumbling back to her cousin and hid next to a wooden barrel full of discarded half eaten shoes. A gaggle of little sharp toothed creatures came over to inspect Vicki as Zaldehyde began speaking with Magra. The little people were all different colors ranging from blues to reds. Some wore old nineteenth century European style clothes while others wore nearly nothing at all. They all gawked at her, some of them whispering to one another while others made sounds of general disapproval.

They were all of them quite strangely proportioned, with heads about two times larger than that of any person and floppy ears that stuck out into great points. Their pug noses twitched and moved around in the air as they discussed the matter of the girl before them. Their different colored eyes all looked large and curious, they were so big in fact that Vicki's reflection danced around in their eyes as they inspected her.

Some of them had hair atop their heads while others had horns or little hats, but all of them shared one key feature. They all had terrible jagged fangs that rivaled anything from her worst nightmares. Vicki was certain that her entire head could fit neatly into one of their mouths but she wasn't interested in the least bit at getting near one of the disturbing little monsters to find out.

"Goblins," said Zaldehyde with undisguised disgust. "Everfall is infested with them, so you may as well get used to the stench of the little pests. Come, my Magra will take you beyond to your destination."

"Mama, I can go with her to Athenaeum? I can help, I can keep her safe," asked Magra.

Zaldehyde motioned to move forward while Magra nestled up to Vicki. The gigantic witch stared down at Vicki without any trace of sympathy in her eyes. "Indeed, little girl, take care. Our part in this is only to bring you alive and safe to that dreadful little house. I wash my hands of anything that befalls you afterward."

Vicki gripped her hands together and averted her eyes from her aunt. "W-what, what does that mean?"

Zaldehyde bent down closer to Vicki. "For the curse to lift you need only accept your fate and go to the Athenaeum, that much is true. What happens after that is the business of the Three Lords." She jabbed her long index finger at Vicki. "I can't enter that wretched mansion and I certainly am not welcome in Everfall *anymore*. Surely I'm not meant to meddle in this affair. So take heed, little Victoria, no one will be coming to save you from the perils of this hungry new world."

Vicki shied away from her aunt, nearly bumping into a passing goblin as she trembled in the shadow of the witch. "B-but, my mom said that the monsters here aren't all bad." She bit her lip and stared at a bandage wrapped mummy as it shambled past, it stared back at her with its dried out blank eyes and seemed to bare its teeth at her.

"You poor little thing. Not even I could lie to you with such ease," said Zaldehyde, standing to her full height. "You have no idea how to get along in *this* world, let alone your *own*. No magic, no knowledge, no friends. How utterly hopeless this all is for you. Imagine if anything were to go wrong, what could you even hope to do?"

"Mi Madre can help you, Prima, this place it is no good for you! She will help because you are family," whispered Magra.

"Oh it's true, how can I deny that last little spark of humanity that refuses to be snuffed out." Zaldehyde removed her clamshell mirror from her dress as she spoke. "Perhaps it's just one last soft spot. I suppose that I *could* come to your rescue, should that need arise. In exchange for the littlest favor from you of course."

"What kind of favor?" Vicki shivered, her knuckles turning white as she gripped her backpack to her shoulders. "Why would I need rescuing?"

"Oh you might not, you might be just fine. Maybe everything will be easy and go your way." Zaldehyde snapped the mirror shut smiling down at Vicki with her horrible grin. "Or maybe they'll find your bones someday, walking around here with all of the other lost souls." The grin became a show of teeth and gums. "Or maybe they won't even leave the bones. A little thing like you wouldn't be so hard to chew."

Vicki let out a whine and turned away from the smiling witch, holding in her tears as best she could. "I think I just want to go! I want to go to the Atha Zappa! I just want to help my mom and dad!"

At this Zaldehyde frowned, giving a fake show of empathy to the girl. "You're afraid of the wrong people on this side of the world. Such a pity. Regardless, I'll be watching and waiting." She turned her attention back to the enormous furnace behind them motioning for her fluttering book to follow her. "I'll leave you to it, best of luck until then little Voland. Magra, you'll join us at Gryphonhelm as soon as you've finished at that *old meat locker*."

The furnace erupted with a fountain of flames shooting upwards into the overcast sky, Zaldehyde vanished in a plume of ash and smog giving one last shark smile to Vicki. A series of sparks and flames shot out from the furnace and other macabre travelers began appearing at the entrance to the alleyway, shoving past the two little girls.

"Here, come with me! We will get you to Athenaeum," said Magra with a broad grin. Her smile dropped as Vicki reluctantly turned to face her. "Prima, I will not hurt you, come with me. You must stay with me, stay safe." Magra beckoned for Vicki to follow alongside her and the two made their way out of the damp alleyway into the bustling streets of the ramshackle half industrialized city.

The buildings of the city were made miniature for the little goblin inhabitants. Everything from the jigsaw stonework to the rickety telephone poles were built and placed in haphazard fashion, sitting at odd angles threatening to topple at any moment. Vicki marveled at a particularly precarious building that swayed left and right against two others, Magra took her by the sleeve dragging her into a noisy bus depot filled with all manner of monstrous commuters.

They entered into the Wytch Elm station, a loud and busy mismatched wreck of a building. Neon blue and pink lights lit the large space full of bizarre mechanisms and architecture. Huge chalkboards lined the glass walls that led out to the departing steam powered busses and a multitude of creatures went zipping to and fro in between the walls and windows, sometimes mistaking one for the other with a loud thud. A goblin wearing a large official hat covered in horns and fur went scurrying past Vicki towards the waiting wooden wheeled busses outside.

"Make way!" The goblin looked back at Vicki's shoes with great disdain shaking his head. He reached for one of the doors and went crashing into one of the glass walls instead.

"Their ears are so big!" Vicki looked out over the bustling station, her eyes coming to rest upon a green goblin conversing with a mummy in the seat next to his. The mummy laughed out so hard that his arm fell off to the great joy of the goblin. The goblin's ears flapped like bird wings as he laughed in his seat. "...and floppy."

"Yes, big ears hear very good, so be careful how you talk. Prima, you have to be more careful here, you will say and do things that are bad to do. What is the word, offense?" Magra turned and gave herself a nod, proud of her grasp on the foreign language. "Yes, offense, you make the goblins unhappy with this!"

"Offensive? But I don't even know what to do or say around here!"

Magra pointed her in the direction of two goblins sitting next to each other on a bench. "Do you see how they are all colors but not pink? They change to many colors, all the colors when they are happy or sad, or hungry and tired. All colors but never pink."

"Like my shoes? They can't change to pink? Why not?"

Magra sidled up to Vicki and shook her head. "No, it's a bad color, it's like a bad word. That's the color for goblins to say when they have to use the toilet but not in a nice way, they are pink when they say that they are going now! It's an angry color."

Vicki looked down at her shoes. "Ew! Oh no, should go to the restroom and change really quick?"

"Oh no, no, don't use the toilets here Prima. Don't do that," said Magra, with a little shudder. "Athenaeum is for the goblins, you must not wear pink, and you must not stare. Everfall is a city too for the goblins."

"But are there other colors and other things I have to watch out for?" Vicki turned around as a young goblin pointed to her squealing with laughter. His mother shook her big pointy eared head at Vicki covering the boy's little bulging eyes as she led him away. "You said I'm going to a goblin city? Is it only goblins there? Do they speak English?"

"Goblins and many others too. You speak Goblicks already now, do not call it English here. You must not wear pink and you must not speak ill of butter. Everfall is beautiful, Abeulo loved his time there, and me too I also love it." Magra pointed up to a giant chalkboard that teetered on one of the glass walls of the station held in place by a delicate system of string and large rusty nails. "That bus is ours! Come we must eat first." She led them to a kiosk near the front of the glass wall.

Vicki stared up at the chalkboard. Two little goblins rode a suspended bicycle along a hanging track that bordered the glass structure of the depot. The goblin peddling the bike wore huge goggles over his head as the goblin hitching a ride on the back of the bike stretched out to the chalkboard with a long piece of chalk in her hand. She scribbled with furious speed marking the departure times for the busses. The peddler zoomed along and the goblin girl left a long white streak of chalk along the boards as they went, both captivated by Vicki's pink shoes.

Vicki trailed behind the little white haired witch, fiddling with Max's ring and taking in the sights of the nightmarish creatures around her. They were all of them quite jarring in appearance but her mother's words about the Ätherbound rang true. All of the monster folk were really just people doing mundane things that people did. A giant ape man went along emptying trash cans into his janitorial cart, as a shadowy man made of wispy tentacles and smoke played a game on his little crystal rectangular handheld device. An exhausted half cat woman read a newspaper while her misbehaving half cat child stuck its tongue out at Vicki before vanishing in a puff of smoke.

The world seemed a little less scary, not at all without its frights but definitely more comfortable than Vicki would have expected. The two of them reached the Kiosk and she let her attention drift from her cousin over to the side of the kiosk wall. Colorful leaflets and posters were plastered all over one another, some of the drawings on the various pieces of paper were animated through magical means waving themselves around to gain the attention of the passersby.

Vicki examined one of the hand drawn leaflets up close. The leaflet proudly straightened itself out for the reading, giving a smug little flick of its edges as the girl reached out to steady it against its flailing comrades. A grand buttering would soon be taking place in the Ing Valley, and all were invited to attend. Fire proof clothing and high yield umbrellas were recommended.

Vicki furrowed her brow at the nonsensical leaflet and turned around from the wall letting her eyes fall upon the restroom doors. A particularly menacing man with red skin and two long black horns on either side of his shiny red head walked past talking into a small coffin shaped device that he held in his clawed hands. The large red man noticed Vicki's stare and returned a dissatisfied glare back to her.

"What! What are you looking at," screamed the red man as he clicked his coffin shaped device closed. "What's the matter?! You never seen a bald guy before?! Go ahead, yuck it up, everyone stare at the freak," he shouted. The man kicked over a garbage can and went running out of the bus station making a crying bleating noise as he went.

The bus station went quiet and all manner of monsters and strange persons peered over their books and various devices to look at the offending little girl that stood staring out over the sea of curious faces. Vicki held her hands up to her mouth, her face went hot and she turned around escaping to her cousin's side. She took a seat next to Magra on a little wobbly stool in front of the kiosk.

"On Ätherside, it's very rude to stare at people," whispered Magra, as she motioned for the kiosk owner's attention.

A hulking hairy behemoth of a man with one singular eye in the middle of his forehead brought forth a couple of wooden bowls from his kitchen. He placed the bowls in front of Vicki and Magra then filled the bowls with strange dark noodles, ladling a glowing purple sauce on top. Magra paid the cyclops a few golden hexagonal coins and pushed Vicki's bowl closer to her.

Vicki frowned at the bowl of glowing purple noodles. "Oh I... I'm, I'm not hungry," she said, politely scooting the bowl back towards the witch. "My stomach is still adjusting."

"You must, the fire walk it makes you hungry, very hungry. You will become sick if you don't eat," Magra replied, pushing the bowl back in front of her. "Eat! It's good!"

Vicki took the bowl into her hands and gave a jiggle to the grotesque lunch. She stuck a wooden fork into the noodles and promptly dropped the bowl back onto the counter. The noodles began squirming around and chittering, they convulsed in the bowl trying to escape with their little wriggly legs. Vicki leaned away as the wiggling noodles began crawling from the bowl. Centipedes.

"Vicki, you must listen to me now, very carefully." Magra tucked into her writhing mass of centipedes and Vicki covered her mouth in disgust. The little white haired witch began spearing some of the wriggly horrible bugs with her fork. "Mi Madre, she is not nice. I want to be the Housekeeper too, for many years she sent me away to learn how to do this from many great brujas, how to be a good Housekeeper. She is very happy today, happy that I am not Housekeeper, she tries to hide it but I know it is the truth!"

"Well, maybe it was supposed to be you, maybe that skeleton will talk to the people in charge and it will all be okay again," said Vicki, her eyes fixed on the centipedes wrapped around Magra's fork. "I mean he said that it was fake so someone must have faked it, I can't be the Housekeeper or whatever!"

"No, Vicki, you can't say that now! You will anger the curse! You are the Housekeeper now, you must be or your madre will always be a pig!" Magra jabbed her fork at Vicki motioning for her to eat as she spoke. "It is now, it's the truth! It's the truth and Mi Madre, I think that she has done this to you! You must be careful, Prima, I see bad things for you. I love Mi Madre, just as you love yours, but she is a scary bruja. So strong and she has so much hatred for you, I can feel it in the air around us now! So much hate, like a cloud that follows you!"

"Me? But I didn't do anything to her! I don't even want to be here, I didn't ask for this!" Vicki scratched at her tail, wondering if she might also grow a snout. She pulled her hoodie down over the curly pigtail as she stared down into her bowl of putrid food. "I don't want anyone to be mad at me or hate me or anything!"

"Then you have bad luck today, her mind is all hate, more hate than I have ever felt. She hides it, but not from me, do you understand? I can feel everyone like this." Magra took a mouthful of the wriggling centipedes. "I love Mi Madre, but she can be a bad bruja when she is mad. She will do many hurtful things to get what she wants, so when she tells you to do this thing for her, you must do it! You must! All around you I see hate! She will hurt you!"

Vicki restrained the contents of her stomach, slyly scooting the bowl further from her as she spoke. "Do what for her, and what is she going to do to me?" Her voice trembled as she envisioned Zaldehyde leveling her horrible black bone wand at her. "I don't even want to be the Housekeeper! She doesn't have to hurt me, can't you tell her?"

"Prima! Stop saying this! I told you, you will be cursed more! Listen to me, whatever she wants you to do, you must do it or you will be hurt! Do you understand, you could die!"

Vicki scratched at her burning back and frowned, her neck went cold and she whimpered. "But, but I didn't do anything to her! I didn't do anything to anyone, I don't know how to do any of this stuff!"

"It does not matter, it is the truth now, you are the Housekeeper! You must be it! Abuelo chose you or Mi Madre chose you, it is done! You must go to Athenaeum and do what you must do, but listen to Mi Madre, Vicki! Do what she tells you to do or she will burn you! She will send you nightmares and bad things! Do not fight her, you cannot win, keep yourself alive!" Magra gripped Vicki by the shoulders and squeezed her hard.

"She has a bad woman, very bad, a wolf! She is a devil, if you don't do what Mi Madre says the wolf will come and get you! I can see this woman all around you too!"

Vicki gave a solemn nod and swallowed, still quaking from imagined acts of witchcraft against her at the hands of her aunt. "D-Do you mean that lady in red? Shucks? She's like a w-werewolf? She came to our house today, I couldn't even move when she looked at me." The memory of the woman's flaring green eyes forced Vicki to hold her hands tightly together to keep them from shaking.

"Ciara Shuck, yes! She is a bad lobo, Prima, Mi Madre keeps her away from me too. She is hungry, always hungry, and she will take you! So you must listen to me, do not fight, just do what she wants you to do when she tells you!" Magra looked away towards the line of busses outside rubbing at one of her little horns as she spoke. "You will be safe in Athenaeum, Athenaeum will love you like a daughter, I can see this too. Maybe abuelo saw this, that is why he chose you to be Housekeeper."

Vicki gave a shiver and hugged her arms together. "What do you mean, is that place like haunted or something?"

Magra returned a sad little grin. "The Athenaeum, she will protect you with strong magic, but first she will test you. You will pass the test, Prima, you are a good person. You have a good heart, and she will see into you..." Magra covered her mouth and a look of panic crossed her eyes. "Oh I shouldn't say these things! Ours is leaving soon." She darted away from the kiosk and motioned for Vicki to follow, her little barbed tail curled up as she jogged towards the bus terminals.

"What kind of tests though? Do you mean like folding sheets and things?" Vicki hurried along wiggling around in her hoodie trying to alleviate her itchy tail.

"Those things, yes! Everything you can do, you are smart! You have your wits!" Magra looked particularly proud of her last bit of vocabulary.

"Oh sure, my wits," said Vicki as they walked out of the bus station and towards one of the clunky looking busses. "At least I have that..."

Magra led the way up into the steaming clunky vehicle. They came upon the first few rows of seats taken up by a large stone man and a glowing translucent specter wearing a sheet over its body. Hammocks hung across the walkway filled with sleeping goblins and witches of all sorts. The two girls began ducking and weaving around the other bus riders. They moved onward to the back where they would find a few empty spots. Vicki passed by various goblins and imps already murmuring to each other about her shoes. The bus sputtered loudly and came to life, steam blasted out of the sides and its heavy wooden wheels began to crunch forward.

She looked out of the window as the bus hissed and moaned out of Wytch Elm. The tall modern buildings began to taper out into quite mundane suburbs. Monsters of all shapes and sizes roamed the streets and sidewalks. Vicki pressed her head against the glass, staring out the window at lumpy hunchbacked children riding their bicycles and gawked at a hodgepodge gang of skeletons and extremely pale children rolling glass eyeballs into a circle on the sidewalk.

"Abuelo would be happy to see you do this. This is very brave. Me too, Vicki, I am happy for you. I think that you will do good, do what Mi Madre asks for and you will go home safe. Be strong for your family!" Magra took her crystal wand out from her dress and tapped it along Vicki's arm. "I wish you good luck, and good courage."

Vicki shrank away from the wand and rubbed at her elbow, a warm tingle ran up her arm and into her neck, the sensation washed over her entire body and she relaxed. Magra smiled, then turned her attention to the landscape passing by in the window. She began to speak about the rolling autumn valleys of Everfall, of the path to the Athenaeum. The words echoed in Vicki's mind, her cousin's thick Spanish accent fell away and she heard the words in her own voice.

"You will go up the cobblestone main street, they call it Marrow Gate. The shops and the houses you will see, they are all quite beautiful and rustic. Everfall always has tourists but especially now. It is but a month from Halloween and all manner of creature will come to see the rolling fields of orange and red. Up to the mountain you will go, high up on the mountainside is Athenaeum. She looks over the town that lies in the valley below."

Vicki rubbed her eyes and yawned. "I have to climb a mountain?"

"It is as easy a journey as your own mountain trail back home, the mountain that you love."

"Mount Diablo," said Vicki, her eyelids became heavier and she looked lazily out the window as the voice in her head began to fade away into a pleasant hum. "I painted it for Grandpa, but I don't think that he ever saw it..."

"I see that mountain again in your future, and your friends are there too. I hear the songs of birds and the wind in the trees..."

The suburbs gave way to rural buildings and a great pumpkin field until the view became only cloudy tall fields of grass and unidentifiable farm crops against the dull green light of the overcast Ätherside sky. The wheels made a hypnotic rumbling sound and Vicki soon found herself struggling to stay awake. She closed her eyes, resting her head against her cousin's shoulder and yawning out one last time.

Chapter six

A horn sounded from the front of the bus as it ground to a halt. Vicki opened her eyes and sat up looking around as the other passengers disembarked from the ride. The horn blared again and she grabbed her backpack, joining the line full of little goblins.

"Everfall! Everfall," exclaimed the bus driver. "Thank you."

Vicki searched around for Magra, expecting to find her waiting near the front of the line. She went into a small panic peering out of every window looking for the girl with the white hair and little horns. Magra had vanished without a trace; the strange new cousin had abandoned Vicki to her fate. She grasped tightly to her bag and filed off of the bus with the other creatures, trying very hard to remain composed.

Vicki stepped down from the noisy steam powered bus onto the cobblestone street that marked the end of her journey to Everfall. She threw her backpack over her shoulder turning towards the little town that lay hidden in the colorful autumn valley. She scanned the area with no small amount of awe, taking in the trees full of picturesque fall colors and sniffing the inviting scent of freshly fallen leaves wafting down from the village toward her. She took one last long scan of the area, hoping to find her cousin and finally resigned that she was alone.

The cobblestone street zig-zagged upwards through the hilly town past the smaller wood and stone store fronts. Small and crooked old European style homes with thatched roofs in the village proper were just beginning to light up for the evening. Far off behind those rickety homes, other farmland buildings began illuminating the dusk sky with their own light sources. White plumes of smoke drifted upwards into the darkening sky from unseen chimneys in the distance, the familiar din and clatter of dinner time began to roll out of the wayward leaning goblin-sized homes.

Except of course these were not the kind of families or dinners that Vicki would have ever been acquainted with. In those tiny wayward albeit sturdy homes there were perhaps monsters and demons and all manner of things that she had yet to imagine. Vicki watched two such creatures walk out of a nearby cobblestone store named Freckle's Toads and Tortoises. A small goblin with mucus green skin and a tall puffy hat closed a creaking wooden storefront door as he and a fish headed man locked up for the day. The goblin squinted back at her, placing his hands on his hips in a vexed display.

She averted her eyes and decided that her first new rule for herself was that she was not, under any circumstances whatsoever, to stare at any of the monsters. Vicki would treat them as normal as possible no matter how terrifying or bizarre these people might appear. She was determined to not repeat her mortifying experience at the bus station.

She let her eyes trail further up the village looking for the mansion described to her by Magra. The sloping mountains that cradled the village with fall foliage began to go dark as the green sun retreated behind the first mountain's peak. The village lit up window by window and Vicki began her trek up the wide cobblestone street.

The village was a far cry from the monster suburbs, it had been kept to look nearly medieval. The homes and businesses were decorated as if the Halloween season had already begun. Jack-o'-lanterns lined the stone fences of the stores, long orange and black ribbons fluttered from old wrought iron light poles, and the skinny little tree stumps were all wrapped in delicate spiderwebs. Almost every corner of every block had a haystack on it with distinctly unique scarecrows stuck into each. The scent of cooking meats gave way to wet fallen leaves mingled with the warm candle wax from within the glowing pumpkins.

Vicki held her grumbling tummy, trying to ignore her hunger. "It's only a couple of days," she told herself, imagining the mutant meats being roasted in the ovens. "I can go a couple days just eating crackers." She reached into one of the empty pockets of her backpack and grimaced. Her stomach rumbled again and she whined, thinking about the centipedes.

She clutched her backpack close, moving upward past the end of the market district towards the quaint rickety thatched roof homes on the terraced village slope, passing by some of the town residents. A couple of real live mummies (but actually probably quite undead mummies) shuffled by her, quieting down their conversation as they approached. She began to feel more and more awkward continuing up the cobblestone street full of glowing pumpkins under the appraising eyes of the goblin townsfolk. Some of the monster folk giggled as she passed by, others went silent and a few even grumbled out.

"Mama, look!" A young girl pointed at Vicki from a large public display of carved pumpkins. The girl looked nearly normal with her dirty blonde head of hair and modern clothing, Vicki wouldn't have thought that there was anything monstrous about her at all if it hadn't been for the girl's one singular gigantic eye in the middle of her forehead. The girl's mother, also with her one great eye in the middle of her own head, focused her gaze upon Vicki with unmasked shock. The girl's father, some strange lumpy potato head shaped man with glasses and a bulbous prickly arm at his side, shushed the girl.

"Don't stare, Petula, don't be rude!" The potato man pushed his wife and daughter down the street chastising them for staring at the less fortunate looking Earthbound girl. "You can't stare at people just because they're different!"

Vicki shrugged off the encounter and continued up the cobblestones. She rounded the street reaching a strange lopsided church surrounded by crooked little fall colored trees. A skeletal bird sang out from one of the many branches. She stopped to listen as the bird sang down its shrill little rhyme.

The bad luck witch, the bad luck witch!

She ate a pie made out of pitch!

A disgusting bucket load of dirty water splashed down on her from high above in the wobbling church steeple and she let out a shriek of surprise and anger. Vicki stood shivering covered in discarded half eaten carrots and cold water. She glowered up at the goblin in the swaying tower. He looked back down at her with huge eyes full of fear.

"Oh! Dah! Uh... Sorry!" He vanished into the steeple and slammed a trap door behind him. The entire tower wobbled heavily to one side before slowly steadying itself.

Vicki wanted to scream but instead just stomped her feet and shook off the vegetable matter from her clothes. She tried her best to wring out her hoodie as the sound of approaching wooden wheels on the cobblestone drew near, and a lantern light swung back and forth on the street around her. She searched around for the source of the sound finding a furry red cow man with huge horns sticking out from the sides of his head dragging a two wheeled rickshaw behind him.

His two beady eyes glowed a dull red, partly obscured by his heavy brow which wriggled as he moved his gaze upon her. He stopped in front of Vicki, looking down at her, standing at about three times her height. The beast looked her up and down then released his grip on the rickshaw's handles. He sniffed the air and gave out a full bodied sneeze flicking his floppy cow ears back and forth as he recovered his breath.

"Cor, it's absolute buttery out, innit," said the beast, in a thick cockney accent.

Vicki stared up at the fuzzy cow creature struggling to understand his words. "What," she asked him as she wrung out her hoodie.

The beast motioned with a clawed thumb back to his rickshaw. "Just having a natter. Still, butter in the air for sure, hint of witchbread as well. Got to be beagles about. Maybe even the start of boggle practice."

Vicki shook her head. "I'm sorry, I don't know what you mean."

The beast let out an exasperated sigh and stood to the side pointing at his rickshaw. "Get in the cart," he said, emphasizing every syllable.

Vicki looked at the rickshaw behind the beast raising her eyebrows high. "For what?"

The beast snorted and narrowed his eyes. "So's I can take you to the hoolie, ya' daffy dink! Whaddya think I'm here for?" He pulled the rickshaw closer to Vicki.

"Nope! No-no-no! I don't know who you are and I'm not going anywhere with any strangers, ever, especially here," exclaimed Vicki as she turned away from the beast and scurried away.

The beast followed dragging the rickshaw along. "Jerry," said the beast as he clomped up the cobblestone street.

Vicki glanced back at him quickening her pace. "What?"

The beast sped up his pursuit following closely. "My name, is Jerry," he said. "And you smell like a beagler."

She turned around hissing from clenched teeth, "well you smell like a giant wet ferret!" Vicki scowled at the red cow man. "And stop following me!"

"What's a ferret? And anyways, I'm sposed to take you to work, you can't fire me for doing my job. I have rights you know."

Vicki peered around at the rickshaw behind Jerry reading the sloppily written words on its side. *Athenaeum Express*. She gave him a small frown.

"I'm sorry," began Vicki, "I didn't know who was supposed to come get me, and my..." Vicki hesitated before taking her backpack off. "My friend disappeared and left me all alone, she didn't say that it was going to be a wagon ride."

"S'alright, can't bring the bus down til the power's back on," said Jerry as he motioned to his rickshaw again. "But if you don't get in, ain't much cause for me to be here, is there?"

"No, I guess not." Vicki approached the large red fuzzy cow. She tested the sturdiness of the cart then climbed into her seat biting her lip and keeping a close eye on the cow as she sat down. "Can you take it slow though, I've had a really bumpy day."

Jerry let out a snort grabbing the rickshaw by the handles. "Slow's the only speed they pay me to go, innit," he said as he began to take her up the cobblestone street. "I'll get ya there boss, no worries."

Vicki sat back in the rickshaw listening to the wheels crunch and crack against the cobblestone until the stone path turned to dirt and grass. The lights of the rickety goblin town disappeared behind them and a stretch of dark woods covered the night sky as they went on. Large dark crimson apples hung off of the tree branches, Vicki reached up to grab one as they rolled onward. The dark, wild woods began clearing out as Jerry huffed along the uphill trek, taking them through rows and rows of an old overgrown apple orchard.

Vicki bit into the dark fruit with a loud crunch, the trees around them began shrieking and shaking their branches. The apple was overly sweet, the flavor reminiscent of a stale lime flavored marshmallow, and the flesh inside a dark glittering orange. Too hungry to throw the strange fruit overboard, she continued snacking on the apple hoping that the rest of the orchard trees wouldn't attack them.

"Never seen anyone eat one of em raw like that, you're straight savage, boss!" Jerry mooed out into a chuckle. "Vampples ain't ripe til October, food's in the house once we get there if you're still hungry."

"Vampples?" Vicki examined the fruit more closely, its orange core began to seep a dark goopy red. She gagged and threw the apple out into the darkness, the fruit splattered against a gravestone leaving a trail of dark red juice as it slid down to the ground.

They rolled through a large hilly graveyard where somber skeletons and spectral phantoms moved around in the shadows. Something groaned far away in the tall grass and thickets. Vines and thorny growths wrapped around some of the graves as fog rose up from the moist loose soil. The rickshaw's wheels slopped over the soil and over the vines, while Jerry crunched through the thorns without much worry.

"They call it the graveyard of If Only," said Jerry as they hurried along. "They're a bunch of donuts, don't even look at 'em."

The rickshaw continued out of the misty graveyard and up a path that took them near the top of the mountainside. The winding path became rocky and quite bumpy. The rickshaw jostled left and right until they turned a corner on the path finding themselves on smoother ground again. They passed a few weeping willows and old twisted trees, finally crossing over into the courtyard of the mansion.

The Athenaeum stood stark white and gray against the dark mountainside. The moonlight hit its many arched windows and its marble Corinthian pillars making the mansion glow in the night. Two large red doors sat in the middle of the building surrounded by ivy that crawled up the outer walls of the mansion. Sheets of moss cascaded down from the main porch awning swinging softly in the night air.

The three storied mansion had one great tower to its right side with a smaller one to its left, the building leaned so heavily to the right that Vicki wondered about its structural safety. Bats came flying up from the old domed top of the roof vanishing into the night sky and leaving a trail of guano on the broken violet tile work. The main porch wrapped most of the way around the building spanning all the way to the left of the huge mansion where a large garage sat hidden behind some dead oak trees. The top of the mansion had a large and precarious telescope poking out from its roof. The hanging moss reached out toward the two of them, caught in a strange breeze that blew out from the mansion walls.

The rickshaw came to a stop and Vicki climbed out. She looked up at the huge red doors and gave a shiver. The ivy rustled and shrank back from the door. The wooden porch creaked, its boards sinking down in front of her. The entire mansion groaned as the girl approached, the arched windows lit up for a brief moment as she put a foot on the first step up to the Athenaeum.

"Dat's a relief. The lights have gone dim ever since your gramp's been out," Jerry said, as he continued further down the yard taking the rickshaw away. "I was worried for a tick. Thought you wasn't witch wise for sure!" He disappeared behind the pillars of the massive mansion.

Vicki crept up the porch to the large red doors. She gulped down her fear, spinning the ring around her thumb. She put her hand up to the pull chain strangled by the ivy and prepared to give it a tug.

"You can do this." Vicki said to herself. "For Mom and Dad and Max." She pulled the rope and a loud gong echoed throughout the massive mansion.

Chapter seven

A lanky teenage girl dressed in a tattered French maid's outfit threw the doors open before the gong even stopped its ringing. She stared down at Vicki with mismatched eyes, the left eye being blue and her right being dark brown. Her body was covered in large stitches that connected a jigsaw pattern of multiple flesh tones along her arms and face. Her wild fluffy white hair and the large goggles that she wore around her neck would have been at home on a mad scientist. The girl's striking green lipstick glinted as she shot Vicki a curt smile.

Before Vicki could even open her mouth to speak, the tall girl grabbed her roughly by the shoulders, pulling her into the mansion, and kicking the large doors closed behind them. She pushed Vicki onward through the main entrance of the Athenaeum, a tall opulent room with an old style caged elevator at its center and a wooden staircase that wrapped itself along the paneled wall. The walls stretched far up into impenetrable darkness, as none of the lights in the mansion seemed to be in good working order.

The entrance was decorated with an ancient statue of Medusa standing over a carved out bookshelf lined with marble scrolls and tomes. Pans and nymphs lined the woodwork leading to the hall, frolicking and dragging a long papyrus scroll out behind them. The black and white tiled floor squeaked under Vicki's running shoes. The teenage patchwork girl led Vicki past the foyer of the Athenaeum and into the main hall where the clean tile work gave way to creaking old floor boards. The walls here were much darker, adorned in paintings that couldn't quite be made out as the inner mansion sat in near pitch darkness.

"I am literally having a heart attack," cried the lanky girl. She huffed along and murmured with her thick Queens New York accent. "I've been through two already! One of them was even new!"

"Hi, I'm here about the Housekeeper," began Vicki as she was pushed through the dark main hall of the Athenaeum.

"Boy you'd better be, or I'm out of a job!" The stitch work girl pushed Vicki further along the main hall. Lamps stuck out all along the wall and reflected their weak gas light on the floor, each flittering dimly as the two girls approached straining to light the path forward. The room came to an abrupt end and split off in three directions. Two of the dark hallways broke off to either end of the mansion while the third opened up into a large dark square room. "We can't even get the toilets to flush without you!"

"What?" Vicki stopped and faced the taller stitched up girl. "I'm not a plumber, and where are you taking me?"

"To the dining room, duh!" The lanky girl continued shoving Vicki down the darkened hallway. "You've got a job to do, shortbread, and you better believe that you're gonna do it!"

The two of them hurried into a noisy square dining room. Many elderly goblins along with other small creatures sat together at large ornate tables mumbling and chatting with one another about the cold temperature in the mansion. A few of the old goblins turned in their seats, gasping at the girl in the scarlet hoodie and bright pink shoes. Soon all of the residents had turned to look at Vicki, and they began bickering amongst themselves.

A tall handsome man with pale brown skin and a meticulously groomed goatee approached Vicki and the lanky teenage girl. His large friendly eyes lit up as he grinned at the two of them. He tipped his red beret to one side as he approached with his arms outstretched. His red and white suit had been dirtied by blue glowing fingerprints and his shoes were covered in flour. He stood in front of the girls with his hands on his hips smiling at them revealing the two sharp elongated fangs in his mouth. Vicki recoiled as he drew near seeing that his skin had undertones of gray, of dead flesh at those thinnest parts of his body.

"Hey," he began, sounding overly cheerful. "There she is! Our new Housekeeper! Let's all welcome..." The vampire motioned over to the lanky girl with a snap of his fingers.

Vicki slid the backpack from her shoulders to the ground with a loud thud. "Vicki. My name is Vicki," she said, "and I'm only here for a couple of days." The lights in the dining hall dimmed further and the residents cried out.

The dapper man put a hand to his chest. "Vicki," he repeated, as he motioned for the lanky girl covered in stitches to join him. "Vicki? Not Magra?"

"That's my cousin," Vicki said, as she looked around the dining hall. The goblins stared back at her. A few smiled through the darkness while others glared.

The man in the red beret and the lanky girl exchanged some heated whispers before she stormed off through some swinging doors at the opposite end of the dining room. The man in the red and white suit turned his attention back to Vicki. He sniffed the air then gave a concerned look to her. "That's great, and just to reaffirm here, you are *the* Housekeeper?"

"Only for a few days, my grandpa left it all in his will, but they're going to choose someone better later." Vicki rubbed her arms and breathed out into the chilly air. "It's all a mistake."

One of the goblins shrieked out with laughter and she wheeled herself back around to face the wall. Soon the entire dining hall was alive with chatter and giggling. The man turned around to the crowd of residents shushing them. He waved his hands out in front of him edging closer to Vicki.

"Okay, okay, we've got this handled! You all enjoy a pudding or some brains, and me and *Vicki* here are gonna have a little powwow, it's all good!" He put a hand on Vicki's shoulder bending down to face her. "Okay sweet corn, what do you mean, this is all a mistake? Is there someone from Wands and Warlocks on their merry way?" The man sniffed the air again staring at Vicki.

Vicki shied away from the man's fangs. She took a loud swallow before speaking. "Well, my aunt, Zaldehyde? She kinda maybe messed with my grandpa's will, and she put me in the will as the next Housekeeper. Except I'm too young to work here, and I can't do magic like my cousin can." Vicki stared at his sharp canines.

The vampire stumbled and looked as if he was about to faint. He removed his beret to reveal a perfectly groomed head of short, slightly graying hair and put a hand up to his forehead, trying to stand up straight as he loosened his tie. "Hold on hold on, just hold on for a second here," he said, going over to a table and loudly dragging a chair back with him. He plopped down onto the chair in front of Vicki, scooting close to her. "Just, let's back up here, you can't do magic as good as your cousin can do- or do you mean that you can't do any magic at all?"

Vicki gave him a grimace. "Uhm, I c-can't do any magic." She looked at the crest fallen vampire and frowned. She pulled her hoodie down tightly over her pigtail trying to sound hopeful as she spoke. "But, but the real Housekeeper will be here just as soon as I'm gone!" The lights fizzled and grew dimmer all around the dining room, the goblins all groaned out in unison.

"Well, that doesn't help us much right now." The vampire leaned forward in his chair, Vicki recoiled a bit. "See, the lights and the furnace, the plumbing, all that good stuff? It runs off of magic, and the guy that controls the magic around here is you, kiddo."

"I'm sorry," exclaimed Vicki.

The vampire raised an eyebrow at her. "For what?" he asked sitting back.

"For not being able to do magic... I guess..."

The vampire crossed his arms, squinting at Vicki. "It ain't like you weren't born a high witch on purpose, it's alright." He was suddenly walking Vicki forward and placing her backpack upon her shoulder in one lightning fast movement, startling her so much that she let out a yelp. "Now, you keep that not doing magic yet thing out of your head, you might just be a late broomer. Plenty of good witches are, we'll figure something out to get the lights back on until then. It'll probably be a little weird, maybe even a little grotesque, but it'll work."

Vicki seized up as the vampire walked her towards two large swinging doors covered in red and black stains. "Wait, I'm not sure that you get it, I'm not a witch at all, and where are we going..." Vicki planted her feet to the floor. "What is this?!"

"The kitchen. We've got about forty goblins and other assorted hungry mouths to feed out there, and we ain't got the magic ovens, so..." He shoved Vicki through the doors.

She went stumbling into the darkened cooking space followed closely by the vampire. The lanky stitchwork girl in the maid outfit sat at a candlelit table inside the large brick and cobblestone kitchen, frantically putting together what Vicki thought might be sandwiches. The platter on the table before her didn't appear to be entirely edible. The taller girl slapped random slices of raw meat, green cheese, and bits of old splintered wood together onto moldy bread. The girl gave a disingenuous grin to Vicki and returned her focus to the culinary monstrosities. The vampire appeared behind the stitch work girl moving with such speed and silence that it made Vicki jump.

"Introductions," said the vampire as he loosened his tie and began to roll up his sleeves. He put a hand on his chest and shot a toothy grin at Vicki as he spoke. "Desmond, I'm the assistant general nurse. Do you know what that means?"

"Sure, I know what a nurse does! My mom is the nurse practitioner at one of the retirement communities in my town. So you're basically in charge of the medical stuff around here, right?"

"No, it means I run around and make sure the residents don't electrocute each other, eat each other, or eat the wrong pills," said Desmond as he put his hands on the lanky stitch work girl's shoulders. "And would you believe it, the currently suspended head nurse is right here!"

"Frank," said the lanky girl in the maid outfit. She slapped Desmond's hands away and shoved a platter full of disgusting sandwiches at him, then turned her full attention to Vicki, narrowing her eyes. "And I'm not allowed around any of the medical stuff. Anymore. For a while."

Desmond motioned for Vicki to sit down at the table, leaving back out of the swinging doors as he spoke. "Be nice, Frank," he said, only half jokingly.

Frank made a little heart with her hands and quickly turned the heart shape into a double thumbs down. The taller girl with the patchwork skin looked down at Vicki and sighed out. She shoved a pile of dried bread and some of the slices of unidentifiable fillings at Vicki. Vicki shifted her backpack off of her shoulders and opened her mouth to make small talk, opting instead to begin the sandwich making, spying the way that Frank squinted at her with unmasked distaste. The two girls sat in the candlelight silently and hastily making sandwiches until the swinging doors opened again.

Vicki looked up to see a completely different person backing into the doors with arms full of little boxes. She got up to help the mustachioed chubby man with his burden and he made a surprised little gasp. The man smiled down at her from behind his full mustache and rosy cheeks. Vicki thought that he looked a lot like the cartoon chef mascot of various canned pastas. He was so pale that he was almost literally white.

"Thank you very much, just don't drop them. Terrible mess if they get out." The chubby man with the mustache had a prim and proper English accent, sounding much the same as her grandfather. He led Vicki over to a counter extending a hand to her. "You must be the new Housekeeper! My name is Belvedere."

"Vicki." She shook his hand. "I'm only the Housekeeper for a couple of days, I'm not really supposed to be here, I think my grandpa meant for my cousin to be the Housekeeper instead."

"Well I certainly hope not," said Belvedere as he gave her a warm smile. "You're a far more welcomed sight than any of those awful cousins of yours. Meaning no offense of course, are you close with them?"

"Not really, I only met one of them today. I don't know her that well… I think she maybe helped my aunt turn my mom my dad and my brother into pigs."

"Hmm, sounds typical." He began to carefully open one of his small boxes. "Your aunt once turned poor Jerry into a handsome prince. Now he's that unfortunate looking red beast that you might have seen skulking around outside."

Frank burst out into a fit of giggles covering her mouth with her gigantic meat cleaver. Belvedere shook his head at her and she returned a grin to him. She went back to chopping her macabre sandwiches into their respective piles.

"Oh I met Jerry, he gave me the ride up here," said Vicki as she turned her attention back to Belvedere. "They really turned him into a prince? Why is he a cow now, what was he before?"

"Basically a frog," said Frank as she popped a stray bit of meat into her mouth. "If you axed me, that big Amazon was on to something good. I think it was a public service giving our eyes a rest like that."

"It wasn't very funny for him, Frank, not one bit!" Belvedere glared at the girl, opening his box and sticking his tongue out in disgust at the contents. "Well these are fresh, no doubt. Jerry is our groundskeeper, so to speak. He keeps the pond full of moss and algae, and beautifies the trees and bushes for the residents."

"You mean those creepy looking twisty trees out there? He made them look like that on purpose?" asked Vicki as she took a peek inside one of the boxes. She let out a whimper dropping the box back onto the counter backing away from the horrible oozing blob inside. "Omigod what is that thing?"

Desmond came sliding in through the swinging doors, stopping at the counter in front of Belvedere. He smiled down at the little creature inside of the box wiggling his fingers at it. The thing in the box squelched around, making a high pitched squeak at him.

"Oooh, who's the tastiest little guy? It's you! It's you," sang Desmond, as he poked at the box. "You're going to be sooooo tasty!"

"Vicki wants to know what's in the box," said Frank as she slammed her cleaver into a sandwich. "What's in the box, Dez?"

Desmond straightened up and grabbed one of the boxes as he spoke. "These are… these things, Vicki, everyone knows what these things are. You've never had one of these before?" He held the open box towards her jiggling the little bluish mound of sentient jelly at her. "It's mood food. Ain't you never had one of these around the holidays?"

"N-No, I've only ever eaten normal food, until I got here," she stammered out. "I've never seen anything like that!"

Belvedere raised an eyebrow and cleared his throat. He began removing the little babbling creatures from their boxes and placing them onto plates. Frank stopped her chopping and leaned back in her seat to listen. Desmond gave a quick glance to both of his coworkers. He frowned and tapped his fingers on the countertop, giving Vicki an appraising stare. He took a huge sniff of the air and bit his lip as he spoke.

"*Got here* as in Everfall?" Desmond asked.

"As in Äther, I'm from Earth... I mean Earthside, isn't that how you say it?"

"Earthside, okay." Desmond put his hand to his forehead again. "Frank, how's them sandwiches coming?"

"Peachy," Frank replied flatly. She made a funny little noise under her breath and went back to the mutilation of her sandwiches.

The mood in the kitchen had changed. Vicki could sense that the three others were surprised at how unprepared she actually was for the role of Housekeeper. She shivered from both the cold air in the kitchen and the anxiety in the room. The awkward moment stretched on for a few more moments before Vicki finally spoke up again.

"I'm sorry," she said. "I thought maybe you all knew that already. I guess not."

Belvedere held out a little blob on a plate for Vicki to take. "We're not really in the loop of information around here." He put the plate in Vicki's waiting hands along with a fork. "I'm just the cook, Desmond is a nurse in title only, and Frank should have been fired years ago."

"Fair's fair," said Frank, as she gave one final whack of the cleaver into her pile of sandwiches.

"I'm not hungry," Vicki said politely refusing the fork. "I ate an apple on the way here. I think I'm good, thank you."

"One cannot live strictly on apples and sweets, I speak from personal experience. Now try it." Belvedere pushed the plate and fork back at her. "You'll be pleasantly surprised and you may want to learn to love it as we don't have much else here at the moment."

Vicki shuddered and took a large gulp of air. The little chortling blob made a rudimentary face of sorts looking up to her. It looked just as pensive as she felt. The blob chirped out a series of wet peeping sounds and dissolved into a puddle. Vicki covered her mouth heaving.

"I can't eat this, it still has a face," she exclaimed. Vicki's stomach turned and she gagged. The blob on her plate rumbled erupting with liquid from its center. The sight was too much for her, she gagged again this time pushing the plate far away from her.

"Oh lord, here it comes," said Desmond. He grabbed his next platter of sandwiches before disappearing through the swinging doors.

Belvedere held a waste basket out in front of Vicki. She grabbed the basket from him, gagging and trying not to think about the little gelatinous mess, but as she looked over at the plate it began mimicking her. The little blob copied her face, letting loose with a torrent of jelly from its mouth making little burbling screaming noises as it began to vomit out its own insides. Vicki lost the battle and she too emptied her insides into the waste basket.

"Good! Get it all out," said Belvedere as he gave her a pat on the back. "I have a terrible notion that you're going to struggle with the salad as well."

"It's fine as long as you wipe the slime off the tentacles," said Frank, unaffected by Vicki's retching. "I'm just joshin' ya, there's no tentacles in the salad! Gawd, can you imagine? Putting a raw tentacle on a salad? How could you even eat it without the bile?"

Vicki heaved again and sobbing out, she shouted at the patchwork girl, "Omigod can you please stop?!"

The lights in the kitchen fizzled and buzzed to life, illuminating the room for a quick moment. Cheers came from the other side of the swinging doors, the kitchen appliances sputtered and powered on. The brief surge came to an abrupt end and the house returned to darkness. The goblins from the other side of the door all groaned out again.

"We had a bit of power from that just now." Belvedere gave Vicki a gentle pat on her shoulder. "Isn't that interesting," he said as he handed a towel to Vicki.

The swinging doors flew open and Desmond came bounding into the kitchen. He searched for another platter of sandwiches, staring at Frank. Frank huffed and returned to her table to finish the makeshift dinner service. Desmond turned his attention to Vicki and Belvedere.

"What was that buzz about," asked Desmond. "It's like we had some real power there for a second!"

"I think that was Vicki." Belvedere gently ushered Vicki forward then retreated back into the storage area of the kitchen. He grabbed some of the tiny mood food boxes speaking as he disappeared into a walk in cooler, "I think there's at least a little bit of magic in those bones! We may have hot water yet."

Desmond scratched his chin looking at the sickly girl in front of him, taking great care when gazing at her head. "Got kind of a big forehead, but I think it can work with that," he said as he grabbed onto one of her hands, lifting her arm up to the shoulder. "I bet you're exactly goblin sized."

Vicki slapped Desmond's hand away and felt at her forehead. "What do you mean *I have a big forehead?* I do not!" She frowned.

"It's a little large," Frank offered up from her table as she smacked another sandwich in half with her cleaver. "He's got an eye for heads."

"Yeah, yeah! I think we have exactly what you need, just got to remember where it is." Desmond made a frame with his hands looking through at Vicki. "At least it might help you to keep the lights on, I'll look for it after you give your address."

Vicki's eyes widened and she clenched up. "My address? You mean like a speech?"

"It'll be easy, just tell them all your name and give them some kind of rundown about how you're going to keep the place up and going," said Desmond. He took a monogrammed white handkerchief from his suit pocket, embroidered with the golden initials DJ, and dabbed it to his forehead. "Just, you know, maybe leave that part out about not being able to do magic yet."

"Well, then what should I tell them, about the lights and the furnaces and that stuff?"

Frank finished her last sandwich and stood up from the table as she spoke. "You could always tell them that the parts are coming, or that the house ate a plumber again."

Vicki stared wide eyed at the stitchwork girl. "The house eats people?"

Desmond pulled Vicki away towards the swinging kitchen doors, pushing her forward into the dining room. "It's more like a very enthusiastic nibble, it hasn't ever actually *eaten* eaten anyone," he said as they entered into the dimly lit room full of goblins and several other odd creatures. "Except for the safe housing inspector, but she don't really count. That witch had it coming."

Chapter eight

Vicki stood at the front of the room, petrified more from the thought of speaking in public than at the terrifying monsters sitting before her. She tensed up, turning away from the crowd of goblins and frowned up at the vampire next to her. The doors to the kitchen swung open as Frank and Belvedere came out with arms full of mood food platters. Vicki took a few quick breaths, turning back to the room full of monsters.

One of the goblins wheeled herself closer to the action, nearly knocking a few of the other residents over in her zeal to see the new girl. An elderly, shaky ape creature brought a wavering hand up to his extremely large ear, cupping his fingers around to have a better listen, while a fat old lizard man simply clicked his tongue in disapproval before returning to his ratty old scroll. A table of glowing ghostly figures hovered staring at Vicki with their dark empty hollows.

"Hi..." began Vicki as her veins turned to ice. She froze staring at the weird creatures before her, breathing in shallow breaths as they all closed in on her position. The elderly goblin in the wheelchair stared up at her smiling a big crooked grin. The large ape creature now cupped two hands around his one ear, quite annoyed with the quiet girl at the front of the room. Another little old goblin crossed his arms glaring at Vicki.

"I've got peanut shells in my pockets older than you," shouted the little old goblin man. He huffed and stomped his little foot. "Get on with it! Most of us are on borrowed time as it is!"

Vicki trembled, trying to control her stage fright. "I-I, I'm Vicki, Vicki Voland. I'm taking over for my grandpa, I'm the new Housekeeper!" The goblins grew quiet. "I can't turn the lights on yet I'm sorry!"

"You're not Zaldehyde's daughter?" asked one of the goblins out in the crowd of dark figures.

"No, I'm sorry, there was like a clerical error or something with my grandpa's will!" Vicki tried to regain her composure. "I'm only temporary! B-but I'm going to do what I can until someone better comes along."

"How long will that be?" One of the goblins poked his floppy ears up above the crowd. "I can't see anyfing going on round here!"

"You're half blind already, what does it matter?!" The goblins all started muttering and arguing with one another, their squeaky voices raised and became more and more panicked. "Let the girl talk!"

Desmond stepped forward and tried to calm the crowd. "Everyone, it's going to be alright, we've been through stickier situations than a new Housekeeper over the years!" He gave Vicki a pat on the head. "And she's working on getting everything up and running, we're just getting a few odds and ends in order, that's all!"

"What sort of odds and ends," demanded one of the tiny old goblins. "It's gettin' right frigid in here!"

"What *can* she do," asked a large hunched over furry creature with glowing yellow eyes. "What sort of witchery can't even make the lights turn on?"

Desmond cleared his throat, he put his hands up and sighed. "I said *we're working on it!* We'll have the lights on by tonight!" He shot a quick glance over to Vicki. "Isn't that a fact," he asked as he gave her a little nudge.

"Uhm, I..." Vicki looked out over the befuddled and angry elderly monsters, making an audible gulp. "We will!"

The residents of the Athenaeum all took to chattering among themselves. Desmond motioned for Frank and Belvedere to distribute their nasty platters. The various goblins and assorted creatures began taking their seats at the large dark tables lit by flickering candles. Desmond put a hand on Vicki's shoulder attempting an awkward show of support.

"That could have gone worse," he said adjusting his tie. He tilted his beret to the other side of his head and pointed Vicki in the direction of an empty table. "You go take a seat, don't worry about helping these two, just sit down."

Vicki bit her lip and left his side without so much as a word. She could feel her face radiating heat as she made her way to the empty table lit by one particularly dim candle. She could sense that many if not all of those little goblin eyes were watching her, following her slow walk with contempt. If not contempt then at least disappointment. She plopped down into the chair at the table with her back to the room, staring at the candle.

The little old goblin in the wheelchair squeaked her way to the side of the table, greeting Vicki in person. She grabbed on to one of Vicki's sleeves shaking it with vigor. "It's so nice to meet you dear, we're so glad that you're here! Your grandad talked about you all of the time!"

"He did?" Vicki asked, genuinely surprised. She smiled back at the little old goblin and tried to keep from wincing at the proximity of her horrid little sharp fangs.

The little goblin lady leaned in close, patting Vicki's hand as she spoke. "Oh yes, yes! You're the one that paints! I've never seen such pretty pastas!"

"Oh... thank you, and it's nice to meet you too," said Vicki, her voice starting to break. She steadied herself and covered her mouth with one hand, shutting her eyes tightly and swallowing down her fear. The little old goblin's eyes put a shiver down Vicki's spine, her two dark pools of blood danced around in those sunken eye sockets reflecting the candle light in a most unnatural way.

"I'm Mrs. Klobbreak," the little old goblin chirped out with a kindly voice. "You mustn't worry dear, every Housekeeper is new at their job for a few days! Even your grandad!" Mrs. Klobbreak gave Vicki another smile and began to wheel herself back to the horde of other goblins. "You'll do fine dear, keep your chin up!"

Vicki watched the old goblin lady go and breathed out a small sigh of relief. At least one of the residents wasn't *completely* dissatisfied with her. The little goblin disappeared into the crowded tables just as Frank came sauntering back carelessly swinging her empty platters around beside her as she went. She sat down across from Vicki letting the platters fall down onto the floor. They clanged against each other, making the residents call out in protest.

Frank leaned back in her seat, setting her gaze upon the smaller girl on the other side of the table. She ruffled her mess of white fluffy hair and in a matter-of-fact tone said, "I don't really like you all that much."

Vicki scowled at the stitchwork girl. "What! You don't even know me! Why do you hate me?"

"I didn't say that I hate you, I just don't like you much," Frank said as she tugged at one of her many stitchings. The long cable that zig zagged around her shoulder and upper arm tightened the patches of blue and green flesh. "Not yet, I mean. Sorry, I get my order of operations messed up sometimes, it's my brains."

Vicki stared at the stitchwork girl, her mouth open in shock as she watched Frank tug on another cable within her neck. She looked on with concern as the cable slid around under the girl's multicolored skins, cinching them all together. Frank looked up from her work then adjusted her collar so that Vicki could no longer see the seam around her neck.

Vicki cleared her throat and shuddered. "What about your brains?" she blurted out, beginning to feel dizzy. "I- I mean," she tried to make some sensible conversation but fell silent. She placed a hand over her mouth and gagged, looking away from the taller teenage girl.

Frank crossed her arms and a silence ensued from both girls, both of them avoiding any eye contact until at last she gave Vicki a glance before adjusting the cables once more. "Well, most of my brains are from Brooklyn, but the fly by night that slapped me together dropped em-"

"You mean your brains? Someone dropped your brains?" Vicki's eyes widened at the thought of bubbling jars filled with human brains. "Did it hurt?"

Frank hissed out in annoyance, "No, ya dumdum, I wasn't even baking in the oven yet." She rolled her eyes yanking on her stitching. Her arm snapped backward and she gave herself a pat on the elbow. She looked back in Vicki's direction then turned her attention to the stitching in her legs. "Anyways, most of my brains are from a girl in Brooklyn that went to juvie but they jellied the talking parts. So they just glued on some spare brains from a goody two shoes in Queens and called it good."

"You have two different brains from two different people? Do they, like, fight or something," asked Vicki.

"No I just say stupid things *very* stupidly sometimes," Frank said as she tugged one last cable into place. "So *I don't like you all that much, yet,* but you're just starting so who knows. You might grow on me. Like a cyst."

Vicki furrowed her brow and sat back in her chair. "But why don't you like me?"

"Don't ax me, shortcake, you're just not very likable for some reason!" Frank threw her arms up into a shrug. "You look like you're always about to scream or cry or something. Makes it tough to like ya, that's all."

Vicki grumbled, turning in her seat to avoid anymore abuse from the other girl, just in time to see Belvedere approaching with a platter full of those awful sandwiches and jiggly blobs. She grimaced at the sight of the food and turned back, choosing to stare at the candle instead. The candle flickered wildly and Desmond suddenly sat down next to Frank, looking back and forth between the two girls with a grin upon his face.

Belvedere placed the platter down onto the table sitting next to Vicki. "You look to be getting along with each other," he said as he offered a sandwich to her.

Vicki recoiled from the sandwich. "Uhm, how are we going to turn on the lights exactly," she asked turning her gaze over to Desmond, ignoring the nasty food.

Desmond reached under the table and produced a pointed hat with a wide stiff brim at its base. It looked like a cheap Halloween witch's costume hat only made of much more ragged material. He placed the hat on the table in front of Vicki edging it toward her.

"Huzzah! Now, this cone of locus ought to do the trick. It *will* do the trick, over time, but there's kind of a catch." Desmond loosened his tie and cleared his throat. "You have to focus really hard with this thing on your head, when you're actually using it. If you let your mind wander too much with this thing on, it's liable to broadcast what you're thinking about to everyone around you. Every weird idea, dirty thoughts, everything."

Vicki looked up from the hat with clenched teeth. "What? You mean like literally? It can literally show people what I'm thinking about?" She gently pushed the hat away. "*Oh sure*, like that's not weird! I don't want people seeing my thoughts! Talk about an invasion of privacy!"

"Well either we're gonna put a cone of locus on top of that head of yours, and it'll unlock some sleeping magic for us, or we're going to have to smother you in ectoplasm." Desmond clenched his fist. "Ain't no magic that a bathtub full of ectoplasm can't bring out, at least for a few days!"

"Ectoplasm?" Vicki looked back and forth between Belvedere and Desmond. "Is that the gross dead ghost stuff? I'm not getting any of that stuff anywhere on me!"

"You won't have to, I'm sure that the cone of locus will work," Belvedere said with a calming tone. He slid one of the mood food blobs towards her. "*If* you stay well nourished and well rested, you should be able to focus on your locus *without* any silly hat."

The sounds of the goblins munching away on their sandwiches and the clatter of forks against plates filled her ears as Vicki stared down at the blob. She focused on the little gelatinous thing whimpering out when it formed a rudimentary face returning her distasteful look back to her. She snatched a fork from the table and held it in her shaking hand. Vicki aimed the prongs of the fork down to the little quivering blob.

"Gah! I can't!" She dropped the fork back onto the table and covered her mouth. "I just can't!"

Belvedere took the mood food back. "Then you had just better wear that hat and hope that you can find more pie and candies to live off of, otherwise I'm afraid it's the ghost bath."

Desmond tapped the table in front of Vicki. "Don't sweat it yet, we're not just gonna toss you in or anything, that hat is gonna work. You just gotta believe." He adjusted his collar and sat back. "I mean you ain't gonna fly over night, but it'll do."

Vicki grabbed the hat from in front of her, lowering it to her head. It felt rather heavy but the brim fit nicely around her ears and forehead. She took a feel around the point of the hat at its top, instantly thinking of her aunt. The real witches weren't as fun and this hat was not at all flattering to the size of her head.

"Nothing's happening," Vicki observed, as she fiddled with the tilt of her new hat. "What if it doesn't work on me? My mom said that we weren't born with magic, what if I'm just normal?"

Desmond clicked his tongue, looking around at the still dim lamps of the dining room. "Sweet corn, ain't no way that anyone in your granddaddy's family came out *normal*. I had kind of hoped for fireworks, but you're still pretty young. It's just gonna take a while that's all, just focus on making things brighter for a start."

"It sure is big," Vicki complained as she tilted the hat backward, letting it rest at a skewed angle.

Frank leaned in giving Vicki a big smile. "And it's just so fashionable too!" She raised her hand just a little above Vicki's head. "At least it adds a few inches up there."

Belvedere chuckled, biting into one of the mood foods. It squelched and wiggled around on his fork. Vicki turned away from the sight, bringing her hands up to her ears as the blob began squealing. The color drained out of her face and she took a few deep breaths. She could feel the room start to spin around her again, and she teetered in her seat until Desmond steadied her by the shoulder.

"Let's get you settled into your room before you keel over," said Desmond. He motioned for Frank to help her up to her feet. "If you're gonna flop around, might as well be on your own bed."

Vicki was led down the dark corridors of the Athenaeum and up to the third story somewhere in one of the corners of the great mansion. She was given a candle to light her way following closely behind Desmond and Frank. The two of them chatted and bickered over things that Vicki found too difficult to keep up with. There were concerns of duties and schedules, talk of the *legal department* with Frank looking back at Vicki every now and then as they spoke in hushed tones.

"Did you hear what I just said," asked Desmond. He snapped his fingers in front of Vicki's face. "I wrote down all of your schedule before you got here so we can start filling you in on how to do the housekeeping tomorrow."

Vicki gave him a few quick nods. "Okay," she replied with a heavy yawn. She rubbed her eyes and frowned. "I don't know why I'm even tired. I slept on the bus all the way here!"

Desmond stopped before a large oak door motioning to it for Vicki. "Mind burst. Probably means that the hat is working." He waved his hand onward showing Vicki the way into her new room. "We're gonna give that cone of locus a little while longer to get going. Don't worry about the lights tonight, just get rested and meet me after breakfast tomorrow."

Vicki peered into the room, glancing over at the antique rotary phone sitting on the darkened desk against the wall. "Can I make a call on that?"

Desmond gave her a shrug. "Making a call to Earthside? I guess you can try, ought to be enough juice to at least make a collect call."

Frank pulled Vicki into the room, throwing her arms around in various directions. "There's your bathroom, it's small. There's your bed, it's smaller, and there's your cabinet. Don't touch the art or the statues." With that she stormed off, grabbing at Desmond's suit as she went.

"We'll see you tomorrow," Desmond called out as Frank dragged him away.

Vicki could hear Frank's voice rise as she and Desmond disappeared down the hallway, the light from their own candles vanishing in the shadows of the long corridor. She could make an educated guess that the tall girl in stitches was giving a piece of her mind to the vampire. No one seemed terribly impressed with Vicki. She sighed and turned her attention back to the room, holding her candle high in front of her.

The scent of the cherry pipe tobacco that her grandfather had so often smoked on his few and far between visits to her home drifted through the darkness. She stepped deeper into the room letting her eyes adjust to what little light her candle cast forth. Creaking along the polished hardwood floor she brought the light up to the walls. They were adorned with an old raspberry colored wall paper in a dark lattice pattern and although the walls showed their age, Vicki felt that they were sturdy and crafted with the greatest workmanship of the era.

Her candle flickered and the hallway behind her sent a slight chill down her back, even through her hoodie. She cleared her throat then made her way to her new bed and dresser, taking her small backpack of belongings with her as she went. Vicki placed the candle down in front of the dresser and stared into the mirror hanging just above. She found it odd that the mirror was exactly at her height when her grandfather absolutely towered over most people.

The entire room looked more comfortable for someone her size in fact, and even the old dusty Victorian era bed seemed scaled down just for her. She wondered if maybe the whole room had magically shrunken itself down just for her arrival. That would have seemed fanciful or silly to her just a few days prior. Now nothing was too improbable.

She stumbled her way over to the old rotary phone pressing down on the numbers within the dial in an effort to contact Max back home. The numbers would not depress, try as hard as she might. It took Vicki a full ten minutes to work out how to use the dial; the spinning motion took an incredibly long time to execute and it nearly brought her to further despair. Finally the line clicked to life and a monotonous voice came from the other end.

"Earthbound numbers are subject to Earth tax. Connecting to your party."

Vicki twirled the springy coiled telephone cord in her fingers waiting for the call to go through, she exhaled with relief at the sound of the dial tone and the ringer. The call clicked through and Vicki gripped the cord tightly around her hand. "Max! Max, I made it to the place, I'm here and alive!"

Max gave a whoop of joy, his voice came over the line sounding distant and tinny. "That's great, I knew you could do it Vicki, I knew it! Are you okay, are you scared?" The phone line cut out and sputtered. "-because it's not, it's okay if you are."

"The call is dropping, I can barely hear you!" Vicki bit her lip, shining her candle around the dark room. "I... I feel weird here, it's so dark and the people are strange... I think that the nurse is a vampire too..."

"Are they treating you okay? The lawyer said you have to..." The phone line filled with static electricity and popping. "You have to be hired I guess, I don't know." Max sighed out from the other end of the line.

"I think I already am, the monster people made me give a speech and everything... I don't think they like me very much." Vicki pressed her ear tightly against the telephone speaker. The popping became louder and louder. "Can you hear me?"

Max replied with some words but his voice was too distant now to hear. "-again tomorrow, see if it's better!" He yelled through the line. "Stay safe okay?" Max shouted into the phone his voice drifted out with the waves of static.

"Max?" The phone line went quiet and the call clicked to an end.

Vicki replaced the phone in its cradle and sat down on the smallish creaking bed. The four posts of the opulent bed frame seemed to bend inward as she put her full weight down in the middle. The springs inside the old dusty mattress gave way with a loud crunch and a slight groan. She shifted uneasily waiting for the imminent collapse of the bed frame, for the terrifying fall to the floor, but it never came. The bed, its dark wooden four post frame, and the heavy drapery attached to the mattress all seemed to give out a collective sigh of relief.

Vicki gave a reassuring pat to the mattress, musing that the bed might have a personality as well. She scanned around the room as her eyes finally adjusted to the darkness, staring wide eyed at the various statues and paintings of religious icons hidden on the walls and in the shadows. She became more and more paranoid as she inspected her new sleeping space.

Crucifixes and strange metal shapes littered the walls of the room, an oil painting of Jesus praying near the sea gave off an especially eerie feeling, and a multiple armed elephant on a sequined tapestry seemed to avert its eyes whenever she looked at it. She carefully stood up from the bed and moved closer to the elephant staring at its eyes to make sure that she wasn't just imagining its movement. Vicki reached out and slid her fingers down the colorful threads of the wall hanging.

"It's very rude to stare," shouted the elephant on the tapestry.

Chapter nine

Vicki let out a shriek, falling down into the creaky old bed and hiding herself beneath the blankets. The paintings and various statues around the room began chuckling and conversing with one another, taking great amusement in her terror. She trembled, covering her ears and hoping against hope that it was all a terrible nightmare, that she would awaken at any moment safe and sound back in her own room.

The oil painting of Jesus rolled his eyes and leaned against a stone resting his chin upon his praying hands. "Of course she's going to stare at you, everyone stares at you! Look at all of those hands you've got, who needs that many hands?"

"Oh just say what you want to say, just say it! Say *she's staring at you because you're a big freaky elephant*," the tapestry barked back.

"You don't know that I was going to say that, when have I ever said that?"

A painting of a tentacle-faced elder god groaned and gave a dramatic yawn. "There it is, master of *I never said that*. It's a miracle that people can even keep your lessons straight, some rabbit you turned out to be." He sprayed his tentacles around the frame of the painting.

"That's Rabbi, they call me the great Rabbi." The painting of Jesus struggled up from his kneeling position at the rocks, his knees creaked and popped as he stood. "Shows what you know!"

An African totem with a blue face shook its head and frowned. "Uh, pretty sure it's the great rabbit, that's why they celebrate your rebirth with the Easter Bunny."

The paintings and statues all began talking over one another arguing over their various monikers and standing within the Earthside communities. The tapestry of the many armed elephant shushed the others and waited for everyone to calm down. The painting of Jesus threw his hands up in despair, accidentally parting the sea behind him. He grumbled out and tucked his hands into his armpits.

"Now then, young girl, who are you?" asked the elephant as he tossed his trunk over his shoulder. "I presume that you are the new Housekeeper?"

Vicki peered up from under the safety of the blanket. "V-Vicki, I'm Vicki... I'm not sure that I'm supposed to be here! My grandpa is, well he was the Housekeeper, but someone mixed something up in his will!"

The bust of a woman in front of a crystal ball spoke dreamily from her pedestal, "you are the Housekeeper, I can see it, for I see all."

The painting of Jesus scoffed and sat down with his back to the rest of the deities in the room. "You couldn't see the future if it lodged itself in your eyeball!"

The bust stuck her nose in the air and ignored the painting. "You are precisely in the place where you are supposed to be. Right where you are is where you are, and rightly so."

The elephant on the tapestry squinted at the bust, shaking his head in dismay. "That doesn't actually mean anything! Anyways, have a look over there, do you see that little monk?" He pointed with his many fingers at a tiny pewter statue sitting in a corner of the room. "To prove that you are the Housekeeper you need only pick up the monk."

Some of the paintings began to stifle snickering and others simply squealed with restraint. They all peered down at Vicki with gleaming eyes and springy tentacles, the elephant motioned with his hands down to the pewter statue again giving her a reassuring nod. The painting of Jesus hovered over his rocks to get a better view of the girl as she reluctantly sat up in the squeaky old bed peeking over the side to see the monk. It was as still as a statue ought to be. Moving with as much caution as she could manage, she stood from the bed and crept her way over to the little pewter statue.

"Go on," said the painting of Jesus with an excited tone.

"Well, do I have to turn it around with some kind of special magic? I can't do magic, I didn't even know it was real until today," said Vicki as she inched closer to the monk.

The elephant raised his many hands into the air around the tapestry. "The magic is in the monk," he said with dramatic flair. "For if you can lift the weight of the monk, you can surely carry the burden of the Housekeeper!" The elephant fell into an excited giggle but quickly regained his composure. "Believe in yourself! Practice makes perfect, start small!"

"Just pick it up? I guess I can try... anything's better than getting dunked in ghost goo."

She put her hands on the Buddha statue's head to turn it around and the little monk lifted its seemingly solid pewter robes over its bare bottom. Vicki recoiled from the statue in terror but not soon enough to escape the vile practical joke. It let off a horrid almost industrial strength blast of pressurized noxious gas straight at her.

Vicki gagged hiding her face fully into her hoodie. The statue turned around giggling at her. Its horrible little laugh screeched out like an angry baby screaming through some distant drainage pipe. The rest of the paintings and statues all joined in with their sickening laughter.

"Oh no!" Vicki reeled and fell to the floor.

She landed on her backside with a thump and the Buddha statue went into hysterics. Its face contorted into a menacing grin as it ran over to kick her foot, it took off out of the open doorway still laughing and making a sort of hollow thudding noise as its pewter feet went running out into the dark hallway. Vicki covered her ears screaming staring at the monk until it vanished into the darkness. The paintings and statues all went quiet, a few last giggles left the deities and they returned to their normal positions, all of them lifeless once more.

Vicki sprawled out paralyzed by both the stench of the room and the hopeless situation that she found herself in. There was no way that she was going to survive this. The stink of the statue's practical joke dissipated and the faintest scent of pipe tobacco returned to the room. The floor boards beneath her creaked and groaned as if they were lodging some sort of complaint at the girl.

The floor boards creaked again a little further into the room and Vicki sat up, scanning around for the intruder. Another slow creak from the other side of the bed then another, little sneaky steps inching closer and closer. Vicki stood up scrambling to grab her candle from the dresser, holding it out in front of her like a shield and nearly dropping it twice as she waved it back and forth. The creaking steps stopped, and she squinted into the corner of the room.

"Who's there? Come out!" The candle flickered and flared against the shadows, it illuminated the entire room for a brief moment and Vicki could see the faint outline of something small standing at the opposite corner of her bed. She brought the candle closer to the figure, hoping to see who or what was haunting her now. Hopping and strutting, the little thing crossed her bed and came into view.

It had a beak like a bird and two huge wet black eyes that stared up at her. It had a blue feathery body, two large long ears on either side of its dark feathered head, and what might have been wings held close to its body. Its body was strange, its forelegs were like the talons of an owl or a hawk but its hind legs, torso, and tail all resembled a wild bunny. The little thing made a chortling sound then spun around on the bed like an excited puppy. It trotted over to Vicki, then quite comfortably and without hesitation knocked the top of its head against her hand. Vicki stepped back from the thing.

"Hello?" Vicki looked down at the creature waiting to see if it would say anything back. The creature sat down on the bed and puffed out its chest. It made a whistling sort of chirp noise at her. She shook her head and waved the creature onward. "Shoo! Go on!"

The creature squawked and flopped down onto the mattress, turning over a few times before coming to a rest atop one of the pillows. The two of them stared at each other for a few moments until the creature gave a huge yawn that ended with a satisfied clacking of its beak. It closed its eyes and let out a contented sigh. Vicki stood there at the side of the bed, marveling at the sight of what she could only understand to be a griffin of old myth and lore.

The candle flame seemed to grow brighter, sending dazzling shadows and shapes onto the walls around the room as it danced around in Vicki's hand. She cautiously reached out to the griffin, the flickering candlelight reflected off of its dark blue quills. Her hand reached the soft little creature and it hardly stirred as she touched the down covering its wingtips. It cooed as she stroked one of the feathers on its tiny wings, knocking its head gently into her outstretched hand with its eyes still closed tight. Vicki let the slightest of smiles cross her face as the feathery griffin nuzzled her hand for a pet on the head. It made its little cooing noise again and buried its face into the pillow.

"You're not that bad at all, are you," asked Vicki gently petting the griffin's head. She stroked its beak and in between its eyes as she talked. "Everyone else seems pretty scary and mean here, but you're okay I guess."

The griffin let out a contented sigh. Vicki grinned and held the candle up to get a better look at the thing. Somehow the candle in Vicki's hand now lit up the entirety of the room. She carefully held the candle aloft surveying the room in the full light of the flame, happy to see that the religious paintings had changed back to inanimate objects. They were devoid of any of the snark or trickery that they were so full of only minutes ago.

The spookiness of the room had dissipated with the growing light source. She noticed that a statue of Kali had moved one of her hands pointing in the direction of the cabinet in the far corner of the room. Vicki walked around her bed over to the old wood and brass cabinet to take a better look at it. The griffin began snoring on her bed as she opened the doors.

The candlelight lit up the inside of the cabinet, glittering off the contents, an absolute treasure trove of strange things had been squirreled away. Strangest of all were the things that Vicki recognized. Through all those months of failed correspondence, her grandfather had actually kept and well cared for the gifts that Vicki had made for him. A watercolor birthday card here, a sloppily made macaroni painting there, so many old things displayed that she had worried never reached him.

Her grandpa had kept everything. A wild thought began to take form in her mind: what if Eckhardt had indeed wanted her to become the next Housekeeper, but not so soon? Might he have actually chosen Vicki, not any of her apparently magically gifted extended family, not anyone else with actual qualifications for the title?

If that was true then it may have been true also that her grandfather had sent the pig curse against her family. She buried those thoughts in her head and continued to look over the photos in front of her. As Vicki shone her light further into the cabinet she spied photos of her cousin at various stages in her life too.

Magra had the most recent photo hanging in the cabinet. She smiled into the camera with her white hair partially covering her horns. She proudly held her simple wand made of clear crystal wrapped in a green bow. Magra had signed the bottom of the photo with a heart to their grandfather. Maybe that wand had been a gift to her cousin celebrating some milestone.

She searched the cabinet for other keepsakes, smiling at one particular old photo of Eckhardt sitting with her newborn mother on his lap. He had never been great at communicating it, but it was clear that her grandfather had loved his family. Only Zaldehyde was excluded from the family photos.

One large empty space in the cabinet remained clear of dust. Vicki held her candle up to the spot. It was large enough for a painting perhaps, or a large portrait. Vicki wondered if this hadn't been the space for her aunt some time ago. She closed the doors and put a hand on the cabinet, feeling warmed by her place amongst the treasures inside.

Turning around to light her way back to the dresser she was surprised to see that the whole room was now lit up quite nicely by lamp light. In fact the whole darkened corridor was now bathed in the warm light of hallway lamps. There came the sounds of murmuring and jubilant cheers from the residents in their rooms.

"Finally, this hat is working!" Vicki adjusted the cone of locus atop her head taking a sigh of relief. Some of the doors down the hallway opened and little old goblins began chattering to each other as she tiptoed to her dresser, placing the candle back on its surface. Vicki grinned to herself and blew out the flame before closing her door for the night.

She settled down into the creaky old bed, kitty-corner from the snoring griffin, pushing it far away with her foot. Exhausted from the events of the day, Vicki didn't find it at all difficult to close her eyes. It felt like a heavy, comforting, warm blanket wrapped around her. She didn't even flinch when the griffin moved its head over to her foot.

She dozed off with the large pointed hat loose on her head and her shoes still on her feet. The griffin inched its way over to Vicki's side and began to snooze away once more as the scent of cherry pipe tobacco drifted away from the room. It was replaced by the scent of warm gingerbread.

It had been a terrible dream, so terrible that it left Vicki wondering where she would have even picked up the stranger parts. Vampires and witches, a Frankenstein girl with a Queens accent, what had she been watching to put such bizarre things in her head? She threw the blankets off from her bed, resting her hands on her ribs.

She pulled her hands away from the hard cardboard set into her chest muffling her scream with her pillow. A familiar colorful little shoebox now grew where her ribs once were and the lid began lifting up with a rhythmic beat. Vicki carefully slid her hands over the box lid, trembling and taking quick panicked breaths. Something from within the box began to pump, thumping against the walls of her chest.

She opened the lid and the thing inside flew up with a great crashing gong.

A loud gong sounded throughout the entire mansion and Vicki awoke to the green sunrise. She startled at the sight of the griffin. It made a discontented noise before jumping off of the bed and sprawling out on the floor. A full nine hours had passed, she was still in the strange monster mansion and she was far more hungry than frightened. She scrambled to her feet, running over to her backpack for a change of clothes.

She was overjoyed to find that her little pigtail had vanished overnight. Vicki turned round and round in front of her mirror, double checking at the back of her hoodie with a wide grin on her face. *If her tail had disappeared so fast, maybe everyone else would be back to normal too!*

"This is going to be easier than I thought," Vicki exclaimed to herself. She looked down at the griffin and hugged her change of clothes tightly to her chest. "See? I didn't have anything to worry about, this is going to be a breeze!"

Vicki's first morning task after breakfast was written out on her chalkboard schedule. It seemed simple enough, *Goblin garden walk with Desmond,* whatever that was. She went down the list and read the daily tasks to herself, hoping to memorize them as best she could. The list was quite small, which was just fine by her. She read the list aloud repeating the words to better remember them.

"Goblin garden walk, lunches and linens, library." Vicki took a breath and closed her eyes, repeating the words to herself. "Goblins, lunches, linens. Lunches, linens, library."

The griffin nestled up to Vicki's knee and grumbled up at her. It wagged its nubby little tail back and forth and stared with its huge black eyes. It knocked its head into her knee and clacked its beak a few times.

"What?" Vicki asked as she edged away from the blue feathered thing. She looked back down at the griffin waiting for any kind of answer, feeling silly for thinking that the creature might speak. "Sorry, almost everything else around here can bark orders at me. I guess I thought you could too maybe." Vicki reached down to give the griffin a pat on its head.

"Breakfast."

Vicki recoiled at the sound of the voice, nearly letting out a shriek. The griffin laid down on the floor and stretched out. The two of them stared at each other for a few moments before Vicki spoke up. "Did you just say breakfast?"

"Yeah! Breakfast! Hurry up and put your pants on or it'll get cold," Frank called through the bedroom door.

Vicki rolled her eyes and sighed, "Okay!" She looked back down at the griffin and shot it a quick smile. "Just don't go telling anyone about this."

After complaining about the weight of the big pointy hat and taking great care to avoid wearing any more pink outfits, she opened the door to the hallway and left along with her new little griffin friend. The two of them crept down the stairwell with Vicki leading the way through the much more brightly lit corridors below. Some of the doors to the resident's rooms were open and Vicki could spy on some of the creature morning activities as she went along.

One goblin in particular had caught her attention. He sat in his large chair rocking back and forth, reading a scroll as if he were reading a newspaper. After his eyes would skim the scroll for some time the elderly goblin would then lick the scroll with his pale sticky tongue. He made a disgusted face, licking the scroll again, seeming to find more joy the second time around. He glanced over to Vicki and the griffin then snorted.

"Butter futures are down this quarter, I can tell you that," the goblin exclaimed with a gravelly voice. "Otter butter, I've never been so insulted in all my lives! It's refreshing to see such a young sorcerer choosing to labor for once," the plump elderly goblin said from behind his scroll. He licked at his roll of paper and sighed, peeking around to look at Vicki. "Your grandad would be proud."

"Oh, I'm not a sauce, a soar chair cha..."

"A *sorcerer*. You've a hat and a beast that say otherwise." The goblin's gravelly voice wavered and thinned out as he spoke. "Do you follow butters much? It's never too early to invest."

Vicki shook her head. "I'm not even sure what that means. I like it on toast I guess?"

The goblin rolled his scroll up and turned a dark blue gray tone. "Young lady, butters are far more substantial than the spread for overcooked bread or merely for a game of beagles and boggles! It's what keeps this country going and it has done for a good one hundred years!" He sat back in his overly large cushy chair, holding his scroll out to her. "Go on, have a taste of those butter reports, tell me what you think of them."

Vicki held her stomach and grimaced. "Oh no, I couldn't right now, I don't want to spoil my breakfast." She gave the old goblin a polite smile. "My dad is really into butter too, he puts it in his coffee!"

"Your father is a wise man! Take heed young sorcerer, and halt all buttering of breads immediately! There's a foul stench to the butters this season. Something is in the air, it's mucked up and ruined the churn!" The old goblin tucked the scroll into a nearby dresser filled with official branded scrolls and wax seals. He turned his dresser lamp off and cozied into his seat. "It has the flavor of old unlucky magic, from the days of old witchcraft. Like the cream has curdled before it ever hit the bucket." He took a big sniff of the air and sighed.

Vicki blinked a few times at the nonsensical words of the elderly goblin then gave him a quick grin before venturing down the hallway. They passed more and more rooms each one holding its own bizarre little morning scene. A cyclops taking great care to curl his last four remaining eyelashes, a giant old lizard man practicing aerobics in front of a mirror, and other oddities that she struggled to look away from.

They continued making their way through the twisty hallways into the main hall of the Athenaeum. Vicki took her time coming down the great wooden stairway to the second floor appreciating the fully illuminated mansion. The softly flickering lamplights reflected up from the shiny wooden floor boards that peaked out from the edges of the ornate carpeting, casting warm tones all around the cracked plaster walls. Giant dull red draperies hung by the tall arched windows. Little particles of dust floated into the greenish sunbeams as they swayed in place.

She could make out the paintings more clearly now, the strange image of a giant frog balancing on a unicycle decorated one side of the stairway while a painting of several fall colored maple leaves hung on the opposite end. Caterpillars ate through the leaves revealing small winter landscapes within each chewed out hole. Vicki startled as one of the caterpillars fell from one of the leaves. It vanished from sight as the other caterpillars chewed on within the confines of the painting.

The rest of the walk to the dining area was also quite scenic. Portraits of Housekeepers and nurses from years gone by hung haphazardly on the walls. Soon the portraits became more modern and she could spy her Grandpa Eckhardt standing among the other staff and goblins. An ugly and terrifying creature always stood at her grandfather's side in those pictures, a menacing horned reptile with a long neck and dark blue scales. She began to recognize the goblins and other creatures as the portraits reached the current day.

Many of the residents were captured in the group photos and paintings. Few of the creatures smiled. Only one elderly goblin woman seemed to always have a pleasant grin on her face, progressing in age throughout the years in the photos along the wall. She remembered the goblin from the night before, the kindly Mrs. Klobbreak. If every group photo had taken place on an annual basis she reasoned out that the old goblin woman with the happy smile must have been in the nursing home for about fifteen years. Only Eckhardt had been there longer.

Vicki came to the final staff portraits seeing her prim and proper grandfather standing with the current roster of weirdos that she had met the day prior. Frank was there, standing in an orange and black nurse's uniform, looking dour. Belvedere smiled into the camera proudly wearing his chef's coat and hat, his arms folded in front of him and holding a spatula off to the side. He had replaced the former cook in the pictures, one of the odd looking half cat people, but he wore the same apron that she had worn. She squinted at a rather handsome man dressed in regal gowns before moving on.

"That must be Jerry," Vicki remarked to herself as she and the griffin crossed the dining room. "No vampire guy though. I thought he'd be in at least a few of those pictures."

The griffin merely sneezed, vigorously shaking its head in response. It sat down in front of the swinging kitchen doors, pawing at them and whining to be let in. It unfurled its little useless wings and squawked.

The door gently pushed open from the other side and Belvedere poked his head out to greet them. He smiled and waved them in. "Vicki! That hat worked miracles! You're in luck today, I just so happened to have found some rations that you'll be familiar with."

"Omigosh, like actual human food," Vicki asked excitedly. "I'd eat a twenty year old piece of toast right now, I'm that hungry!"

"Oh it's much better than toast," said Belvedere as he went to finish his cooking. He went about flipping some pancakes on his griddle, cheerfully singing to himself and performing quick checks of his many ovens. "We'll be ready in ten minutes, then I'll do the morning meal for the residents just after we've finished. I do believe you'll be joining me in the afternoon to help with feeding the more dependent goblins."

"Sounds good to me," Vicki said with a cheerful tone.

Belvedere glanced down at the griffin by Vicki's feet. "Ah, so is that your *gargoyle?*" He wiggled his mustache back and forth in thought. "I can't recall ever seeing one that looked like that exactly, but I suppose this means that you're official now."

"A what?"

"Your gargoyle. Every Housekeeper has one, your grandfather's gargoyle looked like a proper dragon, horribly strict thing as well. From what I understand the gargoyle is often a reflection of the Housekeeper's true nature, as your granddad told it to me anyways." Belvedere reached down and gave the blue griffin a pat on its beak. "It disappeared as soon as he passed away. I suppose this one appeared as you entered the Athenaeum last night."

Vicki reached down and pet the griffin on its head as she spoke. "I thought maybe it was just someone's pet or something and maybe it got lost. It's not so scary looking though, it doesn't have horns or scales or anything! Maybe I should give it a name?"

"Yes, well, maybe it'll grow into those ears. I'll try to find it something to eat as well." Belvedere took another appraising look at the griffin and returned to his cooking.

Vicki sat at the large kitchen table watching as the cook left the black cast iron griddle. She was amazed to see that his pancakes flipped themselves onto a waiting plate. His gigantic bronze cauldron also began to stir itself and a large shaker of pepper lifted into the air sifting its contents into the mix. The old kitchen was either enchanted or Belvedere was some kind of kitchen witch.

"A man witch," Vicki muttered to herself. The griffin placed its head on her shoes and cooed out in agreement. Vicki looked down at the griffin, letting Belvedere's words roll around in her mind. *The gargoyle is often a reflection of the Housekeeper's true nature.* "I guess my true nature *really is* a bird brain," she mused, as she adjusted her heavy pointed hat.

A loud smack came from behind her and she turned her attention over to Frank who stood leaning out of a window on the tips of her toes. She held a large fly swatter in her hand, taking careful aim before smacking the swatter onto an unseen surface just outside. The lanky girl gave a self satisfied nod at her work with one last gentle smack forward.

"There ya go Brisket, don't say I never did nothing for ya," said Frank as she stood back from the window.

Jerry stuck his head in through the window, smiling down at Frank as he spoke. "Tanks Frank," he said grabbing the fly swatter from Frank's waiting hand. "Hey ho, morning boss!" Jerry nodded over at Vicki.

"Oh, hello!" Vicki smiled back. She watched as the red bovine man left the window and began climbing downward out of sight. "Good morning," she called out before he disappeared.

"He gets morning flies," Frank stated as she plopped down in a chair next to Vicki. "It's because he's up all night staring at the farm field down the other side of the mountain, trying to catch a peep of old farmer Herman milking the cows. It's really kind of sick when you think about it."

Vicki shut her eyes tight, focusing hard on not envisioning what she had just been told. The stitchwork girl definitely had a knack for grossing her out. She opened her eyes at the sound of a plate and cup being set down in front of her. She looked around at the scrambled eggs, pancakes, and meats on the plate. She shook her hands and bubbled over with excitement at the feast before her. She wordlessly scooted the glass of milk away from herself then hungrily dug into the scrambled eggs.

Belvedere chuckled putting a plate down for himself and for Frank, then he tossed a bit of meat down to the griffin. "You really were hungry, the good news is that there's plenty of those rations left over from your grandfather's time here," he said as he slurped down something close to coffee from his mug. "The bad news is he was quite the stickler for routine, so eggs and bacon are just about the only things that you're going to see."

Vicki held a bite of scrambled eggs to her mouth and let her eyes fall upon the bacon that sat upon the plate. A rush of chills crept down her spine as she stared at the crispy little bacon strips and she thought of her family back home. She couldn't help but imagine her parents squealing and running away from a crazy goblin butcher. The scent of the bacon hit her nose and her mouth went dry. Vicki lowered the scrambled eggs back down to the table, cringing as she felt at her waistline where the pigtail had been.

"Do the, uhm... *residents* not eat eggs and bacon for breakfast?"

Belvedere shook his head beginning his own unnatural macabre breakfast as he spoke. "The residents are issued specific porridges and breads for the morning meal. It's all that some of them can handle. Outsiders, like the Golem, eat much worse things."

Vicki poked at her plate of eggs again, glancing around at Belvedere and Frank as they ate. Belvedere enjoyed his breakfast of those horrible black wiggling noodles that she had seen before at the bus station. He slurped them down with a smattering of maple syrup and drank the crude brew from his mug. Frank on the other hand ate her food with a comically tiny fork and knife, her pinky extended as she took bite after bite of food. Vicki was pretty sure that from the color and the shape of the thing that was wiggling around on her plate, Frank must have been eating brains.

Her stomach tied itself into a knot and Vicki politely put her fork down. "Is that other guy, Desmond, is he going to eat breakfast with us too? I saw that he wasn't in any of the photos on the wall, does he like being alone or something?"

"Dez is in most of the photos," said Frank as she carved up another bit of gray wobbly meat. "He just doesn't show up all the time, especially at this time of day."

Vicki furrowed her brow then sat forward. "That reminds me, the old paintings and statues in that room were really annoying last night! The little Buddha statue was mean too, do they have to be so rude?"

Belvedere grumbled from behind his mug. "Those paintings, unfortunate as it may be, are there to protect you from any untoward spirits or devils. They ward off plenty of things that might want to do you harm." He stroked his mustache and lowered his eyebrows. "You might be able to talk Desmond into putting in for some shrouds to throw over them, at least they couldn't look at you then."

Vicki adjusted the large pointed hat on her head and ignored the sickening gray jelly on the lanky girl's plate as she spoke, "Well, I think I'm supposed to meet him after breakfast so that I can learn how to do the Housekeeping stuff. It's on my little chalkboard."

Belvedere finished his mug of dark crude and motioned to Vicki's plate. "Well then you had better hurry it up, Desmond eats *his* breakfast just before sunrise," he said pushing her glass of milk back to her. "You're already late."

"But that's crazy! I'm supposed to get up before the sun even comes up?"

"Well, you could always wake up a bit later if you feel that's too early for you. That's your choice I suppose, although it will make feeding the Golem a tad bit more challenging."

"The *Golem?*" Vicki asked as she began to power through her remaining scrambled eggs. "What does he eat?"

Frank clicked her tongue and stabbed her tiny fork into the jiggly meat upon her plate. "Oh boy are you in for some trouble."

Chapter ten

Doubt and worry followed Vicki like a cloud as she crept down the hallway to the back doors of the mansion. It was her first day doing any real kind of job and it had been a long time since anyone had entrusted her with an important task, not since she was still in the scouts. She shoved the thought of gingerbread cookies and dog treats out of her mind, hurrying down the hallway in the hopes of outrunning the memories of her last summer.

The little griffin hopped along beside her making its little squawks of protest at Vicki's speed. It stopped just short of the large oak doors that led to the garden and cocked its head sideways. It gave out a shrill little cry like a howling puppy walking in a circle around Vicki's legs.

"What's the matter?" She went to turn the old iron doorknob and began to strain. The knob wouldn't so much as budge. She tried the other door, throwing her weight against it to no avail. "They're locked!"

She rattled one of the doorknobs again then stood glaring up at the doors with her hands on her hips and her bottom lip sticking out. The griffin cooed and laid its head down between its front legs. Both of them startled at the sound of one of the door knobs twisting and clicking into place. Vicki yanked on the doorknob and pounded on the door.

"Hello!?" She pounded again bending down to peek through the keyhole. She could make out some garden hedges and the sunlight outside but didn't see anyone standing on the other side of the door. She tried the doorknob once more and this time could feel the knob being held in place. "I have to get through here!"

She began to pull on the door with her full weight, grunting with the exertion. The griffin jumped to its feet and grabbed Vicki's hoodie with its beak pulling along with her. The door fought against the two of them, finally opening just a small bit before snapping closed again.

"Hey," Vicki shouted into the air, looking around the hallway. The lamps flickered around them and the mansion groaned. Vicki narrowed her eyes, bringing her pointed hat down tight around her head. She circled the brim of the hat with her fingers then grabbed onto the doorknob one more time. "I'm supposed to be your Housekeeper, aren't I? Well I need to go outside or I'm going to be late!"

The hallway rattled and the lamps shook, sending particles of dust down on their glowing rays. Vicki calmly turned the doorknob, closing her eyes in concentration. She envisioned the door opening and letting her through to the other side. The door shook and trembled before creaking open.

"I did it!" Vicki breathed out a sigh of relief and grinned as she opened the door to the outside. A fresh breeze hit her face and the fallen leaves on the ground began to stir around, kicking up and flying into the hallway. "Let's go," she nudged the griffin with her foot and held the door open.

The hallway shook again and the lamps darkened. The door tugged violently away from Vicki's hand slamming itself shut and locking itself into place with a loud clank. The lamps lit up again and Vicki looked around at the mansion with great concern.

"Okay, I can take a hint," she said as she crept away from the garden doors.

The entire mansion groaned and the hallway trembled as if caught in an earthquake. Dust fell from the ceiling and the creaking of the floor boards moaned out like a person wailing. The garden doors clanked and shuddered, finally flinging open with a gust of wind and leaves. Vicki covered her face from the flying debris and made a run for it towards the garden. The griffin took off after her and the two of them together jumped through the creaking and shaking doors.

Vicki stumbled out of the back doors into the garden, tripping over her own feet and nearly falling down onto the poor griffin. She caught her footing and turned back to glower at the doors of the mansion. They slammed themselves shut sending a gust of air back at her, knocking the large pointed hat right off of her head.

"Thanks a lot! I don't want me here either, you know!" Vicki went running for her hat and came face to face with the well dressed vampire.

"You're late," said Desmond. He stood in the middle of a cobblestone patio, arms behind his back and a walking cane held sideways in his hands. He took out an old style pocket watch from his blue velvet tuxedo and regarded it with a sigh of disappointment. "By almost a whole hour."

A younger goblin in official business attire stood to the side of the vampire. He made a mark on his strange stone tablet squinting at Vicki as he wrote something out. The goblin sat down on a bench holding his tablet to his chest watching her with great focus.

"Well this stupid house has been trying to keep me from getting out here on time," Vicki whined as she pulled the large hat back over her head. "The doors kept locking on me, I swear!"

Desmond held a stick out towards Vicki, motioning for her to take it. He brought her in close as she took the walking stick whispering down to her, "Keep it cool now, that little guy over there is assessing your aptitude for magic. I guess they're trying something new with you, don't know why. He's gonna be here for at least a couple of days. Try and act like you at least want to be here."

She grabbed the walking stick without another word and began to follow Desmond through the overgrown garden behind the Athenaeum. She trampled along, followed closely by the griffin, kicking twigs and stones out of her path as Desmond took them further into the garden where the hedges became a literal maze. She glanced back at the goblin every couple of yards; he followed behind them at a distance writing on his stone.

Desmond came to a stop and motioned around the maze with his cane. "Okay sweet corn, here's where the problem is. You see these old dead vines over here?" He pointed at some overgrown hedges where the leaves had been choked out by brown withered vines. "These are ravenous ivy, and at least once a month some dumb goblin will get too close to one of them and get tangled up, so every morning we have to trim the vines and keep a head count just in case."

"Ravenous ivy? Is it like poison ivy?" Vicki ventured closer to the hedge and the griffin bit into her shoe, stopping her from going any closer. "Hey! Stop!" She gave the griffin a scornful look.

"I just told you, *dumb* goblins get too close to them," said Desmond. He plucked a rock from the ground and tossed it at the ivy. He picked up a few more stones and began to launch them at the withered vines. "Now poison ivy just makes you itch, these little guys are more like me."

"What do you mean?"

The ivy rustled and twitched then sprang away from the hedges wrapping vine after vine around one of the stones that Desmond had tossed. He tossed another rock at the vines and they caught it in mid air tangling around the rock and snapping back towards the hedges with their catch. Vicki grimaced as a bulk of bird skulls and old decayed feathers fell to the ground from the long rotted leaves of the hedge, jostled loose by the sudden movement. The griffin made a concerned hooting noise and Desmond clicked his tongue.

"Now, it would take them about a week to get it done but they could drain a little goblin body if we left them to it. You've got a little goblin sized body yourself, so keep an eye out." Desmond flashed her a small smile. He grabbed his cane and slid the metal end against the rocks causing a spray of sparks to shoot up along behind it. The ivy made a high pitched shrieking noise and retreated into the leaves of the hedge. "Little bit of fire will fix them right up, yessir, fried greens never hurt nobody!" He brandished his cane at the hedge and the ivy shook in fear behind the leaves.

"Has anyone ever, you know, got eaten by them?" asked Vicki, as she followed along behind him. She took great notice of the hedges around them now, keeping an eye out for any more of the ravenous ivy. "Like, totally eaten?"

"Only once. Cute little gardening girl, I think she was half breed, couldn't wolf up with the rest of *those furballs*. The ivy caught her and dragged her all the way back into the garden wall. No one could find her till she was just bones." Desmond grew quiet, sighing and tapping his cane upon an old statue of some nude hero decorated with laurels. "That was way back. Can't even remember her name."

The two of them stopped in front of the statue, the greenish morning sun cast a shadow across the hero's face. Small sparkles glinted in the stonework of the sculpture, flecks of rainbow colors dotted the base where a long faded inscription once was. The griffin huffed and pawed at the base of the statue, sniffing around at the ground. The assessor yawned from far behind them.

"Did you know her?" asked Vicki. "How long ago was that?"

"I knew her, she just wasn't here for very long. I think it was back in the nineties." Desmond tapped his cane on the ground, bringing it forward. "Come on, I'll show you the gathering box."

They walked onward towards the center of the expansive maze, Vicki's mind kept going to the poor gardening girl and to Desmond's age. She wondered if the vampire were perhaps a hundred or more years old, and if so, how long had he been working at the

Athenaeum. She was yanked from her thoughts when the griffin once again bit down on her shoe.

"What is your deal?" Vicki shook the griffin off of her shoe and pushed it away with her foot. "That isn't food and we totally fed you like half an hour ago!"

"I think you got a defective one," laughed out Desmond as he took them into a large clearing. A great derelict white marble fountain full of wheelchairs and pillows stood in the middle of the area. "All of the exits lead right here so we can just scoop up the oldies on the way back after the walk."

Vicki looked around the moss covered fountain and at the maze that surrounded them. "You mean they all just end up here? What do they do when they get here?"

"They just wait. Most of them don't even know time is passing anymore."

"That's awful!" Vicki let out an exasperated breath and slumped her shoulders in disgust. "You just leave the old goblins out here for hours and hours?"

"Some of them. Some of them just stay inside and sleep." Desmond reached into his blue tuxedo pocket and pulled out his watch. He shook it and held it up to his ear. "They don't really want to do much else, as far as I can tell, and no one really comes to visit them. That's the way of goblins."

"Well I think it's terrible, leaving them out here in this cruddy old place!"

The assessor cleared his throat and called out for Desmond. The two of them stayed out of Vicki's earshot while they discussed some apparent private matter. Desmond looked less and less comfortable with whatever was being said before returning to Vicki's side. He gave her a sideways look and straightened his posture.

The assessor raised his stone into the air and called out, "Let the Housekeeper summon the waters to the fountain." The little goblin marked off his stone and sat back on a bench just outside of the gathering box.

Vicki looked up to Desmond. "*Summon the waters?* I can barely summon the light bulbs! I don't know how to do that!"

Desmond whispered back down to her as smoothly as possible so as to not get caught giving her any pointers. "You'll do fine, just say something like, *waters come forth.* Make something up, if it doesn't work I'll see if I can't come up with something on the sly."

Vicki gulped and stepped forward to the fountain, she glanced back at the goblin. He stared back with unflinching concentration. She quietly cleared her throat and put her hand out in front of her.

"Water," she began, "please come forth."

The griffin reared up to its hind legs, screeching and grabbing Vicki by her legs with its talons in order to drag her away from the fountain. The ground beneath them shook and the wheelchairs in the fountain began to roll around crashing onto their sides. The pillows were tossed into the air and Vicki lost her balance, falling on top of the little griffin. Desmond went to help her back up, but before he could even reach out his hand the fountain behind him exploded with a geyser of muddy water. Concrete, wheelchairs, and all manner of rubbish went flying into the air.

Vicki let out a high pitched scream as the column of water burbled and turned to a spout of thick mud full of twigs and dead vines. The spout slammed itself left and right spinning itself around, seemingly intent on crashing into Desmond. The spray of powerful mud and water took him off of his feet, throwing him into the hedges. The large broken bits of concrete came crashing back down to the ground, splashing mud and water everywhere as they landed.

"Get out of there! Run," Desmond yelled from one of the hedges, struggling to break free from its branches.

The mud spout tore away from the base of the fountain, shattering the cobblestone as the mud grew and grew. The griffin bit down on Vicki's shoulder and dragged her away from the menacing mud with all of its might as she kicked away from the spout. The bubbling muddy mess grew and grew, nearly reaching Vicki's feet.

The griffin flapped its wings in an effort to pick her up. The mud seemed to be racing right at them as if it were a living thing with its only aim being to envelop Vicki. The dead vines sloshed around in the muddy mix and whipped out at her legs, trying to wrap themselves around her. Vicki kicked her legs and shrieked. Finally the griffin was able to lift her from the ground enough for Vicki to stand up on her own again.

The ground shook violently once more, and the mud spout turned itself toward her, aiming a torrent of stones and decayed matter in Vicki's direction. Vicki grabbed onto one of the hedges and climbed up the leaves as quickly as she had ever climbed anything in her entire life, only just avoiding the blast of mud and stones. The mud sloshed around with wild intensity as if it were throwing a temper tantrum.

"Stay there! Don't move!" Desmond freed himself from the hedge on the opposite end of the large clearing. He raised his cane into the air and waved it around a few times. A bright pink flare went shooting out of the cane high up into the sky. It floated back down towards the mud, making a high pitched whine as it glowed lighting up the entire area.

The mud gurgled loudly, and with one more quake of the ground that nearly shook Vicki from her hedge, the spout retreated back into the fountain. It drained with a thunderous suction, leaving behind a messy swamp of broken wood and dead vines, disappearing down the large chasm that it had created and giving one last sound of angry gurgling. Vicki could have sworn that something in the fountain had called out an actual word but couldn't quite make out what the word was. It almost sounded like *vitamin*.

Vicki clung tightly to the hedge with the griffin perched close by her side. She called out to Desmond, the pink glow of the flare almost blinding her. "Are you okay," she yelled out.

"Just peachy," Desmond answered with an annoyed tone.

Vicki dropped from the hedge and ran to Desmond. They both surveyed the damage, Vicki could feel the assessor's eyes upon her. She didn't even need to look back, she recognized the sound of chalk on stone quite well.

"One point is deducted for mismanagement of magical properties." The little goblin got up from his bench and calmly went about reviewing his stone tablet.

The gathering box was gone, replaced by a dark hole in the ground filled in with the chunks of concrete and detritus that had once circled the dried out old fountain. A wheelchair went careening into the hole, crashing a few seconds later into a watery grave. Desmond took a deep breath and fished a clean white handkerchief from his pocket handing it off to Vicki. She took it with a grateful smile.

"Well, this is gonna make the day activities a little less exciting for the rest of them," said Desmond as he kicked some mud away from his shoe. "Probably gonna need to get some bingo cards together or something."

"Oh sure, they play bingo at the nursing home that my mom works at," said Vicki, her voice shaking and her heart pounding like a marching drum. She wiped a few specks of mud from her face and held the handkerchief back to Desmond. He walked away towards the hedge maze without even acknowledging the gesture. Vicki bit her lip and followed along behind him. "Uhm, I was going to work there this last summer, but then things kind of- they weren't really gonna work out. You know, because maybe it would have been too much for me. Well, I guess *I* kind of decided that it would be too much for me." She let her voice trail off feeling that the vampire had lost interest in the conversation. She shook her hands and adjusted her pointed hat.

"Sweet corn, you better play it safe for the rest of the day, I got a bad feeling about your grading papers back there," Desmond finally whispered back after a few moments had passed.

"I know." Vicki frowned and looked back at her poor little mud covered griffin, followed closely by the spotless goblin assessor.

Vicki kept up with Desmond all the way back to the mansion, stopping to listen to a curious sound that came from the east. Down past the town of Everfall, a loud trumpeting repeated a few times over, followed by an inaudible voice over loudspeakers. The griffin perked its ears up and stood on its hind legs sniffing the air.

"What is that, what's going on?" asked Vicki.

"The buttered beagle boggle. Come on, let's get back inside before the butterers start churning," said Desmond with a look of disgust on his face. "I thought I kept smelling butter. Man, I hate this time of year."

They all entered the mansion and Desmond momentarily stopped at the doors, looking them up and down. He bent down and ran his fingers across the doorknob, then jiggled the locks. The vampire closed the outside doors and scratched the side of his head with his cane.

"Sticky doors around here lately," he said loudly, so that the assessor could hear him. He motioned for Vicki to follow him down the hallway. "I'll look at it later, come on, it's time for your new favorite part of the day."

"What's that," asked Vicki as she hurried along behind him. "Is it the library?"

Desmond looked back at her with a raised eyebrow. "*Library*," he said. "You must be talking about the *storage* room. Either way that's been broken down for years. It's just storage now, where'd you hear about it?"

"Oh it was written on my schedule. I'm sure it was, it was there on the chalkboard when I woke up this morning."

Desmond shrugged and took her back through the mansion towards the dining area. "Must have been a mistake then, I don't know, best just disregard that." He stopped her by the shoulder and tapped his cane on his muddied shoe. "Come to think of it, might be best for you to take it easy with the magic aptitude for the rest of the day. I'm going to have a little chat with the assessor and the legal department. See if we can't get some kind of written test instead or something. In the meantime you might help Bell Boy if he needs it. Just maybe stay away from the stoves and the sinks, stick to delivering the food to the goblins. You know, stay out of trouble."

"You mean *don't lose any more points* or *explode anything else.*"

"You're smarter than you look. Just hang with Belvedere and follow his lead, he's got plenty of stuff that he needs help with." Desmond gave her an awkward and not at all reassuring pat on the shoulder. "Keep your focus, remember that."

"Oh, okay but," began Vicki. Desmond sped away down the hallway in a blur before she could get anything out. Vicki searched around the dining room. The little goblin assessor had also vanished. "It's just you and me again," she said, looking back to the griffin.

The griffin gave an exasperated little coo and followed behind her into the kitchen, shaking the mud off from its wings.

Chapter eleven

Vicki rummaged through a dusty old cupboard filled with cobwebs and ancient canned goods. She carefully looked over one of the larger cans, inspecting it and whining in disgust as she brushed several years worth of dust from the label. "This can't be it," she said turning back to her little griffin.

She examined the can and turned it in the light of the hanging kitchen lamp. Pickled Fish Fingers. As far as Vicki knew (which wasn't at all too far) fish didn't actually have fingers, and fish fingers as she had come to know them were really just thinly breaded fish sticks. Yet here was proof positive in her hands, a picture of tiny glittering scaled fingers lining the old rusted can.

"Do the goblins really like this stuff?" Vicki hopped off from the kitchen counter and held the can out to Belvedere. She shook the can and stuck her tongue out at the sound of the sloshing fingers. "Or did they do something wrong, like is this their punishment or something?"

"Oh no, no no of course not, pickled fish fingers are somewhat of a delicacy on this side of the world. The trouble is, most people won't touch those fingers unless they're at least five years rotten. Unfortunately, the older residents have to make do with three years or less, it's better for their digestive health to have fresher scales, you see." Belvedere clapped his hands together and his large copper cauldron began marching its way to the stovetop in front of him. "Half of my job is tricking them into thinking that they're eating stinkier food than we can afford."

Vicki sat down on a chair next to her griffin, staring up at the kitchen utensils as they came together for the pudgy cook. "Stinkier?"

"Hmm, usually just toad essences will do. A bit of crow mucus and worm stones can really add some flair for the palate." Belvedere dropped the tin of fingers into the cauldron. The can violently exploded up and out of the cauldron, leaving a jet of awful fish chunks behind. "Well, that will just sit there and boil for the next few minutes. This way," he said, beckoning for Vicki to follow him into the walk-in freezer as the can landed neatly into a waiting waste basket.

"How do you stand the smell? Don't you think it's too much sometimes?" Vicki asked following behind him and holding her nose as she hurried past the boiling fish fingers. "It's making me gag just thinking about it! I thought being around puréed meat and vegetables was gonna gross me out at my mom's nursing home, this is way worse!"

Belvedere brought Vicki around into the freezer and began to shuffle some unidentifiable meats around on the shelves. A look of surprise crossed his face as he spoke. "Oh, were you going into housekeeping back home? To work with your mother?" He unloaded some frozen cold cuts into Vicki's waiting hands and stroked his mustache. "I trained with my mother when she was the cook here for many years, cooking here has been quite the family business. Seems you must take a bit after your own mother too."

Vicki furrowed her brow and struggled to balance the slippery hunks of meat in her arms. "Well, no I... I mean I was going to but I didn't, it's not that I didn't want to! I was just worried that I'd disappoint her even more after I messed everything up with the scouts and Rachel and..." Vicki clenched her teeth together shutting her eyes tight, she grunted at the strain of keeping quiet. "This stupid hat!"

"Hmm." Belvedere seemed lost in his own thoughts. He rearranged a few more items on the shelf in front of them and finally led the way back out into the kitchen. The cauldron boiled and foamed with its sickly green fog and he poured a sparkling purple powder into the mix as they passed by. A puff of dark, shadowy smoke lingered over the cooking fish fingers and a ladle began stirring itself around the rim as Belvedere hummed to himself.

"Uhm, Belvedere? How do you do that, with the spoons and the pots and stuff? Are you like a food wizard?" Vicki plopped down on a chair her arms still full of frozen meat. She cradled the cold cuts in her oversized kitchen apron taking care to keep the meat out of reach from her little blue griffin. The griffin's stomach gurgled as it sat fixing its eyes on the gleaming frozen food. Vicki shooed the griffin away and watched on as the griddle began to scrub itself clean. "I wish I could get my room to clean itself."

"It will, eventually! It seems to me that the Athenaeum is up and running again, and once you have your Housekeeping feet beneath you it should all come together for you." Belvedere took one of the frozen cuts from Vicki's apron and tossed it on a large cutting board set into the stone counter top. Several knives joined him in his slicing as he spoke to her. "The kitchen just sort of does what it's meant to do, it helps me here and there when I need it. I suppose that when I retire the kitchen will be much less organized and much less helpful for the new cook. For a time at least."

"Kind of like how the housekeeping is for me right now." Vicki hugged her frozen meats away from the griffin and it bellowed as she thwarted its sly attempt to grab a large chunk out of the apron. "I can't do anything yet, I can't even make this bird stop trying to eat everything in sight! It's no wonder I couldn't even turn the fountain on."

"And how is the assessment going? I'm not overly fond of the legal department being here, I find both the assessor and the law officer rather bracing."

Vicki squirmed in her seat bringing her hat down tight around her head. "Well... it's going. I maybe didn't do so great with the doors, and the fountain in the garden, it kind of... exploded."

Belvedere turned on his heels and raised his eyebrows at her. "Kind of exploded?"

"It sure chose a bad time to do it, too! The little guy was there watching and everything, he probably thinks that I did it on purpose, but I didn't! I don't know what I'm doing at all, I think that thing just blew up to get me in trouble!" Vicki shook her head and rubbed her hands together for warmth. "Or maybe I did do it, I don't know what to think. I can't ever get anything else right, so it makes sense, I guess."

"It's a good thing that we didn't dip you in ectoplasm then. You might have blown up along with it."

Vicki's back tensed up and she sat forward, her eyes widened and she frowned. "Really? Could that happen?"

"Well, let's not find out. Just in case." Belvedere gave her a weak smile and turned back to his cutting, humming a jolly tune as he worked. He grabbed another frozen cut of meat from Vicki and said, "surely there are some things that you do get right, you mustn't condemn yourself so unfairly."

"Oh sure, like at least I can brush my teeth and tie my shoes the right way. I'm fine with basic stuff, that's what they call me back at home, basic Vicki. Vicki Vacant. Brick brained Vicki." She covered her mouth, surprised at the words that had crept out from her memory. The little nicknames that she had earned from some of the scorned girls in her old troop began to bubble to the surface of her mind. "This hat is making me say stuff I don't mean to say."

"The cone of locus? Yes I suppose it will do that, your locus is all over the place, the hat is pulling from your deep subconscious instead. You have to focus on your being here for a purpose, just think of being in the present moment." He tapped the top of her pointed hat down onto her head with the flat end of his cleaver. "Think. Why are you here?"

Vicki gave him a quick nod and tried to concentrate with great effort on anything but the cookie fiasco. Her mind raced back and forth to her friends and to her family. Vicki began to feel that the hat must have been working. A tingle ran down her neck and her thoughts went to her mother and father. "Okay," she said, giving him another reassuring nod.

"Good, now leave those over there in the sink and I'll show you some of the tricks of the trade." Belvedere flashed her a bright toothy smile and brought her over to his spice rack. "The first thing to know is which ones are expensive. The more expensive, the less shakes we takes!"

Belvedere proudly showed Vicki his rare collection of Earthbound and Ätherbound spices. Seven different kinds of cinnamon, exotic and colorful toad essences from South America, even a small bottle of liquid penguin wax. He instructed her on the stinking up of the goblin dishes, his jars of ogre musk and crushed gnome corns had sent her into a gagging fit but she was glad to be away from the more magical aspects of her temporary job. The cook happily shared his vast knowledge of roots and dried flowers, the art of dehydrating all manner of fruits and berries, and the most important knowledge of all.

"Never take butter lightly around here, the entire economy of the country depends on it. I suppose you don't bother with butter much on Earthside, but here on this side of the world it's absolutely crucial for most everything!" Belvedere beckoned for Vicki to step up to the kettle. "Here the various creameries imbue their respective butters with magical and alchemical properties. Chief among them being taste of course, and this one is the house favorite."

Vicki stepped up onto a stool in front of the cauldron and took a glowing green cube from Belvedere. She immediately disliked how the butter felt in her hand, like a damp warm washcloth. "At least it doesn't smell bad like the fish does. Why is it glowing, is it magic?"

"Indeed it is, it's called Prismemory, very affordable but quite potent! Here drop it in," said Belvedere as he added one last shake of Toad's Twist into the cauldron. "This should be interesting!"

Vicki dropped the hunk of glowing green butter into the bubbling stew, holding her nose as she came close to the horrible concoction. "I don't see how you could make this stuff smell any worse than it already does!" She gagged and hopped off from the stool, shielding her poor nose as she retreated back towards the kitchen window. "I'm not supposed to eat that too, am I?" she asked with a gulp.

"No, I suspect that you'll be stuck with toast and eggs for dinner for quite some time. Now then, the butter that you dropped into the fish fingers will add just a dash of your own palate to the meal."

"My own palate? What does that mean?"

Belvedere stirred the bubbling cauldron. "Prismemory retains the most putrid food scent that you can recall, it adds that memory to its flavor profile. Just a bit mind you, nothing overpowering."

"That's gross! So what, if I imagined steamed broccoli and liver that's what the butter will taste like?" Vicki stuck out her tongue and recalled a time in sixth grade when she and Rachel had bought a sushi making kit from the grocery store.

Vicki had invented a particularly awful piece of sushi for her best friend, and Rachel being the kind soul that she was, indulged Vicki. It wasn't until after they had opened the can of crab meat that the two girls realized that the kit had long since expired. The smell of the crab meat had lingered in her nose for days and poor Rachel never even so much as mentioned sushi ever again. Surely that would have been the worst thing that she had ever smelled, the rotten crab meat.

"No, your imagination has little to do with it, it's more of an imprint. Think of it as nasal trauma. The stinkier the scent was the more of a lasting impression it will leave behind. The more you despised it, the stronger that taste will be." Belvedere finished his stirring and beamed down at her. "Would you care to help deliver some soup?"

The griffin clamored to its feet and stared up at the cauldron as Belvedere brought it over to Vicki. "Sure! That's one thing I definitely can't get wrong!" She traced the brim of her hat with her fingers and sniffed the air, staring at the drink trolley in the corner. A cold pit filled her stomach. "Well... maybe I should just tag along the first time," she said, with a tiny frown.

"Oh of course, I insist on it. I wouldn't leave you to wander the corridors alone, you'd get lost in an instant trying to find the rooms." Belvedere began to spoon the horrific finger stew into little bowls. "Stick close and you should be..." Belvedere sniffed at the air and furrowed his brow. He wiggled his mustache back and forth then sniffed at the stew, a look of relief crossed his face. "Ah, there we go, for a moment I thought the soup had gone off."

"Oh sure, like the goblins could even tell!" Vicki held her nose and helped to load the trolley with the bubbling green bowls of fish sludge. "Why are the goblins so crazy about butter anyways?"

"The discovery of enchanted butter saved this country from starvation and ruin," he began as they left the kitchen. "There's nothing much else of value here you see, the quartz mines dried up years ago, and vampples are almost always out of season. It wasn't until a family of wily goblins went toying around with casting spells on a cow that it all changed. The whole of Äther went crazy for the enchanted butters, and overnight the country was able to pull itself up out of the mud and into the muck."

"Into the muck? That doesn't sound better," said Vicki as she trailed behind holding her nose.

"Ah, that's a goblinism, the muck is richer mud, you see. In any event, the butters from our humble little country of Vania have put us on the map. Even retired goblins are still very passionate about how butter is doing and the advancements made in the schools of churning charms. I suspect that you only have the one type of butter back home?"

"Oh no, we have peanut butter too," Vicki exclaimed as they reached the great spiraling staircase.

A look of disgust crossed Belvedere's face. "Yes, well, let's not mention that too boldly around here."

"Oh, you don't like it? It's like my favorite thing." Vicki gave him a smile. "Haven't you ever had a peanut butter cup?"

Belvedere gagged and motioned for her to shush. "I should think not! I've never even been to prison, let alone the dungeons!"

Vicki followed alongside Belvedere through the Athenaeum with her little blue griffin close behind, more confused than ever about butter. The squeaky wheels of the cart rolled along the carpeted hallways, echoing off of the broken plaster walls. She felt a small tinge of guilt as they walked through one of the many common rooms of the above floors, the goblin residents sat in a circle staring out the window and bemoaning the demise of their fountain. She wondered what the little old things would do to keep occupied now.

They stopped at the common room and Belvedere began to hand a few bowls of the soup out to the goblins. "Tough bit of business about that fountain, Mrs. K. Still, we've got plenty of sewing and reading." He set a bowl of the steaming vile green stuff next to little old Mrs. Klobbreak, taking care to put the bowl within reach of her tiny wheelchair. "Looks as though it could rain this afternoon, maybe it was a blessing in disguise."

The little old goblin shifted her eyes left and right, then looked up to Vicki. "It was that dreadful little girl," she said opening her dull red eyes wide. "I seen her, I did! Sneaking around the garden, casting spells! She's out there right now, cursing our nappy service!" Her old wrinkly skin went from a shade of green to dark brown and she shivered in her seat.

Vicki scrunched her mouth to the side and clasped her hands together. "Oh, I didn't mean to, I'm sorry!" She glanced out the window and frowned at the sight of the great hole in the center of the hedge maze. "It just sort of blew up, I didn't really do anything... at least I don't think I did."

"Beware," the little old goblin lady whispered up to them both. "There's old witchcraft about! She's here you know, The bad luck witch!"

Belvedere scoffed and began handing more soup out to the other residents. "Oh really now, Mrs. K, come off it. Accidents happen." He nudged Vicki in to handing out some of the soup to the residents. "And I highly doubt that anyone would take the time to put a curse on the laundry service."

Vicki handed the soups out to the waiting little people around the room but her mind wandered as she set the bowls down on the tables and chair arms. She smiled at the goblins and imps as they grabbed out at the bowls with shaky little hands and she cautiously helped them back over to their seats. Their grisly little fangs and deep sunken eyes still had an effect on Vicki and she found herself trembling as one of the older goblins smiled back at her. His yellowed fangs stretched from one pointed ear to the other and his eyes glowed an eerie blood red.

Belvedere whispered down to Vicki as he prepared a few more bowls from his great copper cauldron. "They're not as likely to bite as you might think. The last person that bit me was Frank, that was well over a year ago." Belvedere stacked his bowls of soup up on the trolley and handed a few down to her. "You may only be here for a short while, but do try and make friends with the residents. It won't do to have the Housekeeper shying away from all contact."

"I don't mean to, I can't help it that I'm scared," she whispered back. She stacked an armful of the bowls up and she tried to shake out her nerves, wriggling her hands and puffing out quick breaths. She steadied herself and grabbed out for the bowls. "It's not just that I'm afraid of them, I'm also not all that great at making friends anyways, all I ever do is let people down." Vicki scowled and covered her mouth fuming with anger at the stupid cone of locus.

One of the goblins dropped his spoon into his bowl and the room went a little quiet. Vicki tried to ignore the feeling of her face heating up and the sweat gathering at her palms. She wordlessly went about distributing the rest of her soup out to the waiting residents in the common room, missing out on the conversation between Belvedere and an old decrepit cyclops man. She flashed her quick smiles to the goblins and handed them their bowls right up to the last goblin. The little blue griffin made a worried series of chirps and nestled up into Vicki's leg as the girl handed over the bowl to the goblin in front of her.

"Here you are," Vicki sang out, trying to sound as polite as possible while not exactly looking at the goblin's horrible little face. "Do you need help with a spoon?"

The little goblin narrowed his eyes up at Vicki. "Do I look like one of your residents? I'm here to assess your progress, girl, not eat this porridge!" The goblin assessor snatched the bowl from her and grumbled, staring down into the awful green sludge. "What... what is this, is this molasses chili?"

Vicki recoiled and balled her fists up staring down at the goblin. "I'm sorry! I'm sorry, you all kind of look the same to me," she said gripping her hat down around her. She shut her eyes and hissed at her own words.

The residents in the room all called out with distaste and offense at the young girl's words. The assessor shook his head mumbling under his breath sniffing at the fish finger soup. Vicki could hear Mrs. Klobbreak giggle from the crowd and Belvedere's footsteps approaching her from behind.

Belvedere laid a hand down on Vicki's shoulder. "She didn't mean that, it's been a long few days for the young Housekeeper here, she's still adjusting quite a bit." He leaned down over her shoulder and whispered into her ear. "You'll have to watch yourself with that kind of talk, Vicki, you can end up in a lot of trouble otherwise."

"I already am in a lot of trouble," Vicki whispered back to him. She hid her face in her hands and clenched her teeth together before biting her lip and holding her hand out for the goblin assessor's bowl. "I'm sorry! I'm sorry, I wasn't paying attention and I didn't mean to insult anyone."

The assessor brought the bowl back up towards Vicki's hands. "Apology accepted," he said, sounding nonplussed over the offense.

Before Vicki could take the bowl from him one of the goblins threw their own bowl down to the floor, crying out. This was followed by another and another, until even Mrs. Klobbreak whimpered and set her bowl as far away from herself as possible. The goblin assessor snatched the bowl back and sniffed at the sludge, inhaling the vapors from the green fish finger soup.

Belvedere brought a bowl of soup up to his mustache and recoiled at the scent. "Good heavens, it's overpowering!"

Vicki's entire body clenched up, she could feel the color drain out of her face and her feet went cold. "Oh no! What is it! What happened?"

One of the older goblins spat out the soup into his bowl and retched. "My blood sugar! By Crom, I can feel it spiking just tasting this!"

Another resident coughed and gagged, trying to clear her throat as she retreated from the vile soup. "Cursed! Cursed crumb soup! We'll all be cursed!"

The room filled with an uproar and the bowls were flung away from the residents, some of them going so far as to open the windows to toss the soup out bowl and all. Belvedere went around in a panic trying to quell the little riot taking place while Vicki stood frozen to the spot, watching the chaos happen all around them. The goblin assessor cleared his throat and she turned back around to him wearing a grimace that turned into a guilty little grin.

The assessor sniffed the soup again. "Molasses, earth gum, honey of the wood flyer... by Crom. This is cursed. This is Witch's Bread."

The room went quiet save for the few gagging goblins. Vicki stood on her tiptoes looking into the cauldron of soup. The scent had turned from that putrid rotten fish and unnameable stenches into a sweet warm aroma, even the fog had settled into something much less offensive. She knew the smell immediately, for it was a scent that haunted her waking thoughts at least once a week.

"But, but it was supposed to be something gross, like the worst smell ever!" Vicki turned to Belvedere and he returned a concerned look. "Why does it smell like that? Why does it smell like gingerbread?"

The assessor spat out and threw his bowl out of the window with unnatural accuracy. "Mister Belvedere, I suggest that you take this abomination away and fix a proper meal for the residents of the Athenaeum, lest you be put under assessment on the next quarter!" The little goblin pushed past Vicki nearly knocking the trolley over in his haste to get away from the pungent aroma that now filled the common room. "Let the Housekeeper clean this mess! I will add this to your assessment for speed and cleanliness!"

The residents all began to file out of the room, leaving Vicki behind along with Belvedere to clean up the soup from the carpets. The griffin puffed its chest out and sang a little song before pouncing on the lumps of discarded gingerbread and fish finger soup. It happily began gulping down the soup and wagging its little tail.

Vicki picked a few bowls up from the carpet frowning at Belvedere. "I'm sorry! It was me, wasn't it? It's because of the butter that I dropped in, I know it!"

"I'm afraid that I simply don't understand what happened here, I've never seen anything like this, certainly not from Prismemory butter!" Belvedere carefully loaded his trolley with some of the discarded bowls, keeping his voice low as the last goblins left the area. "It was as if the entire pot had turned to a great batch of the stuff, gingerbread, I haven't smelled it in years. It couldn't have been the butter, Vicki, don't worry yourself over it. It must be something in the stock."

"But I- I just, first the doors and then the fountain, now the soup!" Vicki gathered the last of the bowls and hugged them to her apron. "And what did he call it? Witch's Bread? They all said it was cursed!"

"Witch's Bread, gingerbread, it's from olden days and older magic. No one uses it anymore, not in hexes anyways." They gathered the bowls into the cauldron and Belvedere led Vicki back through the mansion. "From what I understand they still make cookies out of it on Earthside, have you ever seen one?"

"I've seen a few." Vicki followed along behind him and shooed her griffin away from the last mound of green sludge. "I guess it's back to sandwiches now?"

The gingerbread weighed heavily on Vicki's mind that night and she hid herself away into her bedroom, smuggling in a dinner of eggs and toast. "Stupid dog treats," she murmured to herself as she winced at the memory of the great cookie fiasco. "Stupid, stupid," she hissed at herself. She sat on the bed sharing her toast with the hungry griffin and staring at the telephone. The line had only given her static for the entire day and she desperately wanted to reach out to Max.

Any voice would have done, anybody to offer her some reassurance. A shadow loomed over Vicki, she could sense that something wasn't right with her being chosen as the Housekeeper. She could sense that the mansion didn't want her and she wondered how much longer it would put up with her. She glanced at the spot where the mischievous little statue had been and felt at her hat.

Maybe, just maybe, the owners were already finding her replacement. Maybe by tomorrow morning she would get the news that she was free to go home. At the very least perhaps by then the phone would work again. Of course it might only be that her home line was the problem... or maybe Max just didn't have the time to call her.

Vicki got up from her bed and plucked the telephone receiver from the cradle. Max would be busy with pig duties, that made sense. She placed her finger into the dial and began to spin the number to her mother's work phone. The call went through straight to her messaging service. Vicki smiled wide and ended the call immediately dialing up her home phone number in the hopes that the static had cleared.

The phone line still buzzed with the fizzle and pop of the static. She pressed her ear to the receiver and waited hoping for any sound to escape from the other end. A small and distant sound came from the other line and she perked up.

"Hello!" Vicki called out loudly into the speaker and shook the telephone violently in an effort to clear it of the static. "Max? Mom?"

An inaudible voice whispered from the phone, line drowned out by the electric popping and hisses. Someone on the other end of the line was holding a full conversation conducting business of some kind. The static washed over the line and the call ended with a click.

Vicki stood with the telephone in her hand, disappointed and near tears after having been so close to talking with someone back home. She put the receiver back and let her hand linger over the dial. The thought of calling Rachel crossed her mind. She might even pick up for a strange phone number before she would pick up for Vicki's.

She began the long process of spinning the dial, taking care not to plug in a wrong number. Halfway through completing the dialing Vicki spotted the time on the old wall clock then sighed as she dropped the phone back into the cradle. It was already past nine in the evening and Vicki didn't want to annoy Rachel by calling her so late and with no real reason to talk. "She probably wouldn't have answered anyways," she told herself.

She went to pick up the receiver again but was startled by the telephone ringing loudly in her hand. The bell rang inside of the telephone and Vicki nearly dropped it to the floor. She clicked the hook on the cradle and listened to the receiver. The griffin whined and laid its head between its talons watching her with large wet eyes.

"Hello," asked Vicki, as she pressed her ear closer to listen. The static buzzed into the phone line and the small voice returned, continuing the conversation from earlier. Only now Vicki could understand what the voice was saying.

The disturbing high pitched cartoony voice went on and on about being hungry, finally it began to say other words. "She only leaves the bones, you know," said the little hissing voice. It smacked its lips and took a large loud gulp of something on the other line. "I wants me steak and kidney pie too, I says to her, leave me at least one kidney for gravy then! Cor, she's greedy innit? She'd eat my legs right out from underneath me if she got the chance!"

Vicki trembled and went to end the call, another familiar voice came over the line just as she tapped the hook of the cradle. "Alive and screaming," said her aunt Zaldehyde. She let out a laugh from the other end of the line that turned into that distant hissing static once again.

Vicki whimpered setting the telephone far away from herself onto the floor, cuddling up next to the griffin on the bed and taking shelter under the bed covers. She couldn't shake the feeling that something dreadful was coming to get her. Something that no one else in the mansion would be too upset about.

From the portraits and statues on the wall the bust of the woman with her crystal ball turned and cracked as she whispered, "I see hate." The statue became inanimate stone once more, her gaze still upon Vicki.

Vicki pet the griffin late into the night, finally falling asleep as she stared at the bedroom door, fixated on the dull glow that came from the keyhole. The griffin stood guard over her, only settling down into the pillows once the glow from the doorway vanished back into the darkness.

Chapter twelve

Vicki burst into a fit of laughter, along with Rachel and the other girls as Jade tried pulling her fondue fork from the pot. The entire pot lifted up with the white cheese as she pulled with all of her might. The girls squealed with delight as Jade let go of the fork and the cheese kept it cemented in place.

"I think we missed a vital step," whined Jade.

Rachel poked her own fork into a small chunk of bread popping it into her mouth before speaking. "Well, at least we still have the other stuff! Does anyone have anything to say about the cookie sales next week? Me and Vicki are going to set up outside of the Costco and we're going to have two fourth graders with us. So somebody else needs to put Erica at their table."

The other girls all grumbled, squirming with unease at the very mention of the girl's name. Jade crossed her fingers in front of her as the other girls in the room began moaning and complaining over who might have to take on the burden. Finally, one girl spoke up over the chorus of complaints.

"It better be where no one can see her, like maybe she can just sit in the back of a van and hand the cookies down to us. You know, out of sight?" The other girls began snickering and nodding in agreement.

"Or where they can't smell her," said Vicki, leaning forward to stick a fork into a bit of bread. "She always sat next to me in math last year, it was so gross! I wish I could have just told her to go take a bath."

Jade giggled laying back on her bed. "See? When the nicey nice says it, you know it's bad!"

"Vicki! Not you too," exclaimed Rachel with an amused look on her face. "Okay, fine, we're just going to have to draw straws for it I guess."

The closet door handle jiggled around and Vicki snapped her attention to the corner of the room. The other girls continued murmuring about the problematic girl. None of them seemed to notice the sound at all. She let her eyes drift back to the laughing girls, returning to the conversation.

Rachel leaned into Vicki's shoulder as she whispered, "No one wants to take her, I don't know what to do!"

Vicki gave a shrug. "Well, no one likes her and she knows it, I don't even know why she's still in the scouts!" The closet door creaked open and a gush of cold air chilled her neck. Vicki turned to stare at the closet. "I don't want to sound mean…"

Rachel frowned looking away. "It's okay Vicki, we get it too. Everyone does."

A loud slap snapped through the air, and a red hand mark appeared on the face of one of the other girls. Vicki's voice rang out through the air, "You big dumb Hippo! If we want to go to the zoo all we have to do is look at you and your family!"

Vicki let out a shriek, covering her mouth as the other girls went on chatting and giggling. She spun around to the closet door just in time to see two shining bits of tinfoil disappear into the darkness, twisted little red fingers wiggled at Vicki as they vanished behind the door. She scrambled to her feet, nearly knocking over the statue of fondue in her panic.

Another snap traveled through the air landing squarely on the chin of a different girl. "You're so gross you need sandpaper to scrape off all those zits!" The angry cartoonish voice broke into a hiss as it traveled around the room. Another slap landed on the girl's cheek. "At least I don't need a rubber bed sheet like you!"

Vicki rushed to the closet door slamming against it with her full weight. The door began to shake and rattle as the little monster on the other side beat his fists against the splintering wood. She screamed, planting her feet against the floor and holding back the unseen assailant from her friends. The door knob rocked back and forth so fast that it began falling apart inside of the door.

Rachel sat in the circle with the other girls, wearing a frown and looking to the floor as she spoke. "Vicki, it's okay, just let it go."

"There's something in here!" Vicki pressed against the door, screaming as it began to split down the middle.

"I know, it's okay! Just come back," said Rachel beckoning for her to rejoin the other girls. "Just try, you have to try it!"

The door exploded behind her, tossing Vicki forward to the floor. She crawled away from the wreckage as quick as a bunny, reaching Rachel just as the other girl began to scream. Vicki turned to face the darkness in the closet. Those two tiny balls of tinfoil stared back at the girls in the room, darting left and right, then slowly lifting higher into the darkness. Higher and higher those little specks of light climbed until they both reached the top of the ruined door frame. The glowing light of those eyes turned to a piercing green as a low snarl ripped from the closet space. A massive amount of sharp teeth opened and glimmered in the doorway. The creature within let loose with a blood chilling howl.

The howl hit Vicki's ears, transforming into the sound of an out of tune trumpet. Vicki swung her feet at the thing in the closet only to find that she had instead kicked her little griffin off from the bed. The loud obnoxious broken trumpet blasted through the mountainside again. She peeked over the bed at the griffin with a tiny frown.

"I'm sorry! Are you okay?" she asked. The griffin stirred then returned to a sleeping position, unconcerned with its new bedding arrangement. Vicki blew a strand of hair from her face unamused by the laziness of the griffin. "Want to get some breakfast?"

The griffin sprang to life and began making a fuss for her to get out of the bed.

"She lives," Desmond laughed out from the kitchen table. He folded a newspaper over in his hands scooting a chair out for Vicki. "Did the trumpets wake you up?"

Vicki collapsed down into the seat, giving him a tired nod, her oversized hoodie spread out around her and the cone of locus toppled forward over her eyes. A plate of scrambled eggs and bacon appeared in front of her and a bit of green meat fell to the floor at the griffin's waiting talons. Vicki slid the plate closer to herself, picking at the eggs.

"Why are they blowing them so loud? What are they doing down there in the town?" she asked with a crabby tone. "Like is it band practice or something? It's so bad."

"The Buttered Beagle Boggle. It's big around these parts, sounds like they're gonna have a match tomorrow." Desmond sipped at an empty teacup, replacing it into a clean saucer with a satisfied look upon his face. "I can get you some earplugs if you need them, gonna get real loud around here tomorrow."

Vicki glanced at the completely spotless teacup and gave him another nod. She rubbed her eyes, searching around the kitchen, wondering where Belvedere might be. "I still think I messed up the soup yesterday," she said pushing the bacon away from her.

"Ain't no way that was you, Belvedere told me the whole thing. It's probably just one of the ghosts around here pranking it up. They get everywhere, you know." Desmond sipped at the empty teacup again. "Belvedere and Jerry went down town talking to the legal department today, she's got some hang up about the overgrown ivy in the front I guess. Good news though, the assessor's still here!"

"Great," said Vicki, as she let her head drop onto the table. The griffin cooed up to her and nudged her in the knee. "What am I messing up today?"

"Laundry! This is an easy win today. Get yourself filled up and we'll head down to the laundry as soon as you're ready." He opened the newspaper and Vicki glanced at the back page. It was another advertisement for an outlandish butter, this one being made from Centaur's milk. "You aren't eating your bacon?" asked Desmond.

"No! I, I mean no, you can have it if you want it." Vicki slid her plate towards Desmond with a grin. He remained silent reading his morning paper.

The morning's breakfast ended in awkward silence and the three of them went traveling through the Athenaeum down to the bottom level. Desmond showed several points of interest to Vicki, one of them being an elevator that didn't quite work, sometimes moving to random locations within the mansion as soon as anyone approached too closely to it. The mansion was littered with strange objects and goings on and he was adamant that Vicki keep her wits about her at all times.

"The elevator is bad enough," began Desmond. "But the old dispensary in the back of the mansion is off limits, you understand? Sometimes the stacks get a little mean, they can turn you around for hours if you aren't careful."

Vicki followed along behind him and gave a nod. "This sure is a weird place. Did you ever get lost in here?"

"Well, it's kind of all up to the mansion itself. I got a feeling it could keep you running down these hallways forever if it didn't much care for your company." Desmond shook his head, his eyes seemed to look far away into the past. "Saw a Roman soldier running between the same two rooms a couple of years back. Kept coming out the same door, yelling a bunch of nonsense. I still wonder if that was just a man in a costume or not. I don't know."

They came to pass a great iron seal upon the wall just before the turn of the corner that would take them to the basement. Etched into the metal were the three great runes that Vicki had seen before on the wax seal of her grandfather's will. Formed together in a circle were the water droplet, the crescent moon, and the thunder bolt.

Desmond tapped Vicki on her shoulder, moving her along from the iron seal. "We don't really talk about the owners much here, it annoys them."

"The Three Lords, right?"

Desmond shushed her and placed his finger to his lips. "They listen in, they see everything. Don't talk about them unless you mean it. Understand?"

She gave him a nod and they walked onward. "Got it."

They arrived into a dark hallway full of steam and damp carpeting, Desmond took a whiff of the heavily chlorinated air around them. "What I wouldn't give for some good old fashioned fabric softener." He motioned Vicki forward into a large, loud room at the end of the hallway. "Guess who," he said sounding amused with himself.

As Vicki entered the steamy doorway, her shoulders slumped down at the sight of Frank. The stitchwork girl sat on an overturned laundry basket with piles and piles of linens surrounding her. Two white rats scurried along between the piles dragging sheets together and hopping over one another helping, to fold and sort the linens as they went. A third rat sat on Frank's shoulder, turning its head along with her to stare up at Vicki.

Frank lifted her large flashy aviator goggles from her eyes, squinting at Vicki. "Cop a squat short stuff, the first load is taking forever." She looked over to Desmond. "Did you hear the *trumpets*, Dez?" she asked waggling her eyebrows up and down.

"I'm so happy for you, Frank. Anyways, Vicki, here's your next job. Hope it doesn't blow up in your face too," said Desmond nudging Vicki toward the piles of linens. "Just joking! You're all good, you're good. I gotta go jive with this assessor guy, you wanna show her the ins and outs of the laundry?"

Frank gave Desmond a salute and the vampire promptly vanished from the doorway. She turned to Vicki smiling a big toothy grin. The stitch work girl had changed her lipstick color to bright orange and she wore a pair of denim overalls. If not for the grotesque stitches and unkempt fluff of white hair, Vicki would have thought the girl quite fashionable.

"Basically, we just stuff the nasty things in here," Frank began, pointing at one of the many sputtering laundry machines in the room. The machines clanked and shook as she scooted her basket along the ground to the other side of the room. One massive drying unit stood in the far end corner. "And we put the wet clean things in there, with me so far?"

"Oh sure." Vicki sat down on a pile of sheets joined by her griffin. "I mean, we have these where I'm from too," she said with a small amount of snark in her tone.

"*Good!*" Frank returned with a condescending flourish, giving the other girl a huge thumb's up. She opened a rusty door on the side of the drying unit to reveal twenty or so rats diligently running in coordination on a great wheel within the machine. The rats all looked up at Frank in unison and squeaked. She gave them a tiny salute before closing the unit door. "As you were," she said as they all went about their duty.

"Why are the rats making it run, can't it run on magic like everything else?" Vicki sat up and involuntarily jumped as one of the white rats hopped over her shoe. She let out a little gasp and brought her knees up to her chest. The griffin also shied away from the rat settling into a higher pile of blankets nearby.

Frank gave Vicki a distasteful look then gave a loving pat to the rat on her shoulder. "It's *ecto friendly.* Plus it gives the rats some purpose and self worth, it's a whole team synergy thing."

Vicki carefully rose to her feet, picking up an armful of sheets. "Well at least I know how to do some laundry, I can't mess this up," she stated proudly. "I wish my assessment guy would grade me on this instead."

"Oh no, you don't do the loading or folding or anything, that's what the rats do. Well, *me* and the rats." Frank put her goggles back down over her eyes. "You do the housekeeping, you bring me the laundry then take it back to the residents. Pretty simple, right?"

Vicki gave her a nod. "Oh sure, I can do that."

"The thing is, usually the Housekeeper *and* the house do it together, you know like you could just magic it down here. You don't really got that going on for you." Frank took the pile of sheets from Vicki's arms. "If you did, you could just make the sheets and curtains and everything march down here all by itself."

Vicki felt at her pointy hat. "Yeah, the assessor tried to make me turn the fountain on, and it exploded. I don't think I'm living up to expectations."

"Well, I didn't expect too much, I don't think a hat and five years of grade school are ever gonna cut it so I wouldn't worry about it too much." Frank threw the pile of sheets into the air and the rats jumped up sorting them into the machines as they fell. "How old are you anyways? Now that I get a good look at ya in the light, I'm beginning to wonder just how much trouble we're really in."

"I'm almost fourteen, and I've had *eight* years of grade school for your information," said Vicki crossing her arms. "And you don't look that much older than me either!"

"I'm plenty older than you," said Frank, throwing another pile of sheets into the air behind her. "Well most of me is. Come on, we're going to have to show you how to do this the old fashioned way." She skipped over to the door waving for Vicki to follow. "This way."

Vicki stood waiting for the little protective griffin to spring forward. It had nestled itself deep into a pile of blankets and dozed off. She glanced back to the stitchwork girl and cringed. Frank smiled wide, petting the rat sitting upon her shoulder.

"Okay," said Vicki as she began shuffling behind Frank. The two of them trekked up the hall in uncomfortable silence. Vicki gripped her hoodie tight staring at the long line of stitching that traced Frank's spine, wondering if the stitches ever got caught in zippers and jewelry.

The second floor was so quiet that it nearly felt abandoned, more paintings lined the old broken walls and the carpets wheezed out dust with their every step. Large creeping ferns spread out like gigantic spiders along the floors lining the paneled doors of each room. It was amazing to Vicki at just how much space there was in the mansion, the hallway seemed to stretch on for longer than a football field or more. Vicki followed the lanky teenager into a large open room full of couches and chairs, worrying that she might have to work with the rude girl all day long.

"I know what you're thinking," said Frank as they came to the commons room of the second floor.

Vicki grabbed onto the brim of her hat fearing that the other girl had indeed been privy to her thoughts. "You do? I'm sorry, I was just- I," she stammered out.

"It's bigger on the inside than the outside. Well sista, you don't know the half of it." Frank put her hand out to the side for Vicki to follow. "Some of the rooms are bigger than the hallway too, it's freaky," she continued, leading Vicki to the first set of rooms.

"Oh... how big is it? Do you know?"

Frank stood at the entrance to one of the resident's rooms. She raised her goggles up placing them around her forehead. "Big enough to get lost in for a while." She took out a large roll of paper from her overalls unfurling it for Vicki to see, she pointed at a place on the scroll. "This will keep you going in the right direction, allegedly, I don't know for sure because I haven't ever had to use it. Some of the rooms are empty now, we don't always know where the residents went. I think Jerry might be snacking on a few of them, ya know, on the sly."

"Gross, why wouldn't he just eat a sandwich?" Vicki grinned at Frank's obvious joke.

Frank stared back at Vicki without any hint of a smile. She held the scroll out to Vicki. "Well, he's not a vegetarian. You watch him now, you're pretty goblin sized yourself." She raised her eyebrows and nodded at Vicki.

Vicki gulped at the idea of being eaten by the red cow and took the scroll from Frank's hands, watching as it filled in with a floor schematic. It was a basic floor plan easily understood even by the likes of her. There was a north facing compass rose in the corner of the scroll and several marked off rectangles resembling the resident's rooms. A shimmering red X showed the current location of the scroll holder.

"Is it just this floor?" She opened more of the scroll. The map extended further into a legend with footage markings and icons of interest. Notes had been hastily scrawled in nearly illegible handwriting. Things like bad smells, wet carpets, and even residents that chatted too much were marked off. Vicki had to tilt the map to the right just to read the highly distorted letters. "I can hardly read this!"

"It'll change floors when you change floors. It's not much good outside or in the basement." Frank pointed to the compass rose. "This will turn red when you're facing the right direction, it just sort of knows where you're supposed to go. The *mansion* knows lots of stuff."

"But what if *I* don't know where I'm supposed to go?"

"That's what a map is for, ya doughnut, geez!" Frank threw her arms up in defeat. "Just follow it to all the rooms and get the laundry then bring it downstairs. Sheets, towels, robes- go go go!" The stitchwork girl clapped her hands together and motioned for Vicki to go about her new job.

"You mean I have to walk all this laundry down by myself? That's gonna take forever!"

"Makes you wish you could just use *magic* or something instead, huh?" Frank stared at Vicki with a wide smile on her face.

Vicki stepped into the first room, briefly spinning around to watch Frank go. The other girl skipped along down the hallway back toward the first floor, gleefully leaving Vicki behind to face the perils of the resident rooms all by her lonesome. She checked the map one more time before rolling it up into her pocket and walking over to the first messy bed in front of her.

"Piece of cake," she said to herself. She lifted the first blanket from the bed only to be met by the naked bottom of the pewter monk statue. She let out a scream as it tried spraying her with its horrible gas attack. She raised the blanket up in front of her blocking the noxious spray. The monk gave an evil little laugh and went thumping out of the room. Vicki held her nose and gagged. "Piece of cake."

Several hours had passed and Vicki now knew without any doubt that she was actually terrible at even the most simple task of gathering sheets and towels. She had guessed that the actual housekeeping part of being the Housekeeper might be easy. It had turned out quite the opposite. She sat slumped against a wall with the cone of locus hanging off her brow and her aching legs turned to jelly.

Vicki had accomplished getting the laundry out of 28 rooms so far, and as time went on it became clear that finishing the laundry before sundown seemed less and less likely. She had 20 more rooms to go and little stamina left, having walked arm loads of laundry down to the first story more times than she cared to keep track of. She adjusted the heavy hat upon her head, sighing before rising back to her feet.

She stumbled into her twenty ninth room, giving a tiny gasp as she spotted a goblin resident. Mrs. Klobbreak sat in her rickety old wheelchair staring out of her window, straining to get a good look from her vantage point. The goblin turned in her chair giving Vicki a warm smile full of jagged little yellow teeth.

"Oh it's you! So nice to see you again dear," said Mrs. Klobbreak as she wheeled herself over to Vicki. She opened her dark red eyes wide, looking the earthbound girl up and down. "That old witch hat suits you! You look just like your mother did when she was about your age."

Vicki smiled and touched the brim of her hat. "What, no my mom isn't a witch, that's Zaldehyde. Zaldehyde is my aunt." She plopped down on the edge of Mrs. Klobbreak's bed and breathed out. "I'm not really a witch at all, even if I was I don't think I'd be very good at it."

Mrs. Klobbreak rolled up to the bed and patted Vicki's knee as she spoke. "Oh no, not Benjamina, I meant *your* mother! *Eleonora,*" she said with a delighted tone. "Oh they both loved running around here, pretending and playing make believe! *Wearing their little hats!*"

Vicki raised her eyebrows and sat up. "They did? My mom did? You knew her when she was a little girl?" Vicki marveled at the idea of her mother running around the same mansion hallways. "She didn't really ever talk about this place..."

"Oh I suppose not. Oh I shouldn't say. It's not my place, dear. Ben and Ellie both used to run around these hallways in their younger days! Then they both stopped coming around as much, I've always wondered how they got on after growing up."

"Who's Ben," asked Vicki, as the goblin lady turned a darker shade of green. "Did you say *Benjamina?*"

"That was her name, your mother's best friend! She was such a nice girl, it's a shame. Your aunt came along and ruined everything for the both of them. I think her name was Ben, I can hardly remember my own names these days." Mrs. Klobbreak shook her head and grimaced. "Oh, but that doesn't matter now, that's for you and your mother to discuss. Now then, how do you like being the *Housekeeper?* Have you seen your grandfather around here yet?"

Vicki gave the old goblin a sad smile. "Oh, Mrs. K, *he passed away a few days ago.* That's why I'm here."

"Yes that's what we heard, he should be wandering in any day now, you'll have to catch him before he leaves for good!"

Vicki gave the goblin a nod. "Okay, I'll keep my eyes peeled," she said with a wistful look out the window.

"Oh oh! Come over here and see!" Mrs. Klobbreak grabbed onto Vicki's hand leading her over to the opened window in the middle of the room. "Did you hear the trumpet earlier this morning? That was them down there!" She pointed out across the hedge maze and toward the far end of Everfall down below.

"Oh sure, Desmond called it the battered beetle something."

Mrs. Klobbreak giggled sitting up straight to get a better look out over the valley. "No no, the Buttered Beagle Boggle!" She pointed back down to the mess of the exploded fountain in the garden. "We all watch it from between the hedges down there, Desmond and the others think we're all just sitting and sleeping." Her voice reached a joyous high pitched whisper. "But we all have our favorite peep holes in the hedge!"

Vicki couldn't help but grin at the older lady's giggling and she looked down at the broken fountain. "That's pretty sneaky! What is it though, is it like a sport?"

"It's the only thing worth watching, that's what it is!" Mrs. Klobbreak smiled and let her eyes close. "And my grandson Derkie is one of the best hammerers in all the world! You'll see, one day he's going to be the biggest star in the whole game!"

"I'm sorry that I kind of blew up the fountain. Can you watch it on the television instead? When is the game?" She turned around at a sudden noise on the bed behind them, relieved to see that the griffin had returned to her. It made a quiet cooing noise. "Is *Derkie* playing in the next one?"

"He is, he is! It's a very special day too, tomorrow! It's his birthday!" Mrs. Klobbreak grasped her hands together opening her eyes wide, staring out the window. "They're playing tomorrow and it's his birthday!"

"Oh! Well maybe he'll visit after the game," said Vicki. She leaned out of the window to view the town with Mrs. Klobbreak. "If he's playing right down there."

"Maybe, maybe!" The old goblin's smile faded just a bit and she wheeled herself away from the window. "Oh, but you should get back to the laundry! I'm keeping you, I'm sorry!"

Vicki went to gather the sheets and blankets from the bed shooing the griffin away. "It's okay, I wanted a break anyways. It's a lot of work going up and down the stairs with all these sheets!"

"The stairs? Why not just use the rat chutes," asked Mrs. Klobbreak. "Every room has a rat chute!" She wheeled herself over to her toilet and pointed to a long pipe that stretched along the wall.

Vicki had assumed that these pipes, of which there had been one in every room so far, were plumbing of some sort. Mrs. Klobbreak knocked on the pipe and a portion of it opened up popping outward like a little door on a submarine. A fat white rat clamored up from the hole in the pipe, puffing its chest out and giving Mrs. Klobbreak a salute.

"You see dear? The old rat service is still going strong!" Mrs. Klobbreak returned the salute to the white rat. "You can send anything anywhere in the house with these! It's how I send letters to all my friends here. I'm surprised that your friend with the white hair didn't tell you about it before."

"What? I could have been using these all along! Frank didn't tell me about any of it!" Vicki clenched her teeth together and blew out a lungful of hot air. "And she is not my friend! Why is she like this? I swear she hates me!"

"No no, not her, the other one with the white hair. Oh I can't remember her name, I'm sorry dear, sometimes I get so confused. Maybe that is her, I don't know." Mrs. Klobbreak pulled on her ears in deep thought. "Oh poor girl, It's her brains dear, she's got odd brains. It's not her fault, she's nice some days and some days she's very frank about things. She's like two different girls."

"She's very, very *Frank*." Vicki stormed over to the chute and began stuffing the bedding into it. She tried her best to salute the rat and it returned a squeak. It stomped the laundry down into the pipe, riding it away into the darkness.

Mrs. Klobbreak wheeled herself back into her room and cackled. "You two are going to be the best of friends, I can see it! Don't forget your gargoyle, dear!"

Vicki looked back at the bed and groaned at the sight of the lazy little griffin. It had made itself perfectly at home on Mrs. Klobbreak's bed stretching out and staring back at her. She cleared her throat, motioning at it, and it clucked out a few times before finally hopping down to the floor to follow Vicki out.

She went about the rest of the rooms with newfound speed, thanks to her knowledge of the laundry chutes. She fumed and obsessed over the stitchwork girl wondering why Frank hated her so much. Those thoughts slowly turned and Vicki began accepting that there was plenty about her to hate. She was so deep in her thoughts that it took her by surprise when they came to the end of the first floor rooms.

"We're almost done! Maybe we can go find some lunch after this is all over," she said down to the griffin. "You have to eat something besides that weirdo meat that you keep gulping down, that can't be good for you, *it was green!* Let's see if Mr. Belvedere can fix us something that isn't any weird colors and…" Vicki entered into one of the rooms and fell silent.

The griffin came bounding into the room and passed in between Vicki's legs. It too came to a stop and stared at the room ahead of them. Vicki held her map up again checking for her location. She had worked her way down from the second story and through most of the first floor. She should have been in the northwest corner of the mansion.

The map didn't show that she was in the mansion at all. The room blocks kept filling in and disappearing on the scroll, depicting various indecipherable symbols and shapes before changing to large black squares. Vicki turned the map over, shaking it to make sure that it was in proper working order.

"Well, this isn't even marked on the map. The clinic and dispensary are right next to here, but we shouldn't even be in this room." She followed the map with her fingers. "There's three more rooms down the hall that way."

The griffin cooed and went running through the darkness deep into the middle of the room. It stopped and turned, looking up at Vicki with an expectant stance. It wagged its little nubby tail, chortling at her, seeing that she was hesitant to follow.

"Where are you going? That's not the way!" Vicki started off after the griffin. "I don't think we're supposed to be in here!"

Vicki chased the griffin into a dark corner and through a hole in the back wall, suddenly finding herself in a different area of the mansion altogether. The griffin happily pranced around in the well lit room full of pills and medical supplies. It squawked and raced to the other end of the room where a large plate of fruits and kibble had been placed.

"Is this the dispensary?" she asked herself. She pulled the scroll out and whimpered. The scroll had replaced the floor plan with an image of a skull and crossbones. No mansion layout, no words at all, just the macabre image filling itself in with the magical ink. The ring on her thumb glittered with a purple light then went dark. "We should go," she said, staring at her hand and making a bee-line back to the hole in the wall.

The hole had vanished. Vicki slammed her hands against the wall where the hole had been. She spun around to the griffin; it remained at the plate of food gobbling down the treats that had been laid out. Someone had put the food there on purpose, someone had led them into the strange room. Her breaths quickened and her heart began to beat faster and faster.

Vicki ran up to the door framed on its sides and top by an opaque white glass wall. She tried the door handle, finding it locked. The handle wouldn't even twist in the slightest. She put her hands on the sides of her head and shut her eyes tight, wishing with all her might for the door to unlock. It seemed that the hat was not overly effective at granting wishes either.

The griffin stopped its eating and blinked a few times. It gave a hiccup and stumbled around, knocking into one of the medicine delivery carts and sending it crashing to the floor. Pills went flying onto the ground. The griffin clucked and fought its way over to Vicki before collapsing onto its side and passing out.

"Oh no!" Vicki cradled the griffin up into her arms and backed into the corner of the room. "Hello! Is anyone there," she cried out. Vicki gave a piercing scream at the top of her lungs, kicking at the door as hard as she could. "Anybody!"

The mansion shook and groaned around her, and the lights in the dispensary began fading away to darkness. Vicki and the griffin were left in the dark save for a tiny bit of light that came from the wall behind them. She felt around at the wall surprised to find that a new door had appeared. Light glimmered out from its keyhole and she could hear distant old timey music playing from the new room behind the mysterious door.

"Hello?" Vicki peered into the keyhole, still cradling the griffin in her arms. She could just make out a crackling fire in an old brickwork fireplace and an old record player spinning a tiny disc in the corner. A writing desk sat facing the keyhole, and an ink pot had been precariously placed at the edge of the desk with a feather quill pen sticking up from it. Far off into the corner of the room she could just barely spy a dark red cloak drifting back and forth as if caught in a breeze. The room looked familiar, though she couldn't quite recollect when or where she had seen the room before. "Is someone there?"

No answer came from the new mysterious room, but a sudden low growl came from behind the door to the hallway. Vicki hugged the griffin close to her chest, sneaking away into the corner of the room and hiding behind the downed medicine cart. She watched in horror, holding her breath as a large shadow appeared on the white glass windows that framed the door.

"Who's in there? You're not supposed to be in here," came the voice of the goblin assessor from the other side of the glass.

"It's me! It's me, I got stuck in here and I can't get out," Vicki shouted clamoring over the cart and running up to the door. "Please help!"

"Okay, okay! Stand back!"

Vicki held the griffin close, backing away from the door expecting it to get kicked in. The door unlatched and the goblin assessor peeked inside. He stared at the two of them, giving her a confused look.

"I thought you said that the door was locked."

"It was! I swear it was and then this door over here..." Vicki turned to face the wall with the mysterious door, it had vanished. The large hole in the wall had returned in the corner of the room. She turned back to face the assessor. "I'm not crazy! This room trapped me inside, and that hole over there just completely disappeared, and then a weird door just showed up on that wall! There was a whole other room in there!" Vicki hugged her griffin. "And somebody poisoned my griffin!" She sat down and began huffing out quick panicked breaths, rocking herself back and forth on the cold linoleum floor.

The assessor backed away from the hyperventilating girl, finally setting his stone tablet down to help her back to her feet. "Well, it won't do us any good to sit here and shout about it, come on, let's get that bird to the house doctor!"

"Okay," Vicki said as she took the goblin's hand. "*Where are we going to find a doctor around here?*"

Chapter thirteen

Frank examined the little griffin, stretching open its beak to get a closer look at its tongue. She opened its eyes, shining a light into them and frowning at the response that she got. She looked over to Vicki and gave the griffin a few unsympathetic pats on its face.

"So what'd you feed it," asked Frank.

Vicki gripped her hands wringing them together and sighing as she stared down at the little griffin. "I don't know, someone put a bunch of food out in the pill room and she ate almost all of it. I feel so stupid, I should have stopped her! Is she going to be okay?"

"*Her?* I don't know, we're talking about a magically powered gargoyle here, magically powered gargoyles are kind of shaky. I mostly deal with normal toads and above average rats. You know if it dies, the mansion will just make a different one for you, it's no big loss." Frank said with a shrug of her shoulders. "It takes like a day tops!"

Vicki shook her head and rubbed the griffin's face, ignoring Frank. "I don't want a different gargoyle, I can't just throw her away like that! I don't even know what her name is yet."

Frank huffed, gesturing for Vicki to step back into the hallway. "Well, I'll work my magic on *her* and see what I can do. Don't expect miracles."

Vicki shuffled out of the bare bones clinic with its singular bed and broken down examination table. She moped the entire way through the upstairs, stopping at one of the large windows overlooking the front yard of the Athenaeum. The goblin assessor conversed with Desmond and another unseen person on the patchy lawn outside.

They all seemed to be giving some spirited opinions, probably about her performance. Desmond shook his head back and forth, aggressively motioning with his hands as he spoke. He gestured over to the hedge maze and all over the mansion's windows. Vicki pressed herself up against the glass, sighing and leaving a little vapor cloud on the window. She watched on as the assessor shook his stone tablet at Desmond and the person hidden by the front porch awning.

The unseen third person finally walked away from the building and took a look back at the mansion. Vicki gasped and hid herself to the side of the window. She carefully peeked out from behind the dusty old tattered curtain, watching the tall strawberry blonde woman.

Ciara Shuck froze in her tracks sniffing the air around her. The horrible woman twisted around, looking directly up to Vicki and wearing a grin so unnatural that it sent ice into the girl's veins. Vicki ran away from the window all the way back to her bedroom. She slammed the door shut, leaning against it with all her weight and holding her breath.

She sat against the door tucking her knees under her chin, envisioning the horrible lawyer's misshapen nails and teeth. The long fingernails scraping down the front door burned into Vicki's memory. The hungry growl of Ciara's stomach and the way that she had looked at Vicki haunted her. She began to sniffle and shiver wondering if her family had been cured yet. A light knock came from the door and she sprang to her feet ready to flee.

Desmond's voice came from the hallway. "Vicki, you in there? How are you feeling?"

Vicki opened the door, looking past him down both ends of the hall. She breathed a sigh of relief and reached out to Desmond's hand trying to drag him into the room. A blue flash emanated out from the doorframe and Desmond leaned back from the threshold.

"Hey careful now, I can't come in there!" Desmond adjusted his collar looking down at Vicki with great concern on his face. "You got pretty shaken up this morning, are you doing okay?"

"What was that woman doing here! That Ciara Shuck lady?"

"You call *that* a lady? Do you *know* what she is?"

Vicki leaned her head against the doorframe. "She came to my house and she was really creepy. My mom and dad hate her, I don't know what she wanted, I think she... I think she was going to try to kidnap me... or something worse..."

"Oh it's something worse. That old hound is asking lots of questions about you. Made me a little uncomfortable." Desmond checked both sides before waving her into the hallway. "Come on downstairs, Bellboy and Jerry are waiting for us."

"My cousin Magra said that she's a werewolf," whispered Vicki as she followed behind Desmond.

"Your cousin is right, and then some. All of them lady lawyers are werewolves, same big company, same name. Shuck has some other serious issues though, all on her own. She's all twisted and wrong, everyone knows that she's bad news, that you don't leave your babies out if she's around."

Vicki gave a shudder and stuck close behind him. "She works for my aunt."

"That makes sense. Birds of a feather. Now look, no one in this here house is gonna try to hurt you, but Ciara Shuck is a different story. She can come and go as she pleases right now too, so you better keep your wits about you, you know what I'm saying?" Desmond turned to face Vicki. "Do not, and I mean *do not*, find yourself alone with her."

Vicki gave him an emphatic nod and they continued down through the mansion. "Well, why is she even allowed in the mansion? My Aunt Zaldehyde can't come in, couldn't you just make another magic force field thing to keep her out too?"

"That's tricky. The Company of Wolves handles all the legal stuff here, just about everywhere else too. She's got to be allowed in for all the official testing. *She's* the legal department. You're in a tough spot, but you're the Housekeeper. The mansion should still protect you well enough."

"But my griffin is poisoned now!" Vicki stopped at the realization gripping the brim of her hat and frowning. "Omigod, it's her! She did it, she poisoned her! I know she did!"

Desmond ushered her forward through the dining room. "Okay, but let's not say it too loud, she *is* a lawyer. You start making accusations like that and she's liable to get litigious." They made their way into the kitchen area where Belvedere and Jerry were waiting. He gave her a pat on the shoulder. "Take a seat, we're gonna have a house meeting, just assessing out the situation."

Vicki sat at the large kitchen table, exhausted and worried, resting her head on her forearms. She was absolutely uncomfortable with the idea that Frank, of all people, turned out to be the only suitable medical professional in the Athenaeum. Surely there had to be better options, a witch doctor somewhere down in the town, perhaps. A veterinarian one hundred miles away would be a more viable prospect any other day, but today Frank was her only hope.

Desmond, Belvedere, and Jerry all stood around the table. They spoke on the matter of the griffin to each other letting Vicki have some time to herself. The conversation hadn't escaped her completely, however, and she was able to follow along with their hushed discussion.

Desmond in particular wondered if Vicki hadn't succumbed to an over abundance of stress or if the mansion was playing a nasty trick on her. Belvedere began to agree, stating that she shouldn't continue most of the responsibilities any longer, and that she would soon return home anyways. Jerry simply kept quiet, save for his convictions that there was far too much of Ciara Shuck's stench in the air.

Vicki perked up when Frank entered in through the swinging doors of the kitchen. The stitchwork girl wore a smug expression on her face as she made her way over to the group. She gave a proud little smile to Vicki and sat down next to her.

"She's gonna be okay, I petrified her and the poison will wear off by the time she un-stones."

Vicki let out a heavy sigh of relief covering her face. "Thank you," she said with a small tremble in her voice. "I can't believe *that woman* did that! Who could poison an animal like that? Why didn't I stop her from eating it, I'm so stupid."

Desmond took a seat next to Vicki and leaned down to her eye level. "It's not your fault, that thing is pretty young yet, it ain't the sharpest tool in the shed. It would have probably gone back for seconds if you let it."

Vicki raised her head up from the table. "I should have fed her she was probably starving." She swallowed down a lump in her throat and sat up in her seat. "She was supposed to be protecting me and I almost let her die."

Desmond shot a glance at Belvedere and cupped his hands together. "On that note, we were thinking that maybe it's better if you just take it easy here from now on, just to stay on the safe side." He gave a nod to Belvedere and Jerry. "The residents need some company, so there's always that! They'll need something to keep themselves occupied especially tomorrow with the garden out of order. We were thinking that you could just get to know them all, maybe hand out some of their snacks."

"But what about that weird room? And the doors locking on me? It really happened, you know, I didn't make that up!"

Belvedere stroked his mustache as he spoke. "No one is saying that you did, Vicki. Only, this mansion can be a strange place for anyone, it can make you think that something is right in front of you when it's really just an illusion. It can play awful tricks on people, who knows why."

Desmond nudged Vicki on her arm. "It's like I told you, sweet corn, that dispensary is bad news. The mansion just likes to play around sometimes, that's the fact," he said with a wide smile. "But if it's really freaking you out, I'll personally go check on it tomorrow. I'm even gonna go around and check all the doors, make sure that they don't keep locking up on you by mistake."

Vicki gave him a small frown, feeling at the brim of her hat. "I don't know if this hat is really helping all that much. *None* of the doors want to open for me, even when I really try to focus on it." She looked up to Belvedere and the others. "Do you think maybe the Athenaeum doesn't like me? Like it knows that I'm not the real Housekeeper, and that's why it's locking doors and tricking me? Maybe it wants me to leave?"

Desmond remained quiet for a few moments before rising out of his chair. "Nah, get that out of your head, it would never do that. Not to one of Eckhardt's kids." The dapper vampire left the kitchen carrying a glum expression on his face.

"I wouldn't think so either. Don't dwell on thoughts like that too much, Vicki, they have a habit of becoming self fulfilling prophecies." Belvedere waved Jerry onward and started out of the kitchen behind the big red cow. "We all have bad days here." The two of them left Vicki alone with the stitchwork girl.

Vicki hunched over in her seat holding her knees to her chest. She darted her eyes over to Frank and back down to the table a few times wondering when the horrible girl might start in with her never ending poking. Vicki tensed herself and readied for whatever abuse might be thrown her way.

Frank got up from her seat. "It would have chewed you up for sure by now. If it didn't like you we'd already be scraping you up out of the basement," she said, giving a wink to Vicki. Frank smiled and grabbed onto Vicki's hands pulling her up out of her seat. "Come on, there's something the rats put together for you upstairs!" She dragged Vicki along behind her.

"The rats?"

Frank led the way through the mansion, her lanky legs quickly outpacing Vicki with ease. "They've been watchin' ya, I think Fyodor is in love, but don't worry I've told him how it is. He's a Scorpio, you're obviously an air sign, it just isn't going to work out."

Vicki followed behind the stitchwork girl, her legs still burning with the effort of the laundry. The two girls reached Vicki's third story room and Frank pointed to her bed.

Vicki reached out to the neatly wrapped package that sat upon the bed pillow, turning it over in her hands.

"They like ya, they said you got some moxie, and smarts too," said Frank as she joined Vicki over by the bed. "I helped make it. Because I'm good with a needle and some thread. Also I guess because I felt a little bad for being a tuna head to ya earlier."

"A *tuna* head?"

Frank narrowed her eyes at Vicki. "*Mostly* because I'm good with a needle and thread, so don't get *too* excited, I don't wanna hold your hand or anything like that. I just get a little stupid sometimes. *Sorry.*" The words seemed uncomfortable for her. She kicked her foot at Vicki's bed frame. "Go on! Open it up!"

Vicki tore at the packaging. She pulled out a soft and fluffy bathrobe fit perfectly to her size. She stood up and breathed out in fascination at its luminescent cloth, radiating a green hue like glow in the dark paint. Vicki wrapped the robe around her body and grinned at the stitchwork girl.

"It's glowing! Is it magic?"

"It's to help you see in the dark at night. Not a bad thing if that hat fizzles out! We made it out of wisp wool."

"I really like it!" Vicki hugged the robe around herself. "I love it! Thank you so much," she said as she sat back down on the bed. "Oh, it's really amazing!"

Frank sat on the edge of Vicki's bed helping to bring the robe's sash around her waist. "You wanna know something, I'm a little jealous of ya."

"Well, couldn't you and the rats make one of these for yourself too? They must *love* you, you're like their queen!"

Frank adjusted the robe around the collar, satisfied with her handiwork. "No, I mean that you get to go back home in a day or two. I'm stuck here pretty much forever. I'll be doing the laundry and changing diapers until this place finally falls down around me."

Vicki frowned. "What do you mean? You can't leave here ever? Can't you just quit here like a normal job?"

"Nope, it's a contract. Me and Dez, all the rest of us are stuck here until our contracts are up. I've been here for almost six years now," Frank counted upon her fingers making sure of her math. "Dez, he's been here for about forty. He's got another hundred and sixty to go!"

"Two hundred years!" Vicki shook her head trying to imagine what the world would be like in two centuries. "Why? What kind of contract did you guys sign?"

"Same as you. The three you know whos has all the contracts for this place. All of us were kind of roped into it." She itched the side of her arm bringing one of her stitchings loose. She sighed and hid the cable from Vicki. "It's keeping us all out of the dungeon. Community service, you know the drill. Now I'm not saying this to pique your curiosity, I just think that you should know it, it turns out that you're the only one that can even touch those contracts. It's not just little contracts like mine either, your grandpa told me there's some whoppers in there, you know what I mean?"

"Like what kind of contracts? Did he say?"

Frank leaned in close. "Powerful stuff, real bad stuff. That's why no one else can touch them, not even the you know who. Plenty of bad people would love to get their grubby little mitts on those things." She put a hand on Vicki's knee. "So it's best to not even know where the cookie jar *is*, you follow me? In case someone thinks you know how to score those cookies later on."

Vicki gave a quick nod. "Especially if I'm going home in a day or two," she whispered back. "Don't go snooping around."

"Exactly. You just need to stay safe and get home to your mom and dad. Don't go talking too loud about any weird doors you find around here. You'll be okay." She tugged at the cable under her overalls and darted her eyes back to Vicki a few times before heading for the door. "Well, I better go get pretending to work. It looks good on ya, I'll tell the rats you like it."

Vicki got up from her bed and tied off her robe into a neat bow as she walked with Frank back to her bedroom door. "I do, and thanks for taking care of my griffin!"

She watched Frank go, standing in her door frame peering out over the dimly lit hallway outside with a grin across her face. Her smile faded as she began wondering about the implication of those contracts. She wondered about what favor Zaldehyde might ask for, what heinous thing Vicki might unleash by fulfilling her aunt's wish.

She let those thoughts tumble around in her head for a few more moments before turning on her heels towards her dresser. She grabbed the old rotary telephone from its cradle and spun the dial around to her lengthy phone number, the receiver made a few musical tones beginning to ring through to the other side after a full minute had passed. A buzz of electricity ran from the cord of the telephone and into Vicki's hands, making her fingers tingle and sending a small spark between her lips and the speaker.

"Hello," answered a small and pained voice from the other side. The person on the other end oinked and coughed. "Excuse me, sorry."

Vicki held a hand over her mouth and suppressed a tiny yelp. Her mother's voice was nearly unrecognizable yet Vicki knew it immediately. Her mother sounded strained and exhausted, in much the same way she would sound after one of her work meetings. So tired, so worn out and weak.

"Mom? It's me," Vicki's voice broke and she stifled her oncoming tears. "I had to come over here, I- I'm sorry!"

Mrs. Voland oinked again and her voice strained even more as she spoke, sounding as though she might also be restraining some tears of her own. "Vicki! Are you okay?" She squealed and returned to the phone. "We're all getting better! We're going to be there soon to get you out of there!"

"I'm okay, it's okay here, I think I'm mostly just going to stay in my room for a while." Vicki gulped down the lump in her throat, weighing the notion of whether or not to tell her mother about the weirdness going on at the Athenaeum. "How's Dad, and Max?"

Her mother snorted a few times into the phone then cleared her throat. "Your father has hands again, but he can't come to the phone yet. He's still got that terrible snout." She oinked and the sound of hooves scraping against the plastic of the receiver filled the line until she eventually succeeded in securing the phone again. "And Max is fine too! He's finally getting some sleep now that we're up and walking again."

"Well that's great! Uhm, do you know when you'll come to get me then?"

The line went quiet for a few moments with Mrs. Voland talking to someone else in the background. She came back to the call. "One more day Vicki! One more and we'll be able to come get you. The lawyer says that you going over there did most of the work to get us out of this." The line went silent again for a moment before she oinked into the phone. "Max said that you were so brave, that you just went running into it."

Vicki frowned, yearning to be back home in her own bed. She pursed her lips together and tried to sound as positive as she could about staying in the mansion for one more day. "It isn't so scary here!" She twirled the phone line in between her fingers. "I think most of the people here even like me, so I barely had anything to be afraid of!"

"That's great, Vicki, we're so proud of you! You're more grown up everyday..." Mrs. Voland made a terrible squealing noise that ended in a sob. "I'm so sorry that you were thrown into this, it must be so scary, I wish that none of this happened! It's not what we wanted for you. Are the people there being nice to you? Is Zaldehyde leaving you alone?"

Vicki remained quiet holding her hand to her mouth again. "It's okay," she said at last. "I think I made a friend or two... and my first days went pretty good." A heavy tone sounded through the line.

A slow metallic voice came over the phone call speaking in monotone. "One minute left. Earthside tax, one Gorgoln."

Mrs. Voland made a panicked squeal. "Well, I'm going to have your Father call you tomorrow when he's a little less piggy! I love you so much Vicki! We all do!" She sniffled into the phone line. "You be careful, you promise to stay out of trouble and you stay safe!"

Vicki bit her lip. "I will! I promise, and I love you too!" She wiped her nose on the back of her hoodie collar. "Tell Dad and Max I'm okay, and that I love them too," she said as static began to fill the other end of the line.

"Vicki?" Mrs. Voland called out from the other end of the line. "Vicki," the voice became too quiet to hear and static crackled loudly into Vicki's ear.

Vicki set the phone receiver back down into its ancient cradle. The bedroom was quiet, even the dull hum of the residents and their chatter seemed muffled to near silence. She reclined on the mattress, letting her mind wander over the day's events as she wiped some tears away from her eyes.

She simply could not get the mysterious locked door out of her head. The writing desk, the fireplace, and the feathered quill all danced around in her mind's eye. Vicki pictured herself in front of that warm fireplace and let out a long yawn. The old phone rang and she shot up from the blankets. She put her hand out to the phone waiting for it to ring again but it fell silent.

Vicki lifted the phone from the cradle slowly bringing the receiver to her ear. "Hello," she asked with a worried tone. "Hello? Mom?"

The other girl's voice crackled through the static, "Vicki? It's Rachel. I tried to call but... did something happen?"

Vicki trembled hugging the phone tightly to her ear, overjoyed to hear the voice on the other end of the call. "Rachel! I'm okay, I'm sorry I didn't call you, my parents are kind of sick with stuff. I'm not even at home... it's been a weird couple of days."

"The troop leader said that they found you in a shoebox. Is that all that was left?" asked Rachel. She let out a tiny sob and took a heavy breath. "No one got to see you, you just disappeared. You and your whole family."

Vicki's stomach went cold and the hairs on her arms stood up. "Rachel," she asked, sitting up slowly. She inspected the phone in her hand. "I'm... I'm right here, what are you talking about?"

"I just, Vicki, I just wanted to say goodbye. I didn't get to say it to you when you were still here. I know everyone else hated you, and I get it, you did ruin everything last year. It's just that I have to move on I guess, and everything is a whole lot easier now that you're gone." Rachel sighed out in relief. "Okay, so this is it. I think I'm the only one going to the funeral. I can't believe how tiny that box is. God, what did they do to you, Vicki?" Her voice became distant and the static on the line was replaced by the fluttering of papers against the speaker. The phone let out an awful shriek and the line went dead.

Vicki yanked the phone cord out from the wall shivering and holding her scream in as she jumped back into the bed. She curled up into a ball, throwing the blankets over herself. She laid there for what seemed like an eternity staring into the wall thinking about how the phone was probably right, that things were a great deal easier without her being in the way. The warmth of the blankets eventually overtook her frigid thoughts and she let her eyes close for just a few moments.

Her nap turned into a full slumber, only waking from her sleep at the rumbling of her stomach. She reached down and held her griping abdomen, turning over and trying to get back to sleep. The hunger pains resumed and she stumbled away from her little nap. Several hours had passed, the nap taking her long past dinner. Vicki reasoned out that the others had let her sleep instead of waking her for whatever macabre dish might be available for the night.

She left her tall pointy hat on the dresser and bumbled out of the room, bringing her new glow in the dark robe up around her. Making her way through the dilapidated halls and down through the mansion stairwells, she was delighted to see that the robe indeed provided enough light to keep her going in the right direction. Its hazy green glow lit up the walls and floors around her without disturbing any of the sleeping goblins that she passed.

The nocturnal residents were far stranger than the run of the mill goblins that she had become accustomed to. Ghostly figures in glowing shrouds of their own floated between the halls of the Athenaeum, some of them wearing the classic cut out bedsheets that might be worn as a Halloween costume. Only a few days prior, Vicki would have run screaming from the mansion at the sight of the ghosts and spirits. The abnormal was quickly becoming the norm. She waved at one of the passing spirits, and it bowed its head to her before vanishing into the floor boards beneath. She pressed on into the dining room, spotting Desmond sitting alone with a steel flask in his hand.

Desmond put his flask away into his glitzy blue velvet dinner jacket and smiled at her as she crossed into the dining room. Vicki yawned and rubbed her eyes, hardly able to keep from bouncing into the buffets. She came to a rest at the table across from Desmond then fell into the chair, dropping her head down onto the table with a thud. Her hair cascaded all around the table and covered her face. A few moments passed with Vicki slumped over the table and Desmond twiddling his thumbs as he rested his hands on the plate in front of him.

"Couldn't sleep?" he asked looking down at the mess of a girl in front of him.

Vicki lifted her head up, peeping out at the immaculately dressed vampire. "I keep having nightmares here. Like nothing but nightmares." She pressed against the sides of her head sitting up in the chair. "I woke up really hungry too. I haven't eaten anything since breakfast but I'm too tired to find anything to eat," she mumbled as she moved her hair back behind her ears. Her eyes adjusted to the light and she looked down at Desmond's empty plate. "Desmond... what do you keep using the empty plates for?"

"You caught me." He shot a perfectly white fanged smile at her then retrieved his flask from his coat pocket. He placed the flask on the plate putting his hand back into another pocket, grabbing from it a shining set of cutlery. He placed the cutlery to the sides of the plate with practiced care then pulled a monogrammed napkin from within his collar. He wore the napkin over his shirt, patting it down. "I still like to pretend sometimes."

"Oh... oh. Ew, is that blood?" Vicki recoiled, staring at the flask and gathering up her glowing bathrobe around her. Her face went a little cold and she clenched her teeth together as Desmond simply smiled that toothy grin at her. Vicki watched with bated breath as the vampire moved a crystal wine glass toward himself, tapping the rim of the glass with the tip of his fingernail. The glass rang out and he inhaled the air. Deafening silence fell across the table until it became too much for Vicki to bear any longer. "Is it, though? I mean, you are kind of... you're a vampire, right?"

"Sweet corn, before I became like this," began Desmond as he drew his hand up and down his face and body. "I was like this," he said opening his hands wide over the table set up.

Vicki looked over the set up. "Fancy?" She looked up to him with an almost hopeful expression.

Desmond laughed and began swirling the flask around in his hand. "High class. I was high class," he said looking wistfully at the shining cutlery. "Man, I was top dog in Atlantic City, Branson, they even called me *His royal finesse* in Vegas. Lord, I miss Las Vegas. You ever been?"

She shook her head staring at the flask in his hand, then looked back up to him. "I think the longest from home I ever got was San Diego." Images of the San Diego zoo and a cart full of dog biscuits popped into her head, making her wince. *She never did get to see those tigers, and neither did Rachel.* "Danville is kind of far away from everywhere else, I've never even seen another state," she said, forcing the cookie fiasco out of her head. "My dad built a few mini malls in Reno once but I never visited him there..."

Desmond stopped swirling the flask. "Wow, Danville. Ain't heard of that one yet," he said with a smile. "Been to Reno a couple times. Too many cowboys and too much of the old UV. You ever see a sore thumb? That was me out there. I don't know how many other vampires were out there trying to make a living on the night life in little Vegas, but sure wasn't enough. I was the best *concierge* the Peppermill ever did see." Desmond smiled at some memory that came drifting in from the past, he slowed the swirling of the flask in his hand.

Vicki stared at the flask with apprehension. "Do you want me to leave," she asked before he could open the flask. "I don't think I want to see this anyways," she added as she scooted off from the seat.

"It's magic you know," said Desmond as he opened the flask, sniffing the liquid inside. "The blood. I *do* drink it to survive but it's not really about just the red stuff."

Vicki turned to face him partially hiding her eyes behind her hands. "Well whatever it is, it's going to gross me out, no offense."

"You don't know what you're missing," said Desmond. He poured the dark red liquid into the crystal cup. Vicki gasped and put her hands over her eyes as Desmond gave a light chuckle. "You think this is just plain old nasty blood?"

Vicki gave him a nod without uncovering her eyes. "It is! It is nasty," she said with a frown. She opened her fingers a little bit peeking out at the cup for a brief second before wrapping her eyes tight again. "That's real live human blood?"

Desmond sat back with the cup inhaling the air around it. "As real as it gets. Live? I don't know about that, and this isn't nasty. It's Penelope."

Vicki lowered her fingers peeking over just a tiny bit to see. "Penelope?"

Desmond gave a nod bringing his ornate steel fork over to the rim of his glass clinking it against the crystal as if to give a toast. "Penelope," he exclaimed out. Desmond brought the cup to his nose and held it there. He spoke as if going into a dream, "Penelope, a girl from a little town in Illinois, from a little Greek neighborhood... she wore lavender behind her ear, she had a champagne laugh and all the boys loved her... and *she* loved carnivals. She loved the yellow strings of lights and the smell of the popcorn and the way that her bare feet felt upon the warm metal of the carousel."

Vicki gave a tiny whimper lowering her hands a little bit more. "You... you can really tell all that from smelling it?"

Desmond closed his eyes and sniffed the cup again. "Hmm... and she was black haired and green eyed... and she worked at the First Kingdom Bank of Vania."

Vicki's mouth dropped open and her hands fell away from her eyes. "That's amazing!" She gripped her fingers together stepping back from the vampire. "You can tell all that just by smelling the b-blood, like, with anybody's blood," she asked with raised eyebrows.

"What's the matter, you afraid I can smell all that stuff on you too," he asked with a wicked smile.

"Maybe a little bit." She bumped into the buffet behind her and squeaked out in surprise.

Desmond leaned forward laughing, sniffing the air deeply. "Well I can't! If I try to get a sniff of you... All that I get is... cheap lip balm, banana shampoo, and cloves." Desmond sat with a huge smile on his face turning the flask around so that Vicki could read the words on the back of its label.

She read the words aloud. "Penelope number 9, our perfected texture of a little greek flavor with hints of a fun night at the circus, made with extra virgin Chicago red, lavender and... You tricked me!" Vicki dropped her hands and gave the vampire a scowl. "Is that even real people blood," she asked as she hugged her robe around her.

"It's mostly an elixir and some high dollar willing donor blood from a bloodery here in Vania, you ever drink orange juice from the store? The good stuff out of the can, and then get home and try real orange juice?"

Vicki gave him a nod. "Sure, I like the store orange juice better."

"That's because they add all sorts of stuff to the OJ in the store. Saves on oranges and makes it sweeter. People don't like the real stuff." He put the flask back into his pocket and wiggled the crystal glass in front of her. "Same idea. Me, I *like* the good stuff but I still *need* the real stuff too."

"Oh sure." Vicki gripped her hands together wincing at the glass full of glimmering red liquid. "Well, what else did they put into your stuff?"

"The magic," said Desmond as he gently placed the cup back down onto his plate. "Penelope's magic. You know how you keep saying that you don't have any? Well that ain't exactly true, everybody's got a little bit somewhere deep down in those bones."

"Do you mean like a soul?"

"I mean magic. The soul is a whole other thing," said Desmond, the smile fading from his face. "And I would know. Nope, all that real stuff, that's the magic. The carnival lights, the lavender, the *feeling* that she got when she'd watch the fireworks. The *happiness, the sorrow*. That's all pure magic, grade A. *That's powerful stuff. The real stuff*. All carried in that sweet red-red wine."

Vicki stared at the crystal cup biting her lip. "Does it have to be human blood? Like you can't get it from a goblin or anyone else?"

"Not just a human, has to be Earthbound. Can't be a witch, or a werewolf, or a zombie. I got pretty sick once from biting a werewolf." Desmond trembled and stuck out his tongue. "Nastiest thing I ever tasted." He brought the cup up to his mouth and gulped down the entirety of the contents in one swallow.

Vicki covered her eyes and turned around towards the buffet. She peeked through her fingers and caught her reflection in its ornate mirror. Desmond's translucent body became more and more solid as she peered into the dusty old surface.

"Desmond, your reflection," Vicki exclaimed whipping around. "That stuff, I think it cured you! Look!"

"Nope, that's just Penelope, carrying me along for a while. Letting me borrow a little of that good life." Desmond held his hands out in front of him smiling to himself. "Putting some color back in these veins." He gathered up his plate and fancy cutlery.

"Sorry, I didn't mean it like that... Like I didn't mean you're sick or something. I just got too excited." She hugged her bathrobe close to her watching as the vampire came over to inspect the mirror.

"It only lasts for a little time anyways, you didn't hurt my feelings none, you're good." Desmond stared at his reflection thinking for a long while before speaking again. "Somewhere in Indiana, there's some photos locked away, maybe hanging on the wall. I'm there in those photos again for just a little bit, until this all wears off. Then I'll be invisible again in every picture, in every mirror, everywhere."

"That's awful." Vicki looked into the mirror along with him. "So when you became a vampire even your old pictures changed? So no one even knows that you were ever there?"

"In their memories too. Just now, maybe a few of my old friends and family suddenly thought about me again and almost remembered my face. Almost."

Vicki frowned and stared at both of their reflections. "I bet they miss you," she said.

Desmond turned away from the buffet and shook his dinner jacket straightening out his sleeves and collar as he walked away. "It ain't gonna be a full course meal, but I know where Belvedere keeps the old breakfast stuff, I can make toast with the best of them," he said beckoning for Vicki to follow. "If you're feeling *really* brave we can even steal a piece of the leftover feetloaf from earlier."

Chapter fourteen

The scout leader continued speaking to Mrs. Voland as Vicki sat slumped down in her chair. They conversed in some bizarre language that she couldn't begin to understand. The scout leader finally addressed Vicki, giving her a frown and clicking her tongue. She handed a tissue to Vicki.

"It was just a shock for everyone, that's all. Poor thing. There's going to be other sales and other trips, really Vicki, you should stay." The scout leader finally began speaking in English. "Those other girls are going to put this behind them so long as you apologize for all those things that you said. I'm sure they want to apologize to you too! Mistakes happen, friends have fights all the time, this is going to be a thing of the past before you know it."

Vicki's mother sat forward in her chair. "You listen to her, Vicki, this is very important."

"Granted, it was a very, very stupid mistake. All that you needed to do was make sure that the dog biscuit boxes were separated from the gingersnaps. Any monkey with half a brain should have been able to do the job, but that's on me. I'm the one that trusted you to see an obvious dog bone on the box. I'll probably end up losing my position over this. Can you imagine what all of those customers who ate the dog snacks are writing online?" The scout leader laughed out, her smile quickly fell into a frown of great sorrow, her face turned gray. "Now, do you want to stay? You can stay and we can all start healing, wouldn't that be nice?"

Vicki shook her head and hid her face into the palms of her hands. Mrs. Voland let out a sigh and rubbed Vicki's shoulder. She checked her watch and gave the scouts leader a smile.

"Okay Vicki, you wait here then, I'm going to go pull the car around so none of the girls see you leaving. We have to get round the store to get your shoebox anyways." Mrs. Voland gave a kiss to the top of Vicki's forehead.

The scouts leader's eyes widened. "Well, Victoria, I'm glad that you decided to quit instead of sticking it out. I know the other den mothers wanted you to stay, but we both know what happened. We both know all the things that you said." The scout mother leaned in close. "God, can you imagine if you did stick around, if you *did* try again? What a disaster!"

Vicki whimpered and turned to her mother.

"She has a point, Vicki," said Mrs. Voland. "You aren't wanted here. You aren't wanted anywhere."

The scout mother stood from her chair, growing in size as she spoke. "Poor Rachel tried and tried to defend you, and look where it got her? You really threw her to the wolves, didn't you?" The scout mother's head reached to the top of the ceiling. "Think about it, really think about it. Wouldn't everything have been better if you had just given up and left sooner? Everyone else would have been happy, but you... you!" The scout mother's eyes turned black with rage, she pointed her pencil length finger at Vicki. "You just had to try!"

A gong sounded throughout the mansion stirring Vicki from her nightmare. She moaned, feeling at her forehead. The gong rang again and she sprang into action. She picked out her last change of clothes, turning to her bathroom. The little goblin assessor stood at the bedroom door with his stone tablet at the ready. Vicki screamed and threw her shower bag at him.

"The relic of Budai has been captured. It caused an event at the cyclops outreach center, you can thank your white haired friend for its return," he said as he dodged the bag. "One point is deducted for gross inadequacy of performance."

"Get out of here you little creeper! Omigod!" She threw her pillow this time hitting the goblin's feet. "Leave!"

The assessor placed the familiar little pewter statue down on the pillow next to the petrified griffin in the corner, exiting out the door without another word. Vicki stared down at the statue fuming that the goblin might continue to come and go as he pleased. She scowled down at the statue of Buddha.

"Thanks a lot," she said to the little monk.

The tapestry of the multi armed elephant gave a tiny amount of applause and smiled at her. "Oh well done, young Vicki! You've returned him at last!"

Vicki grumbled and tied her robe up as tightly as she could. "No thanks to any of you! Aren't you supposed to keep everyone out? I think that little creep counts as a bad guy," she said with folded arms.

The tapestry spread his arms wide and smiled down to her. "Ganesh only wards off those that might harm you, this is his task," he said with a small amount of pride.

"Well... who's Ganesh?"

"I am! I am Ganesh," the elephant swung his trunk about trumpeting and snorting in indignation. "The goblin means you no harm, I can see it clearly. He is a friend to the Housekeeper."

"Well what about Desmond? You didn't let him in, and he wouldn't hurt me!" Vicki motioned down to the petrified little griffin. "And he wouldn't have hurt her either! Isn't he my *friend?*"

Ganesh put a thumb to his chin giving her an appraising look. "You are angry because *I* didn't let your *friend* enter?"

"Yes, I am! And I'm mad that you let that little weirdo in while I was sleeping," exclaimed Vicki.

"Then Ganesh has done his task well!" The elephant brought his hands together in a prayer. "And so have you. You have collected more friends than you will admit... entrance to and love for."

Vicki scrunched her mouth to the side. "What? What does that even mean," she asked. The elephant remained still and silent. She waved her hand in front of the tapestry and sighed. She kicked her foot at the monk and turned to her bathroom.

The morning shower had been cold and quick, Vicki didn't want to waste any time in reaching the dining room. She marched through the mansion with her hat firmly on her head and her dark navy blue sundress flowing out behind her. She stomped down the stairs with such force that dust flew up from the wooden boards.

She blasted through the dining room, flashing a quick smile to the residents then throwing the kitchen doors open. Vicki crossed her arms, facing her coworkers Desmond and Belvedere and sticking her chin up in the air. "That stupid goblin was in my room, trying to take a peek at me!"

"What goblin," asked Desmond rising from his seat. "Which one!"

"The assessor!"

Desmond sat back down. "Yeah, he'll do that. Sorry."

"*Sorry?* He was being a total weirdo, he was just standing there watching me sleep and everything without saying a word! That's harassment!" Vicki looked up at Belvedere and put her hands on her hips. "Well, can't we do something about it! I don't feel safe!"

"You shouldn't feel safe. You're failing, kiddo," said Desmond. He offered a seat to Vicki and she fell into it with an exasperated huff. "We gotta do better today, keep you out of the bigger things. No more magic, no more mansion stuff."

"Am I really doing that badly?"

"Bad enough. You got three more points and we're out!" Desmond gave her a little nod.

Vicki tucked her hair behind her ear, frowning down at the table. "Well, even if I get kicked out and fired, at least my mom and my dad are still getting better. I mean, I don't *want* to get fired. I can't do anything right around here anyways. It's just that maybe it wouldn't be the end of the world."

Belvedere sipped from his mug, settling down in a chair across from Vicki. "Not to put any more pressure on you, Vicki, but it *would* be for *us.*"

"It would? What do you mean?"

Desmond shook his head and leaned back in his chair. "Nah, don't worry about that, let's worry about you for now."

"But what would happen? What's wrong?"

Belvedere set his mug down. "It's a very precarious situation. Without a Housekeeper to keep the mansion running, and without one in legacy, the Athenaeum would be evicted. Evicted, evacuated and exorcised. All of the residents will be thrown out into the caves and all house contracts will go into default."

"*What?* No one ever said anything about that! That's crazy!" Vicki sat forward with wide eyes.

Desmond grabbed her wrist. "Just concentrate on today, we're gonna sneak you out of the mansion on a day break sort of thing. Maybe you can go get candies or something for the residents, something to make them happy, I don't know. No matter what though, you keep away from doing anything in here. Just in case the old house *does* have it in for you."

Vicki sat in silence mulling over the facts in her head. "I'm just not cut out for any of this, am I? I mean, I'm not doing any good here at all! How many points do I have? Three?"

"Three for now, but even if you lose a couple more you can gain a lot of leniency with resident report cards!" Desmond loosened his collar. "We just have to be a little more careful is all."

"Resident report cards? Like all of the old folks are going to grade me too?"

Belvedere slurped loudly from his mug. "If you can make some of the residents happy today before the assessment ends, it'll help towards your ending grade." He rubbed his mustache and let his eyes wander out to the window. "You only need to keep the one point. We'll just have to find a way to make a good number of the residents happy today."

"It's gonna be harder to do with the hedge maze out of order." Desmond sat back in his chair and sighed. "They ain't got nowhere to go, and half of them don't like each other. Makes getting them out of the mansion a pretty tall order. We need to find something."

Vicki sat staring at her hands, drowning in her thoughts of failure and imminent doom. She was going to fail, she knew it without any doubt. She was going to get everyone in the mansion evicted.

She wondered where all of her new friends would end up or if they would end up anywhere at all. What did Belvedere mean when he said that *the contracts would go into default?* Vicki wasn't entirely sure that she wanted to know the details because she was almost certain that she would still fail to appease the assessor no matter what she tried. The goblins would all be thrown into the street and now her new friends would forever remember her as the girl that failed. Just like everyone back home.

Vicki slouched forward, missing the conversation happening between Desmond and Belvedere. She focused only on the dread of the inevitable future. Everyone would pay the price for her stupidity, *again*. Her thoughts went to poor Mrs. Klobbreak sitting by her window crying little goblin tears as hulking men in police uniforms came to evict her from the room. She'd never see Derkie play again.

"*Derkie!!*" Vicki shot up from her seat, hopping up and down on her heels. "Derkie!"

Desmond remained silent for a moment blinking at Vicki. *"Derkie?"*

"The buttery beagles brothers," exclaimed Vicki.

Belvedere also blinked at her. "Do you mean the Buttered Beagle Boggle?"

"Yes! Yes! The Buttered Beagle Boggle! Mrs. Klobbreak said that they all watch it being played from the fountain, when you all aren't looking!" She wrung her hands together in glee. "I can take a few of them to the game! Or is that a stupid idea?"

Desmond clapped his hands together and grinned. "That's about the smartest idea in the whole wide room! You got this, ain't she got this, Belvedere?"

Belvedere grinned from under his bristling mustache. "I do believe she does!" He took a sip from his mug and gave her an approving nod. "We'll see if that old bus out back is working. It'll give those young folks quite a shock, maybe it will do *them* some good as well, finally having to see their elders!"

Desmond stood up and gave Vicki a bump on her shoulder. "You done *good* kid. I'm gonna stick around here and pick up some of the slack, we'll get Jerry to help you out. If you're gonna go see the game, you're gonna have to wear the right colors too." He bent down to whisper into her ear. *"The assessor is still creeping around here, so he's definitely gonna be watching you get everyone together. He'll be looking for you to open those doors with magic, get the goblins on the bus with magic, everything magic. We wanna make sure that today all goes smoothly in front of the old camera. You understand?"*

"So we gotta be sneaky, got it." She gave him a nod.

"If you wait to get them out of here until my signal I can buy you some time." Desmond raised his voice loud enough for the little goblin assessor to hear. "So maybe let's shoot for two! The game starts at four, so if you get them all loaded up in our old wreck it would be about perfect timing."

"Two?" Vicki asked, almost shouting.

Belvedere chimed in. "Yes, two o' clock is when you should start rounding up the goblins."

Vicki held in a giggle and Desmond turned her around to face back in the direction of the dining room doors. The two of them left the kitchen, making their way out into the mansion hall, taking count of the goblins and creatures in the commons areas. Vicki gripped the brim of her hat, taking in a heavy breath.

"It's just one more day," she breathed out to herself.

"Just one more." Desmond gave her a nod. "You've got this. Go on then, you go get Frank up to speed and we'll get everything else going."

Vicki rushed off to the laundry room stopping in the halls a few times to greet some of the residents as she passed by. She slyly mentioned the Buttered Beagle Boggle to a few of them seeing if it piqued their interest. By the time Vicki reached Frank she had three goblins in waiting for the day trip. Giddiness filled her every step, propelling her forward with newfound zeal. Vicki burst into the laundry room, startling the stitchwork girl.

"Frank! How would you like to take me and some of the residents to the Beagle Boggle game?" Vicki stood in the doorway bubbling over with excitement. She put her hands together and squirmed as she spoke. "It's under the radar, Desmond and Belvedere are going to sneak us all out so we can take them before the little goblin man can test me!"

Frank didn't seem as excited. She folded a few sheets in front of her, letting one of the rats sleep upon her lap. "Calm down, *bubbles,* what's this all about?" She set her folded sheets down and eyed Vicki looking her up and down. "Geez, there's color in your cheeks and everything, what happened?"

"I'm failing the assessment, well I might fai- I'll probably fail it, but I can still make it with some good resident reviews from the goblins! Then no one has to get kicked out or anything!" Vicki sat down in front of Frank helping her to fold one of the sheets. "And Mrs. Klobbreak told me that all of her friends watch the Buttered Beagle Boggle with her outside at the fountain. So I thought that maybe we could take them there! There's that old bus outside right, can you drive it to the game for us?"

Frank twirled a bit of her white hair between her fingers. "That's not a bad plan, I can see it," she said throwing her towels into the washing machines. "You sure ya want me to go along? Jerry and Belvedere can drive that thing too, probably a little better than me."

"Well yeah I'm sure! All of the goblins love you! Plus it doesn't hurt that the doors don't try to lock you out at like every turn."

"Kiddo, look," began Frank as she placed her hands on her hips. "My brains can kind of switch around sometimes. It makes my body do funny things too, so I don't want ya to think that I don't wanna go and help you, but it's embarrassing when it happens in public."

"When what happens? You mean when they switch?"

"It's *humiliating*. My stitches get all loose and my parts go everywhere, everyone can just see me scatter. One time my whole butt fell down right in the middle of the Séance and Salsa. I almost died again of embarrassment, I can't imagine having something like that happen in a stadium full of people." Frank threw her hands in the air. "Anyways, I can get kinda unpleasant."

Vicki furrowed her brow, helping her load the laundry into the machines. "*More* unpleasant than when I first met you?"

"Whattya mean, *more unpleasant than when I first met you,* I was being a perfect joy to be around!" Frank grinned down at her. "I just don't wanna be the thing that loses you the next point."

"But you're like the best person here that can help us... you helped my griffin and me, and Mrs. Klobbreak thinks you're nice. It would get you away from the laundry today!"

"Kid you had me at the griffin, but you can keep laying it on if ya want."

"So you'll go?" Vicki hopped up and down. "You'll come with?"

"Sure, I'll go with ya. How are you gonna get all these goblins together anyhow?"

Vicki pointed to the massive pipes along the back wall. "We're gonna use the chutes! I'm going to have Mrs. Klobbreak invite her friends to go and see the game!"

"You got it all figured out pretty good! You got this, Vicki!"

Vicki gave a grin and straightened her posture. She gave Frank a big nod. "I got this," she said with confidence.

The goblin assessor eyed the large group of elderly goblins in the main hall with suspicion. Vicki circled the wheelchairs at the doors waiting for Desmond's signal. The assessor focused on Vicki as she glanced over her shoulder at him. They both knew that those doors were not going to listen to Vicki's commands.

Anything to keep the assessment going, that was the name of the game now, and Vicki was determined to win the game. Frank led her own gaggle of waddling little old goblins towards the main doors of the Athenaeum, lining them up for the dispensing of the Everfall team colors. Vicki had donned the orange and black team colors as well.

She wore an orange band around the brim of her black pointed hat, decorated with black and orange beads. Her dark navy dress looked black enough and Frank had bestowed upon her a pair of striking orange tights. Vicki was particularly taken with the colorful tights as they reminded her of one of her favorite musical artists back home.

Flags, scarves, and hats adorned in orange and black were all passed out to the excited goblins. Jerry stood in wait just outside of the mansion, ready to load the game fans onto the bus. The goblin assessor moved his stone tablet into view, ready to mark his grades.

Frank turned round and round in her gaudy black and orange jumpsuit, wowing her goblins with her fashion sense. She pulled out an orange ribbon waving it in the air.

Desmond leaned over the railing of the second floor, leaping into action as soon as the ribbon went up. He dashed down the stairs waving a small booklet of papers at the goblin assessor. "Hey, mister man, hold on for one minute!" He reached the assessor weighing the booklet in his hands. "Hey, we gotta have a talk."

"That would be impertinent at this moment, I'm in the middle of observing the prospective at her duties," said the assessor as he turned back to watch Vicki and Frank.

Desmond caught him by the shoulder. "Uh huh, yeah, sounds like you were doing a little observing already this morning." Desmond shook the booklet at the goblin. "How up to date are you on your cross species sensitivity and avoiding harassment in the workplace courses?"

"Sensitivity courses?! What preposterous nonsense!"

"*Preposterous, nonsense,*" Desmond repeated the words as he wrote them down onto his booklet. He waved Frank and Vicki onward as he attained the assessor's full attention. "Sir, do you have any idea how much litigation can be brought against this institution in a court of law if we get accused of allowing voyeurism on the work site?"

"*Voyeurism?* I don't even understand what that means."

Desmond smacked the booklet down into his hands feigning anger at the little goblin. "You don't know what it means, lemme tell you what it means, it means you're all up in here staring at the little new hire sleeping and all sorts of creepy things! You know what a peeping Tom is?"

The goblin flushed bright red and his skin began to change to dull yellow. *"A peeping Tom? Me!"*

Jerry opened the doors for the two girls inside and they began to pile out onto the lawn. "Lemme get the doors this time, boss. Told you there was beagles about, din't I?"

Vicki wheeled Mrs. Klobbreak past and she smiled up at Jerry. "I guess you did! I like your horns!"

The red beast felt at his horns, one painted orange and the other black. He hid his face and galloped back to the mansion, making a funny mooing sound as he went. He tried to mumble something and nearly lost his footing up the porch.

"I think ya made him blush," said Frank, pushing her cranky old goblin along in her wheelchair. The old goblin in the housecat skin gown grumbled, trying to adjust the oversized helmet on her head. "God forbid you ever pay him a compliment, he runs away so fast you'd think he was prize Bessie at a barbecue."

Mrs. Klobbreak bobbed her head along quite happily to the music playing in her mind. The fall wind blew a chill air at the little goblin lady in the wheelchair and she covered up with her lap blanket. The residents all chatted and grumbled, as one by one they entered the waiting bus.

"Are you too cold Mrs. Klobbreak?" asked Vicki, as the small old goblin woman wiggled her feet back and forth under her orange fuzzy blanket. Vicki adjusted the blanket on Mrs. Klobbreak's feet. "I hope it's warmer at the stadium!"

"You look nice in that hat, dearie," said the little old goblin back to her. Vicki smiled pulling her pointy hat covered in Everfall colors tighter upon her head. "And don't you worry, your ears will come in soon! You're still just a young girl!"

Frank came up from behind Mrs. Klobbreak's wheelchair taking the chair handles. "I hope she grows a little tail too," she said as she began to wheel the goblin onto the bus with the other residents. Frank leaned over Mrs. Klobbreak's shoulder to speak closer to her good ear. "What do you think, Mrs. K? Wouldn't she look good with a little waggily tail?"

"Oh that sounds lovely dear! I used to put fox tails in the Macy's pies for Christmas," Mrs. Klobbreak giggled out. Vicki twisted around looking down at her backside, worrying that her pigtail might have grown back without her noticing. She did a quick pat around and breathed a sigh of relief.

"This is pretty bang up, boss," came Jerry's voice from behind Vicki. "Better'n just letting all the old geezers go to waste!"

"Go to waste?" She tucked some of her wavy hair behind an ear, adjusting the pointed hat upon her head and taking extra care to make sure that her black and orange beaded band was still tight to the brim. "What do you mean by that?"

"Well, they're just lying about elsewise," he said as they reached the bus. He gently placed a hoof onto the steps, making it squeak with his weight. "That's not how us ogres treat our old, no way!" They both got on and the door closed behind them with a loud squeal.

"Oh! *Ogre*? I noticed that there aren't any other *ogres* in the house, do they all live at home or something when they get old?"

"Course not! We eat em on their big sixty."

"Je... what, are you kidding? Jerry! That's not funny, ew!" Vicki gave a cringe.

"Well, we don't do em in raw, we're not savages."

Vicki's mouth hung open and she stared at him. "Omigod, you're not kidding at all are you!?"

"Whattya do with your elders?"

"Well we don't eat them when they turn sixty," Vicki hollered. She poked Jerry in the belly moving him backwards into the seats full of old people as she spoke at him. "And you better not even think about eating any of these old people while I'm around!"

Jerry landed in a seat next to a shriveled up old lizard man, scooting away from the angry little human. "It's a time honored tradition, I ate me own Gram last year at her sixtieth, I woulda been udders up not to! Ask Frank she was there! She knows all about it!"

Frank leaned out of the driver's seat and popped her head out from behind the cushion giving a sympathetic nod to Vicki. "*I didn't go back for seconds.*"

Vicki's stomach went cold and she covered her mouth. The color drained from her face as she went to go sit next to Mrs. Klobbreak. She took a deep breath out. "I think we can go now."

Frank smiled and gave her a thumbs up, pulling the goggles atop her forehead down over her eyes. The engine steamed to life with a violent blast and shudder. A loud bang erupted from the back of the bus as it lurched forward.

Mrs. Klobbreak patted Vicki's knee reassuringly. "I'm sixty eight," she said with a tiny squeal of joy.

Chapter fifteen

The old bus clanked over the cobblestone road through the overgrown graveyard and out of the dark thorny vampple orchard. The residents sat in the bus chatting and looking out the windows as the old thing sputtered its way through the cozy little goblin town of Everfall. Creatures of every kind ventured out of their homes, marching together down the Marrowgate Avenue in two equally excited groups. There were the gangs in black and orange going to show support for Everfall and the little hooligans in red and green going through the cobblestone streets to cheer for the rival team from Hammertwerk.

The droves of goblins, imps, and other assorted folk all converged at the east end of the valley town. The noisy bus sputtered alongside the walking masses past the beautiful fall foliage of striking red and golden hues. Vicki couldn't help but feel a little giddy as the old goblin in the seat next to her began giggling and clapping with the destination ever closer. The bus reached the haphazard wooden creamery arena, coming to a sudden halt out in the colorful red, yellow, and purple leaved trees. The old folk livened up at the sight of the Everfall creamery's two large potted towers dressed up in the team colors at opposite ends to each other. The towers rocked and swayed with a great rumble as they churned the butters within.

Chain link fencing wrapped round and round the rickety walls of the arena, stacked wooden planks of mismatched size and color made the base of the unstable looking mess. Great stones and lumps of clay buttressed the teetering walls in such a way that should the arena groan too far one way or the other the other side would remain weighted in place. Each stone had been selected without any care as to size or matching aesthetic. Vicki wondered how the thing could survive even one singular goblin sitting against any of the arena walls.

The creamery was abuzz with activity. Gigantic beagles rushed around the well trimmed grass of the playing field, playing and barking as the two great towers churned their respective butters. As Vicki and Frank began unloading their excited passengers fireworks began exploding overhead. Vicki looked up in awe as she wheeled Mrs. Klobbreak towards the stone archway main entrance of the spectator's bleachers. The fireworks were shining and fizzling against the graying overcast sky, their lingering team colors floating in the clouds above. Frank kept glancing over and smiling as she watched the distracted girl nearly wheel Mrs. Klobbreak into a group of slower moving goblins.

"They're enchanted cranberry crashes," said Frank, as she wheeled her own giddy old goblin woman forward.

Vicki marveled up at the sky watching more of the colorful exploding berries. They blasted off from inside the creamery's open air playing field scattering into sparkling patterns with a loud pop. Frank stopped to let her old goblin look up at the displays too.

The residents of the Athenaeum limped and rolled their way into the creamery stadium where they were met with loud pregame revelry. Goblins and imps shouted songs and rhymes at each other all while enchanted glowing cranberry bits fell from the sky above. The old people stuck out like sore thumbs, and some of the other sports fans quieted down watching on with curiosity as Vicki and Frank rolled their two elder goblins towards their seats. *Others watched on in scorn.* Jerry led the rest of the twenty residents to their seats amid a small buzz of discontent and confusion from the stands.

Vicki sat down right next to Mrs. Klobbreak nestling up beside her, wrapping the old goblin up in an Everfall scarf of black and orange stripes. A minuscule goblin child a few rows down from Vicki looked over her seat at the old people up in the chairs behind her giving them all a big toothy grin. The little goblin's mother forcibly spun the child around and berated her for staring. The noise picked up again and the seats around them began to fill in with creatures of all sorts.

Frank came hopping over a few seats down to Vicki's row sitting down next to her. "See the cranberry bog moat around the playing field?" asked Frank as she leaned over towards Vicki. "The rules are different for every Boggle, but the cranberries are always the same. It's always on a cranberry bog."

Vicki scanned the area tracing the cranberry bog that encircled the floating playing field. "It's always played on cranberries? Is that why it's called a Boggle?" She tucked her knees up to her chest and leaned closer to the stitchwork girl, listening intently.

Frank smiled and talked on about the game with no small amount of knowledge, directing Vicki to the various parts of the creamery. "You got your two big butter towers, they each got four butters for each team at random. So the beaglers go and get buttered up whenever they feel like it, or if they drop in the bog, stuff like that. It's all magic butter too, so some of it is super slippery or makes you sort of sticky or floaty." Frank slapped Vicki's knee pointing over to a pair of goblins on beagleback wearing colorful wooden armor and carrying large shields resembling slices of toast. "That guy with the big butter knife lance and the toast shield, he's the lancer. He's the only guy that gets to score a beaglet and only by whacking the boggle into the net with his toast shield. Anybody else even thinks about scoring and they get thrown out!"

Vicki gave her a nod and pointed down to a goblin with a massive spongey hammer. "And that one does what, whacks the other goblins?"

"Exactly, they can hit the boggle too but not for anything that can be useful or beneficial. It's a rule. They gotta hit that boggle in a random direction." Frank shot up from her seat and jabbed Vicki in the arm as she set her eyes upon the next goblin. "And that guy with the hook cane? He's the herder! They have to wear those big dumb goggles so they can't make any accurate shots! They can smack the boggle anywhere they want if they can even see where they're going! I was gonna be a herder way back when."

"You were?" Vicki furrowed her brow, staring down at the stumbling goblin with the huge goggles atop his head. "What happened, why did you quit?"

"Allergic to beagles." Frank sat back in her seat with a shrug.

"The beagles sure are big here, they're like giants," Vicki hugged her hat down over her ears. "Imagine how much food they eat!"

Mrs. Klobbreak leaned over to Vicki waving her little orange and black flag along with the rest of the nearby crowd. "My grandson is one of the Hammerers for Everfall," she exclaimed beaming.

Vicki smiled back at her and adjusted the old goblin's scarf once more. "I know Mrs. K! That's why we're here, remember? You told me it's his birthday today too!"

A gigantic brass tuba blared out. The bass reverberated in Vicki's chest and the bleating of the tuba continued so loudly that she had to cover her ears. She was pretty sure that she had screamed out as well but no one, not even her, would have been able to hear it.

The goblins on beagleback charged towards the middle of the playing field kicking up butter and loose cranberries as they whooped and hollered. The beagles bayed and bucked, slipping along the unstable ground as they all converged on the little green blob in the middle of the arena. The little blob almost looked excited, its little black eyes widening and focusing on the approaching Herders of Hammertwerk.

The little green ball made a happy gurgling sound just before the first Herder wearing the red and green colors violently smacked the blob into the air with his hooked cane. The little jiggling ball screamed out in a high pitched squeal. The boggle ball flew through the air and tumbled down straight into the shield of one of Everfall's Lancers.

"The game is on," shouted a goblin from the press box. The boggle ball bounced back and forth between two Lancers on the Everfall team until a rival Hammerer came swinging his giant sponge on a stick at the Lancers. Both of the Everfall Lancers went sliding off of their beagles, one slipping all the way into the cranberry bog and the other coming to a stop only when he smacked into another rider.

Mrs. Klobbreak grabbed Vicki's arm and pointed down at a dark purple goblin. "See! There he is, that's my little Derkstahl!"

The purple goblin Derkstahl went charging ahead into the fray, he swung his mighty spongy hammer into the cranberry bog as he went along. He met the rival Hammerer in combat slapping his soaking wet sponge hammer against the opposing beagle. The hammer splashed against the giant dog and washed away the sticky butter that had kept the other rider stable, the Hammertwerk Hammerer went sliding off of his beagle onto the playing field.

The boggle meanwhile bounced along the ground straight into one of the Hammertwerk Herders who caught the boggle with her cane, promptly throwing it at one of the referees. The crowd cheered as the boggle smacked into the back of the referee's head. The little goblin went tumbling into the bog and another referee blew a tiny tin whistle expelling the other referee with a hand gesture to throw him out of the bog.

"Out! No taking Boggles to the back of the head," yelled the referee. The crowd erupted with applause, another herder from Everfall caught the boggle in his cane.

Vicki gave a confused look to Frank. "That doesn't make any sense!" She turned her attention back to the game and watched as Derkstahl slammed his hammer against his own teammate sending the Herder flying forward into the Hammertwerk tower. The boggle slipped from the Herder's cane and into one of the nets, the stadium went wild.

"I thought you said that the hammer guys can't make points?" Vicki yelled to Frank over the swell of the crowd.

"Oh, that's only if the referees are watching though, look!" Frank pointed down at the three remaining referees on the field, they were all playing a card game on the ground. "It looks like a round of hearts."

Vicki sat back in her seat confused and lost. She brought her hat down tighter on her head and crossed her arms, trying to follow the rest of the game. She glanced around at the residents and smiled seeing that they all seemed to be enjoying themselves at last, especially Mrs. Klobbreak. She nudged the little old goblin and pointed down towards the field.

"Would you like to get a closer look down by the front? Maybe your grandson could see you," said Vicki. Mrs. Klobbreak gave her a nod and a big smile still waving her little orange and black flag. "You can even wish him a happy birthday!"

Vicki wheeled the old goblin down the stadium slope, past the cheering crowds all the way down to the front of the stadium wall. The enchanted cranberry bog splashed around from the action on the floating playfield, a gaggle of various small creatures lined the wall jumping up and down in an effort to get the attention of the beaglers. The little creatures dispersed with a strange sort of haste as the two of them approached, Vicki wondered what could make the creatures depart with such speed and purpose.

"Ooh, there he is!" Mrs. Klobbreak cheered out. The game continued on and the two of them got splashed with the bog as another Everfall Lancer went sliding off of the arena. Derkstahl went riding past swinging his hammer over his head giving a side glance at the two of them. "Look at him go!"

A goblin wearing a snorkel popped up out of the cranberry bog giving a scornful look at Vicki and the old goblin woman. "Step back from the wall," he yelled out as he brought a whistle up to his mouth and blew into it. It produced a bubbling noise and he pointed down to Mrs. Klobbreak. "And you! Too old! Go away!"

"Don't be such a crab!" Vicki scowled at the goblin as she wrung out her dress from the soaking cranberry moat. "She just wants to see her grandson, he's playing for Everfall, he's that purple one over there." She pointed out towards the field. She looked for the purple goblin and gulped, he had dismounted from his beagle and had begun stomping over towards them.

"Happy Birthday, Derkie!" Mrs. Klobbreak sang out happily, as the goblin approached the two of them. She waved her little flag at him and smiled.

Derkstahl stepped right onto the head of the snorkel wearing goblin pushing him back under the water. He came to a stop on the wall where he stood with his hands on his hips glowering down at Vicki. His color changed from purple to a bright red, his pointed ears pressed back against the sides of his head.

"What are you doing here," Derkstahl barked out. He looked back and forth between his grandmother and Vicki. "I assume you're to blame for this, you're the one that brought all of these bodies down from the home? What kind of witch are you?"

"Oh I'm not... I'm not a witch, this is just my-"

"Stuff it! I can't believe that you'd have the nerve to cart my grandmother down here like this! How dare you!" He pointed down at them both the game still going on behind him. "I could sue you for this! This is harassment!"

"Harassment? She just wanted to come see you and say hello, that isn't a crime," said Vicki shielding herself from more of the splashing.

"I pay good money to keep her locked up in that old looney bin, and this is what I get?! I should have just paid to put you in the retire caves," Derkstahl yelled.

Mrs. Klobbreak waved her flag again at Derkstahl. "You're doing so good Derkie, I'm so proud of you!" She grabbed onto Vicki's arm and smiled up at her grandson. "This is my new friend, Vicki," she exclaimed.

"You're too old to be here," Derkstahl shouted down at Mrs. Klobbreak. Then he turned to Vicki. "And you, *Vicki*, you need to take all of these old broken down geezers back to that wormwood shed and leave them there! That's what you get paid to do, do your job!" He kicked the wall splashing water at the two of them.

"You don't have to be so cruel," Vicki yelled out as she shielded the old goblin woman from the water wheeling her back away from the wall. "She's not broken just because she's old!"

"You pixie brain! You don't know anything about anything!" Derkstahl pointed up to the stadium entrance and motioned for them to leave. "Old goblins are bad luck! Just having one here is a bad omen and you brought a whole bunch! You're just too stupid to know what you've done!"

Vicki spun Mrs. Klobbreak around and began wheeling her back towards the other residents. The seething goblin on the wall gave a few more jeers and returned his attention to the game behind him. "I'm sorry, Mrs. Klobbreak," Vicki whispered down to her.

"Oh I haven't seen him for such a long time! Thank you, dearie," Mrs. Klobbreak replied with a happy little chuckle.

"Didn't you hear what he was saying though? He wasn't being very nice."

"That's the most that he's talked to me in years! I couldn't have asked for a better day!" Mrs. Klobbreak shut her eyes and smiled up at the sky. "He used to chat at me all day before it was my time. I always said that he would be a famous beagler one day, and I was right! I'm so proud of him."

Vicki's lip trembled and she stifled back her anger as she brought the old goblin woman back to the other retirees. Some of the goblins in the crowd began tossing cranberries at them as they ascended the stadium. Vicki could feel her face getting hot and she crossed her arms as she took her seat.

"How'd that go," asked Frank. She looked down at Vicki pushing the pointed hat back so that she could see her face. "Whatsamatter?"

"He was awful!" Vicki grumbled and sat up trying to keep her composure. "He said we were bad luck."

"Well, hopefully bad luck for the away team." Frank shot up out of her seat shouting. "Down with Hammertwerk!"

Down on the cranberry bog Derkstahl pointed up towards the group of elderly residents. Vicki sat up paying close attention to the goblins on the field. All of the goblin riders on both teams sat listening to the instructions of the furious star Hammerer. The riders all faced in the direction of Vicki and the residents.

"Oh no." Vicki grabbed out for Frank's shoulder. "Frank!"

"Hmm. Never seen this in the rules before." Frank shielded her eyes from the sun focusing her attention on the field.

The riders all began galloping towards the butter towers whooping and hollering as they charged into the massive churning centers. Goblins from the tops of the towers fled, some of them even choosing to dive from the tops of the churns down into the bog below. The crowd began to cheer and sing as the action unfolded. Derkstahl emerged from one of the towers standing at its top and staring out over the crowd until he found the residents once again.

"Frank, I think we should go!"

"I can't believe they're churning it that fast, the butters could blast right outta there and into the stands!" Frank lowered her hand from her brow and nudged Vicki in the shoulder. "You know what, I think I'm beginning to see things from your perspective, we should go."

The two girls jumped out of their seats and began rounding up the elderly goblins. The great butter churning tower of Everfall spun round and round picking up speed as the goblin riders on top of the tower hopped up and down in unison. Referees began blowing their whistles and arguing down on the bog.

Vicki wheeled Mrs. Klobbreak around to the stadium slope pushing as hard as she could. "I'm sorry Mrs. Klobbreak, but we have to go!" The wheels squeaked and groaned as Vicki pushed on.

"Oh? Is it about to rain? I see everyone has their umbrellas up!"

Vicki looked around at the stands, the other goblins all began opening their butter umbrellas and hiding underneath them. "Omigod, do you have an umbrella too?" Vicki searched the old goblin's bag. "I think we better find one!" Vicki pushed the wheelchair as hard as she could up the ramp.

The referees blew the whistle again and all at once shouted, "Fire!"

The great churners rocked back and forth sending a massive amount of butter flying through the air, puddles of butter landed on the crowds down below. The small mountain of butter slammed into the stands, aimed largely at the residents, it spread to all the seats nearby splattering the game fans. The fans cheered out from the other side of the stadium laughing and applauding.

The warm and obnoxiously stinky butter struck Vicki on her back and covered Mrs. Klobbreak's wheelchair. The chair wobbled and Vicki pushed it forward again. She found that it moved much easier with the butter having greased the wheels for her.

"Fire!" The referees all shouted out again, blowing their whistles and holding onto one another's shoulders. They kicked their legs out dancing in unison and performing a little routine for the crowd.

A huge blast of butter from the other tower hit Vicki and the rest of the residents. The stadium broke into hysterics. Mrs. Klobbreak's chair began to rise in the air. Vicki held onto the chair crying out as she too began to float away from the ground.

"Vicki!" Frank came running down the slope grabbing onto her shoe. "Stop! Get that stuff off ya, it'll carry you all the way up to the sky!"

"I can't, I can't! What about Mrs. Klobbreak?"

Mrs. Klobbreak began rising higher away into the sky giggling and laughing as they floated upward. Vicki's shoe came off landing smack dab on Frank's head. Frank pulled on the cable that cinched her arm to her shoulder yanking it out of place. Her arm fell down to her side unraveled and sitting in pieces on the ground. Her cables slithered upward and her connected arm segments went flying into the air. Her mostly detached hand grabbed onto Vicki's leg.

Vicki looked down at the pieces wrapping themselves around her leg and screamed out. Franks other arm came away from itself. She flung her other hand up to catch the wheelchair. Frank stood under Vicki, her cabled arms stretching up some twenty feet high.

"I got you, short stuff, just let go of her and get that butter off of you first!" Frank's leg cables began to loosen at her waist, she glanced down the cables and grimaced. "Real quick like if you can, okay!"

Vicki let go of the wheelchair floating upward even higher. She went to work wiping the butter off from her backside and from her arms. The butter floated down and away from her and she stopped her ascent. She reached towards the wheelchair wiping the glop off of Mrs. Klobbreak, hurrying as fast as she could.

"I can see the mansion from here, dear!" Mrs. Klobbreak pointed to the Athenaeum on the mountain. "Oh and look down there!"

Vicki looked down below at the stands. The little goblin assessor stared up at her with a disapproving look on his face. He wore a funny little umbrella hat on his head shaking the butter off of it as he marked on his little stone tablet. Mrs. Klobbreak began settling back down to the ground as Vicki tried wiping the rest of the butter off from herself.

"Vicki, hurry!" Frank's leg slipped and she stumbled to the side. Vicki kicked her butter covered shoe off from her other foot and began pulling the butter out of her hair. "I have to let go!" Frank's leg gave out and she fell over into the crowd releasing Vicki with a cry of pain.

Vicki let out a shriek and continued dropping butter onto the crowd below. She looked out back towards the other residents, Jerry hopped up catching one of the small old goblins taking them under his arm. He looked over at her.

"Stay there boss, I can get ya down, just wait!"

Vicki's hat drifted up and away from her head and she began to lower into the crowd. She spied Jerry leaping through the air just as she vanished into the goblins below. Covered in butter and mortified as the hooligans around her heaved and laughed at her, she went dashing away from the crowd. She stopped in a row of seats that seemed empty enough and sat down to clear the rest of the butter away.

She wiped the butter from her face and rubbed a few tears off from her cheek. The goblin assessor had definitely marked off at least one point for this latest failure. She sniffled and tried to collect herself.

"Rah rah rah. We're going to smash the oinks." The prim and proper English woman waved her orange and black flag in the air with hardly any emotion behind her words. "Such a missed opportunity. You could have just done away with half of your bothersome little devils. Mind you, I would have hoped for better aim from the churners but what can you expect these days. They let just about anyone on to the teams now."

Vicki gripped her hands together shrinking back into the seat. Her palms became hot and moist, the back of her neck went cold. Soon her whole back was as chilled as a winter's rain. She swallowed the excess saliva that gathered in the roof of her mouth and she closed her eyes, wishing the gigantic woman away.

"I never thought that I'd see the day when that horrible little mansion was so close to being purified of its goblin filth." Zaldehyde leaned forward wearing a large pointed hat much like Vicki's covered in orange and black feathers. "Yet you've done it with such ease... and how are you enjoying your time here, my darling little niece?"

Vicki sprang from the stands and spun around. Her aunt sat up and smiled at her in the same fashion that an alligator might smile at a baby deer. Vicki stumbled nearly falling into the seats below.

"I'll scream! If you try anything, I swear! Leave me alone!"

"You've been listening to far too many lies, my dear. Why would I try anything here, in full view of the public?" Zaldehyde sat back and spread her arms out to the crowded seats around them. "Don't you know that we have laws here? We're not in your savage little world anymore. Sit."

Vicki shook her head, searching around for the quickest escape route through the crowd. She cried out and hopped over the seats below her, landing with a thud. Fire went blazing up her shins as she ran between the cheering goblins and beasts. She squeezed through an opening in the crowd and clamored over another row before coming to a stop to catch her breath.

Vicki gasped and fell back into a seat behind her, staring in disbelief at her aunt who sat firmly in place as if neither of them had moved the slightest bit. The eight feet and nine inches tall witch stood from her seat and cheered along with the rest of the crowd around her as Hammertwerk scored a point. Vicki whimpered and turned to see who in the crowd might be able to help her. Zaldehyde sat back down offering the young girl a familiar looking shoe box filled with roasted nuts.

"Please do be careful, I don't want you hurting yourself on these seats." Zaldehyde sighed and shook the box at Vicki then returned her attention to the game, disappointed at the girl's refusal to take a handful. "This stadium used to be state of the art. Look at the state of it now."

Vicki curled herself up in a seat as far away from her aunt as she could get. "What do you want?" she cried out, trembling and wide eyed.

"I want you to stay safe, of course. Oh, if only your mother had listened to me, you wouldn't be in this danger. It chills my blood to think of you stuck there in that rotting old shack. Living there amongst all those godless monsters." Zaldehyde clapped along with the crowd and she motioned for Vicki to come sit closer. "Come, talk with me. I'm not going to bite."

"I-I think I'm good right here."

"Suit yourself. Anyways, it's not me that you have to worry about. Especially with the biting." Zaldehyde began to pick out a few choice bits from the box of roasted nuts. "Now, I can keep my dog on her chain to a point, but you have to understand the politics surrounding your situation."

Vicki sat up in her chair keeping an eye on a hole that was beginning to appear in the crowd. "W-what situation, do you mean the housekeeping?"

"Oh that's just the icing on the cake. No the real meat of it, the good chewy center, that's you. Go on, take a look." Zaldehyde tilted her head towards the upper rows of the stadium. "Look."

Vicki turned her head up in the direction of Zaldehyde's, gaze following along until her eyes met with the strawberry blonde haired woman's piercing stare. She gasped and snapped her attention back to her aunt. Zaldehyde popped one of the roasted nuts into her mouth.

"I view Miss Shuck as a valuable asset. One of my greatest, even. She is obedient to a tee. Would you like to know how I maintain control over such a creature?"

Vicki shook her head, putting all of her focus on the spacing between the crowds. "Is she here for me? Can you make her go away?" she asked with a full bodied shiver. She didn't dare turn her attention to Ciara for fear that she might see the horrible woman coming down the rows of seats.

"She is, and I could." Zaldehyde crunched loudly on a hazelnut. "But that wouldn't be very fair to her now, would it?"

"Why not?"

"I have to throw her a bone every now and then. A piece of steak here and there." She brought another hazelnut up to her mouth. "Something warm and chewy. She has expensive tastes but I'm happy to pay them, considering all that she's doing for me in return."

Vicki glanced back to the spot in the rows far above, searching for Zaldehyde's lawyer. She had vanished. Vicki stood up from her seat, scanning the stadium. Panic filled her body and she lost her breath as she lost the woman in red.

"Please make her stop!" Vicki turned back to her aunt her eyes beginning to mist over. "What do you want with me, why are you doing this?"

Zaldehyde stood up from her seat, towering over the girl, casting a long shadow down upon her. "Oh, it's quite simple, so easy. Even for a girl like you. You poor little frightened rabbit, this is all too much for you!" Zaldehyde bent down closer to Vicki's height. "I told you that there was one little thing that you might do for me and here it is. Quit. Quit the position of Housekeeper, enter the library of contracts and tear yours up. Tear up every contract in there for all that I care, but quit today. Quit and make sure that you rip the Housekeeper's contract to shreds."

Vicki cowered in the cold shadow of Zaldehyde. There was an oppressive weight from the shadow. Pins and needles tingled along Vicki's body. Her thumbs tickled and complained as she brought her hands up to shield herself from the looming witch.

"But I can't quit! If I quit, my mom and dad will become pigs again!" Vicki swallowed hard stepping a few feet back. "And, and all the old people will get kicked out and they won't have anywhere to go! I can't!"

Zaldehyde's eyes went dark. Her pupils seemed to overtake the whites of her eyes as she sneered down at Vicki. "People? People, Victoria? Do you know what the Golem eats? Have you seen the way that stinking vampire looks at you? Really looks at you? You bother to worry about them? They'd eat you as soon as look at you given the chance." She slapped her hands together in front of Vicki's face making the small girl shriek and stumble backward onto the ground. "Do you know who owns the Athenaeum? Scum of the Ätherside, that's who! They know how inept you are and they're more than ready to sign your death warrant, one more slip up that's all it will take. One more and they'll let the Company of Wolves send out a termination decree, and then my little hungry dog will carry it out!"

"What, what termination?! What does that mean?!" Vicki scooted away from Zaldehyde her legs turning to jelly. "They, they're going to send a replacement for me, our lawyer said so! I just need more time! Please!"

"Time is up, little Victoria. If you fail to perform your next duty they'll have no choice! You'll become a liability, too dangerous to keep around, too useless." She narrowed her eyes and hushed her tone. "Ciara has been keeping a close eye on your progress. She's responsible for carrying out all terminations at the Company of Wolves, she's ever so good at it. She's absolutely salivating at the thought of your next flop, it's all that she can talk about. Oh, you'll fail just as you always have, young one. You'll mess up again and again and you'll be thrown out of that house. You'll fail and you'll scream for her, just like she wants you to!"

Vicki wrapped her hands around her ears and shouted out, "Stop! Go away! Go away!" She kicked at the air finally scrambling back to her feet. "Get away from me!"

Zaldehyde smiled that horrible shark smile, her obsidian eyes sparkled with wicked glee. Her words pierced through Vicki's hands, past her ears, straight into her mind. "Quit! Destroy your contract and save yourself! Leave the Athenaeum or she'll start with your kidneys." Zaldehyde shook the shoe box of roasted nuts turning it upside down. Squirming bits of pink and pulsating flesh fell from the upturned box, slipping over one another on the ground as they landed with sickening splatters. "She'll start with your kidneys then slurp out your little liver! She's going to chew out your insides and she'll eat your legs while you're still **ALIVE AND SCREAMING!**"

The contents of the box spilled out completely, a quivering mass of pink organ tissue plopped out onto the ground. A quake ran through Vicki's legs as she trembled staring in horror at the beating heart with a large sharp bite taken out of it. Zaldehyde let out a horrible laugh, a laugh that could frighten a ghost back into its tomb, a laugh that could put storm sirens to shame. The words bounced around the crowd and gained power as they echoed in Vicki's ears. *ALIVE AND SCREAMING!*

Vicki ran through the crowd, crying out, knocking over a smaller goblin and crashing into a throng of giant catlike creatures. She jumped over discarded cups and slipped around on the stadium bleachers. With one last push through the bustling crowd, Vicki bumbled out onto the stairway between the bleachers, checking back at the seats to ensure that she wasn't being chased. The screaming in her ears finally stopped, those terrible echoing words dissipated into the air. The gargantuan witch had vanished and a pile of roasted nuts littered the floor where the beating heart had twitched.

Frank waved at her from the top of the stairs, her arms tightened back to her shoulders. "Vicki! Up here!" She started down to greet her. "What happened, are you..." Frank reached the small out of breath girl grabbing onto her before she collapsed down the stairs. "Stand up short bread, come on get up!"

Vicki covered her mouth and heaved, sobbing as quietly as she could into her hands, she buried her head into the taller stitchwork girl's shoulder. Her face grew hot and she took sharp breaths trying to control the tears. She reached down to the ripped up spots on her new tights bringing her hand up to the back of her dress, she winced and she broke into full tears.

Vicki's dress had split down the back and opened up for all the world to see. Frank skillfully cinched the rip together with a bit of stapling that she tore from her own arm. Vicki sobbed reaching down behind her feeling at the wiggling little velvety curly tail that had reappeared and broken free of the tights. The crowd went wild around them as the action on the bog continued. The goblins around them began pelting them with cranberries and garbage laughing and making oinking noises.

"Don't feed into them," said Frank as she hoisted Vicki up by the shoulders. She shook the sobbing girl. "Don't feed into them."

Vicki's face glowed hot red, she gave a single nod to Frank catching her breath. "Okay." She broke down again wrapping her arms around herself.

Frank hugged her around the shoulder and began to lead her back up the stairs of the stadium. Vicki melted into the stitchwork girl as they climbed the stadium together. The crowd continued to erupt around them jeering and throwing cups, but the two girls went on in silence.

Chapter sixteen

The goblins chattered the entire bus ride home and Vicki did her absolute best to smile with them. She ended the bus ride by letting her head rest against the window. Her eyes stared out into the village and the trees. Vicki wondered how it would end for her.

She felt at her bare legs, trying to think of anything else but Ciara Shuck. She thought of her friends back home, Rachel and the others. Vicki was going to become one of those kids on the missing posters. Her claim to fame would be that she really and truly had disappeared. The invisible girl of Danville would never be seen again.

The poor old residents would be tossed out, and Frank and Desmond, everyone else would be thrown out too. Vicki rubbed one single tear off of her cheek as the bus came to a steaming halt in front of the mansion. The doors opened and Frank along with Jerry began helping the goblins off of the bus.

The excited little old people waddled out, each of them smiling and waving their little flags at Vicki as they passed by. The last goblin wheeled up to Vicki and she patted her on the knee. Mrs. Klobbreak smiled at the forlorn girl.

"Oh, don't be so upset dearie, we lost this game but there's always next season!"

"I know. I'm sorry about the butter-flight. I hope Derkie didn't upset you too much."

Mrs. Klobbreak chuckled and wheeled herself to the door. "That was the most excitement I've had in years! I hope we can go again next season!"

Vicki stood from her seat and followed the goblins out of the bus. The gaggle of goblins gathered around the front yard, Jerry performed a head count and Frank corralled all of the wheelchairs in the direction of the mansion. Desmond stood in the doorway with a hopeful expression. He caught Vicki's eye and gestured her forward.

The walk past the goblins seemed to take forever. The residents were more happy than not and still full of excitement from the game. Vicki approached Desmond, hiding her tears in front of the goblins. She made her way up to him still covered in butter and biting her lip.

He put a hand on her shoulder and brought her into the mansion. "It's okay, hey it's okay," he said, as she tried to push past him. "You've still got the resident points and you're done at nine sharp! Those goblins look pretty happy to me-"

Vicki spun around to face him, wringing her hands together and sputtering. "My aunt wants me to rip up my contract and she said that Ciara Shuck is going to eat me if I fail the assessment." She sat down on the floor hugging her arms. "And she's right! She's gonna get me!"

"Well, we're not gonna let that happen, no one's going to let her get you." Desmond knelt down and offered his hand out to her. "And you aren't going to fail, the old folks loved getting out! They're all going crazy over you!"

"I, I let it get out of hand, a little." Vicki gulped and ignored his gesture. She breathed out a long sigh and looked up to Desmond. "Derkie was so terrible! I shouldn't have taken her down to the cranberry bog, he got so mad and they all sprayed us with butter!"

"I can see that."

"And the goblin man was there and he saw everything! Me and Mrs. Klobbreak floating up and everything! He looked so mad and my aunt told me that I'm going to fail the next test! And my curse came back, my pigtail, my stupid pigtail came back!" Vicki trembled and shivered hugging her arms together.

Desmond frowned down at her wiping some of the butter from her shoulder. "Well look, even if all that's true, the assessor is out there right now talking to all the goblins, they look like they had a blast! Now you only got a little bit more than an hour to go before the whole assessment ends, there isn't too much more they can throw at you. You're gonna be fine!"

"Can you tell my mom and my dad, and Max too, because I can't tell them I can't..." She whimpered out hiding her face in her hands. "Don't let them know that I got... don't tell them what happened! Just tell them I disappeared!"

Desmond sat down on the floor next to her giving her an awkward side hug around the shoulders. He sighed and lifted his fedora from his head. "Alright, listen. I know it all seems pretty dire right now, but don't give up. Nothing is set in stone yet."

"The assessment is *literally* set in stone!"

"Okay, you got me there, but what I said is true. Don't just sit there and wallow in despair, just in case something crazy does happen we have one last trick to get you home safe. That door-"

Frank came running into the hall from the outside motioning for Vicki to stand to her feet. "Dez, the pit bull is here! She's coming in, Vicki you stay away from her, get behind us!"

Loud clopping footsteps came echoing from the front of the mansion. Stiletto heels on hardwood floor boards boomed out with every step forward. Vicki lifted her eyes from her hand up to the intruder. Those long skinny legs came walking towards her, tufts of black hair still hidden into the red shining heels.

Ciara Shuck bent down at her waist looking deep into Vicki's eyes giving her a smile full of abnormally long white teeth. "Oh, well there she is! Hello Vicki, do you remember me from the other day? *Ciara Shuck*, we met only briefly." She extended her hand to Vicki her red nails glistened curling into sharp points at their tips, her tone was overly pleasant and cheerful. "It's good to see you again! I've been watching your progress pretty closely, you know, as part of the assessment team. It's been very exciting, I'm here to oversee the last test! I hope you're ready!"

Vicki began taking in quick breaths, she jumped to her feet and leaned away from Ciara Shuck's terrible red claws. "It-It's not done! I'm not ready!" She stumbled backwards and fell into Frank. "It isn't time!"

Frank hid the girl behind her shoulder and crossed her arms standing directly between Vicki and the woman in red. "Dez, I gotta borrow Vicki for a couple of minutes, I think there's something wrong with the toilets." Frank tugged on one of the stitches in her arm glaring at Ciara Shuck. "Something *stinks* in here, I wanna show her how to deal with any hairballs or whatever got caught in the pipes."

Desmond stood up from the floor adjusting the fedora on his head and giving the stitch work girl a wink on the sly. "You go ahead, I'll hammer out the details back here." He gave a quick glance to Vicki. "Maybe show her where to find the cleaning supplies, over by the dispensary."

"I'll catch you later Vicki!" Ciara sang out her words in a playful tone giving Vicki a little wave of her hand as Frank turned the girl away and began marching her forward. Ciara turned back to talk to Desmond, speaking loud enough for Vicki to hear, relishing her every syllable. "Isn't she just the cutest thing you've ever seen? *Couldn't you just eat her up with a spoon?*"

Vicki's chest heaved and she began sniffling. Frank rested her hands upon Vicki's shoulders walking her forward through the hallway of the mansion. They reached the dispensary and Frank took a peek back to the main hall making sure that they were out of Ciara's hearing range.

"Listen short stuff, it's time to get real. I don't like the way that old basset hound is looking at you," Frank whispered as she opened the dispensary door. She continued to whisper as she searched for the light switch, *"You did real good today, you're gonna pass whatever stupid little test she has planned for you, and she's just gonna have to turn tail and leave!"*

"She wants to eat me! Like for real eat me! My aunt even promised that she was going to eat my legs!" Vicki's whisper reached to a panicked pitch and she shuddered. *"What if I don't pass the test?"*

Frank found the light switch clicking it up and down to make sure that the room stayed dark. "Good, it's working!" She closed the door behind them and brought Vicki forward to the table, sitting her down upon it. "Okay, let's say that you don't. She's gonna come after ya and she's gonna be fast and hungry. You can't fight her like this."

"Like what? You mean because I'm not magic?" Vicki frowned and hugged her knees up to her chin. "I was actually starting to think that maybe I could... I don't know what I was thinking. I don't even have the hat now. I'm not magic at all!"

Frank smacked the tops of Vicki's knees. "You don't need all that stuff anyways, magic and wands, it turns people real sour. What you need is your life and limbs intact!" She turned to the wall giving it a solid kick. The room shook and the floorboards groaned. A small glowing keyhole appeared on the wall behind her. "You need to open that door."

"It's the same one from yesterday! You knew about it!" The ring on Vicki's thumb began to glow along with the eerie light from behind the door.

"We all know about it, it's the library. That's where all of our contracts are, mine and Dez's, and yours." Frank ushered her off of the table forward to the glowing light. "We stay away from it because of all the bad juju that it puts off. This door shows up all around the mansion, it's freaky. I know it's hard and it's scary, but this is for keeps this time! You gotta open this door! You gotta do it like your grandpa used to do it!"

Vicki clenched her teeth clutching her hands together. "But Frank, I don't know how to open any of the doors around here! I can't do anything without that magic hat!"

"Kitten, trust me, I know how hard it is to believe in yourself. I get it, but you have to believe that you're the Housekeeper and start believing it real quick! I'm starting to think that it's the only way the door will open! It's gotta work, that's all we got!"

"But how's opening the door even going to help me! Are you gonna hide me in there?"

"You're getting in there and you're finding your contract!" Frank shoved her forward towards the mysterious door. "And you're gonna rip it up just like that giant hag wants!"

Vicki spun around and shook her head. "No! Belvedere said everyone would get thrown out into the caves if I quit!"

"Caves is better than graves, now get in there!" Frank shoved her forward again but Vicki stood her ground.

"And you'll get sent back to the dungeons! And Belvedere and Desmond, all of you! Don't you care?"

"Vicki, your whole life is flashing before my eyes and it involves a lot of sharp teeth at the end! Do you want to have the contract ready to go or not! Whattabout your mom and dad back home? Whattabout them?"

Vicki hugged her arms and bit her lip. She turned back around to the door and shivered. "I wish they were here to tell me what to do!"

"Tough luck sista, sometimes you have to tell yourself!" Frank threw her arms up in despair and opened the dispensary door. "You stay here, either just stand here staring at that door until your eyes fall out or try actually doing something, I don't care which! I'm going to go get a pry bar and some hammers and I'm coming back and we're getting that contract out of there one way or the other!" She slammed the door shut behind her and went storming off into the hallway.

Vicki grasped her hair in her hands, turning back to the mysterious door. Her parents were mostly back to normal by now, her mother had told her so. How long would it possibly take for them to fully recover after her time in the Athenaeum? A few weeks at the most? Or had the curse returned for them too, just as her tail had returned?

Just how bad could those dungeons be, how horrible would that place be that her new friends would be thrown into? How dark and cold was it? Where would those goblins find themselves tomorrow, in the caves, somewhere worse? What would happen to Desmond and to Belvedere? Vicki couldn't even begin to imagine living with the guilt for the rest of her life.

The rest of her life might only be tonight. Ciara Shuck had smiled at her like a starving cat might smile at a mouse. She wasn't going to rip up the contract really, she would only take it just in case. *Just in case she failed.*

Vicki looked up into the ceiling and around the room. "I know you don't like me, and I know that you wanted someone else to be your housekeeper, but I could really use a break right now." She put her hands together and begged up to the ceiling. "Just this once, please?"

She walked to the mysterious door and twisted the doorknob. It slipped to the left and pulled away from her. Vicki leaned her head against the door and began to cry. Her tears dropped down onto the floor below leaving dark wet spots on the dusty linoleum.

"Please!" Vicki begged, pressing her hands up against the door.

A shadow fell across the white glass of the dispensary door, coming up to the window. Vicki gulped and hid herself into the corner of the room. The person rapped on the door and a sweet little voice came from the other side.

"Vicki? It's me. I want to help you!" The little girl spoke through the door with her heavy Spanish accent and a hopeful tone. "*Prima,* I can help... I can try to help. We can open that door together!"

Vicki stood from her hiding spot taking a step towards the dispensary door. "Magra?"

"Yes it's me! I've been here, Vicki, been here trying to help! I'm so sorry, I tried."

Vicki whimpered out and backed away into the wall. "You... you just disappeared on me and your mother is trying to kill me! I don't trust you!"

"Vicki, I'm sorry about before! I'm not a *bad bruja,* I tried to help you but I couldn't! The fountain was so old, it just broke, I don't know why." Magra sighed out and laid her horns against the door. "Please let me try to help, I don't want that lobo to hurt you either!"

Vicki rubbed her arms and stared at the mysterious door. "It, It won't open, none of the doors will open for me."

"I know prima, I know. The doors are strong here, too strong for me, too! I tried to help open them for you, but no! They stayed closed, the house she's strong! Strong like old brujeria!"

The goblin assessor's words came back to Vicki like a bolt of lightning. *You can thank your white haired friend for its return.* Mrs. Klobbreak had also spoken of another white haired girl running around the mansion. Was it possible that Magra really had been here the whole time? Vicki crept up to the door twisting its handle with great apprehension.

Magra stood in the hallway wearing a light green cloak over her body. Her white hair poked out from around her little horns, her soft brown eyes stared back at Vicki. The girl with the horns and the devil's tail gave her a nervous smile and pressed past her into the room.

"Come, we must work fast! My mother is soon here, she wants your contract, your contract or your life!" Magra looked up and down at the mysterious door. "Come, hurry, please!" She waved her hand taking out her crystal wand from her cloak.

"Why are you helping me?" Vicki joined her cousin, remaining at arm's length and nervously rubbing her hands together. "Your mom wants me to fail."

"No, no Vicki, she wants you to bring her this contract!" Magra pressed her ear up to the door and tapped her wand on the doorknob. Her eyes darted around the room as she listened. "Mi Madre, she hates the people, do you know them? *The Three Lords.* She wants to hurt them all, very much. Very deeply. Everything in life now for her is this and this only!"

Vicki gave the other girl a nod. "I don't know who they are, but I know they own the mansion. Why does she hate them?"

Magra stepped back from the door and raised her wand up in the air, she waved it around in several directions before shaking it and trying again. "She will never tell me why. The Lords, they have many contracts. Here and other places too. Some contracts they keep old magics locked away, magics like this door. I think she wants the old magics! But maybe it's something else." Magra moved her wand around again, distraught at its performance. "Aya, it doesn't want to do it! This is dark magic!"

"Well, they probably keep those things locked up for a reason, and what do you mean, dark magic? I thought we were just opening this door."

Magra raised her wand up and held her hand out for Vicki. "We are! First you need a key! Put your hand here! Quickly!"

Vicki put her hand out looking away. Magra placed her wand tip over Vicki's hand hissing out words that sounded like *All dolls then*. Salt crystals began to pour out from the wand's end, dancing around in the palm of her hand, coming together in the shape of a key. Vicki opened her eyes, staring down at the glowing white light of Magra's wand.

"This is a skeleton key, it will hurt the house, make it into bones. No more magic. Take your contract and give it to my mother. This will hurt the Lords, poison them. You must do it soon or they will come to stop you." Magra turned her head away in shame. "Only the Earthbound can use this key. It will kill all the magic that touches it."

"Kill the house? I don't want to kill the house or anyone in it!" Vicki shoved the key back to her and Magra backed away into the corner shielding herself from Vicki's hand.

"You must, Vicki, you must! The door will open when Athenaeum lays dead! I don't know why the house doesn't like you, but you will die if you don't do as mi madre says! You must get that contract for my mother... or else..."

"But what will happen to everyone else in the house?"

"*Prima,* if I tell you, you will not do what must be done! I don't want to kill Athenaeum, I love this place too...." Magra lowered her hood down over her shoulders and she gave the door a gentle caress. "Abuelo let me run down these hallways, I feel her in these walls. She is like our *abuela,* our grandmother."

Vicki looked down at the key in her hand, its salt crystalline structure caught the light through the keyhole glowing a warm pink hue. "Then... then I shouldn't do this! You shouldn't give me this!" Vicki held the key towards Magra.

"No! No, I can't touch it, it's my own magic! It will come back to me, much much worse!" Magra fled from Vicki and the key, she made her way back to the hallway and turned around. "I want you to live even more, more than Athenaeum! We are family, primas... please live! Live for me too!"

Magra ran out of the dispensary looking around the hallway. She threw her hood up over her head frowning at Vicki. She shrank into her cloak, looking down at the floor.

"Vicki, if you don't get your contract, if you don't use that key... you have to run... my mother... she's a bad bruja. So bad. I love her, but she is bad, so you must run! Do you understand? She will do very bad things to you!" She took off for the opposite end of the hallway and vanished into the corner, a gust of wind flew up from the corner tossing Vicki's hair back.

Vicki gripped the skeleton key in her hand turning back to the glowing library door. She edged closer to the keyhole and sighed out. The Athenaeum didn't want Vicki, that much was clear. It had held the doors closed on her, kept the lights low, and even tried to sabotage her assessment with an exploding pile of mud. Not even Magra could make the Athenaeum behave, and she was a real witch *with real magic.* The house had done everything to bring her to this point, locked every door and dimmed every light, it had perhaps even been the one to poison her little griffin.

If the key would kill the Athenaeum, wouldn't that be enough for Zaldehyde? Why did she want Vicki's contract so badly? Vicki's hands began shaking, she closed her eyes and brought the key to the door holding it at the glowing keyhole. Wasn't her life more important than some weird old monster house? Who back home would ever really know? Who would even care about goblins and vampires and stitchwork girls?

Vicki covered her mouth with one hand and gripped the key firmly in the other. She screamed out through her fingers, clenching the key tight. What if her life *wasn't* worth more? What if her existence hardly even mattered in the greater scheme of things? What if she didn't deserve the vampire or stitchwork girl at all, or anyone for that matter?

With one simple turn of the key Vicki could go back home and disappear from this place. She didn't belong here and she wasn't wanted here, so that simple turn should be quite easy. Killing a living thing wouldn't be so hard for someone as despicable and hateful as her. She could go back home, back to where she could continue being invisible. She could just fail and go back to where she belonged.

It was, in fact, what anyone should have expected out of Vicki, with how stupid and useless she really was. Whoever had selected her for the role of Housekeeper had either done so out of morbid humor or with intent purpose to see the Athenaeum die. She was the perfect person for the job then if the entire reason for her being here was to fail and let everything fall apart. Really, she would only be doing what came natural to her, the only thing that she would ever be good at. Letting everyone else suffer.

She trembled and brought the key into the glowing hole on the door, biting her lip and whimpering as the light from the doorway caught the salt crystals in the key. The light pulsed as the key drew closer, it was as if the keyhole were an eye and it opened wide to look up at her as she drove the killing instrument forward. Vicki couldn't help anyone but at least she could help herself and be done with this stupid sick old house. She could let it die and someone would bury it and she could just forget about it.

Vicki screamed out and pulled the key away from the door. She threw it to the floor and stomped on it crushing it into tiny grains of salt rock. Her last hope crumbled and fizzled away into the air, and the keyhole disappeared leaving her in the darkness of the dispensary once again. She fell back onto the floor behind her, resting against the wall. She hid her face in her hands, calling out to anyone who might have been able to hear her.

"I'm sorry!" She curled up into a ball in front of the door and began wailing.

Vicki walked past the portraits of the Housekeepers that had come before her. She slumped past them exhausted and disinterested in the legacy that she did not share. The lights dimmed behind her as she went, the darkness followed her all the way to the main hall.

"She passed the assessment! It's right there on the stone! This is crazy, you can't do this!" Desmond threw the goblin assessor's stone tablet down to Ciara Shuck's feet.

"She has the points, certainly, but I don't see any aptitudes for defense and strategy. I'm sorry, but the law is quite clear here, the Housekeeper must be assessed in every category!" Ciara put her bright red stiletto on the stone tablet. "The Company of Wolves can't recognize this assessment until it's completed!"

"This is clearly a targeted attack on a girl that is obviously incapable of defending this house! You can't let this happen, you're in control here, not her!" Belvedere pointed down to the goblin assessor. "What about the resident recommendations? They're absolutely sterling!"

Frank turned around and frowned as Vicki came creeping up to the little group. "Short stuff, get outta here! We're running outta time!" She rushed to Vicki's side and tried pushing her back into the hallway. "What are you doing out here, you know what she wants!"

"I couldn't do it! I can't kill the Athenaeum, I can't do it!" Vicki fell into Frank. "My aunt wants me to kill it! She made my cousin give me a key to the room but it was going to kill everything! I can't!"

"Well it's not like the house is making it any easier on you," hissed Frank. "It's gonna suck being back in a dungeon, but it's better than you getting snuffed! Go back and do what you gotta do!"

"I can't, I just can't!" Vicki whimpered and shivered. "I don't want to let everyone down anymore, my grandpa loved this place and he'd never let anything happen to anyone in here!"

Frank gave her a sad little smile. "Stupid kid, you coulda got away with it, coulda gone back home!" She grabbed Vicki's chin and gave her a quick pinch. "Stupidest kid I ever met."

Vicki's eyes fell to the floor as she nodded in agreement. Her shoulders hung low and she sighed. "I know." She wiped her nose with the back of her sleeve and rubbed her arms shivering in the cold evening air.

Frank latched on to her, giving Vicki a quick hug. "Stupidly stupid." She spun around to the horrible woman in red and shot her a look of total disdain.

Ciara leaned her head to the side smiling at Vicki. "I don't see a contract in that hand. Your aunt seems to think that you shouldn't be here, she wants you to be released from the contract for the position of Housekeeper." She pulled out a slip of paper from her jacket. "Now we can achieve that in one of two ways, you can come with me to my office and we can sign a declaration of no confidence, or we can stay here and let you finish your assessment."

Vicki shook her head at Ciara, she gulped down her fear stepping out in front of Frank and Desmond. "I want to finish the assessment!"

Desmond put his arm out in front of Vicki sliding in front of her. "Vicki! No, don't!"

Ciara Shuck made a clicking noise with her tongue and folded her dark red suit coat over her arm. "Well, if we're going to be honest, just between you and me, I'm glad that you decided not to quit. It saves me from getting it all over my car, you wouldn't believe how hard it is to get a little thing like you out of the upholstery." She placed her coat on the floor and began to unbutton her shirt. "I know your aunt hoped that you'd be smart enough to listen to her, but I was rooting for you this whole time! I knew you wouldn't be able to do it."

Desmond stepped in front of Vicki, followed by Frank and Belvedere. Vicki shook with fright, the woman's piercing green eyes followed her no matter how hard she hid behind her friends. Ciara dropped her skirt from her waist standing perfectly at ease in her undergarments. The goblin assessor scrunched his face up and sighed.

"Well? Begin the assessment," Ciara snapped out. She bared her teeth at the assessor and her voice dropped unnaturally low as she growled at him. "What are you waiting for?"

The goblin assessor marked his stone tablet. "The Housekeeper will defend the house." He put his tablet down and turned away, his face full of self disgust and sorrow.

Frank spun around gripping Vicki by her shoulders. "Run!" She pushed her away tugging on the long cable sticking out from her arm. All of her stitching loosened up. "Run, go on! Get out of here! Go hide!"

"But what about you!" Vicki grabbed out for Frank's arm.

Belvedere pulled her away. "We're going to have to stop her, but that means that you have to go! She's right, you need to stay hidden, she wants *you!*"

Desmond threw his fedora to the ground and rolled up his sleeves. He began taking his tie off, turning to face Vicki as he spoke. "We'll slow her down long as we can. You run and you hide, you only have to make it to seven o'clock, the assessment ends at seven."

"But that's so long! How are you gonna stop her for that long?" Vicki gripped her hair in her hands, the look on Desmond's face was answer enough. "I can't just leave you guys behind!"

Ciara's head snapped backward and her neck bent at an angle so steep that it made Vicki cover her eyes. The terrible woman hunched forward. Her head swung loosely over her shoulder, and wet popping sounds began to erupt all over the woman's body. Hair slithered out from her pores in great black masses covering her legs.

The woman's skull cracked, her face scrunched inward to an unrecognizable lump of tissue while the hair continued its growth all over the woman's abdomen and arms. Ciara's entire body began to jerk and quake, every body part wiggling independent from one another. She whined and cried out in pain, her voice distorted into an animalistic holler.

Her hands twisted and her fingers grew longer, her torso stretched and her back became a mass of twisting muscle and fur, she tore off her last remaining bits of clothing with an angry and pained shout. Vicki watched in terror as Ciara Shuck's mouth and nose forced themselves outward. Her teeth became a row of slobbering fangs set into a dripping maw. Her ears stretched far up above her head pressing themselves into Vicki's direction.

Those skinny legs distorted into long wolf legs, muscular and slender. A tail pushed out from her spine and began to flick around as the terrifying creature opened her eyes. Ciara set those glowing green dots upon Vicki, they paralyzed her with some unknown power.

The pitch black mass of hair and fangs opened her mouth as far as it could extend, she puffed out her chest letting loose with a blood chilling noise that made everyone in the room shiver. The howling made Vicki clench up, her legs locked together and she opened her mouth to scream but no air could escape her lungs. The wolf gnashed her fangs together and made an odd coughing sound as if to laugh at the little group.

"Hide!" Frank shoved her arms toward the werewolf. Her stitches loosened themselves and her arms extended to Ciara Shuck's legs, wrapping themselves like a lasso around her feet. Ciara tumbled to the ground catching her fall with her front claws. "Go Vicki, just go!"

Vicki turned and sped down the corridor, crossing the main hall and running for the front doors. The doors were wide open but her aunt sat out in the lawn on an unusually large briefcase. She looked back at Vicki with a smile on her face raising a tea cup at her. The briefcase was in the shape of a small coffin, small enough for Vicki. Zaldehyde winked and her origami bird of magic spells came diving down from the sky straight at Vicki, the doors to the Athenaeum slammed shut. She took off for the spiral staircase behind her.

The werewolf howled out and Desmond let loose with some choice words. Glass shattered down below as large heavy objects were thrown against the walls. Vicki sprinted up the stairs running to the open doors of the residents rooms and they all began slamming shut before she could reach them.

"This way! Come this way," pleaded one of the goblins as Vicki came dashing down the hallway. The goblin's door pulled itself shut and the goblin began rattling the door handle. "It locked itself! By Crom it locked itself!"

More and more doors began crashing and creaking shut down the hallway. Vicki screamed with each door slam, her legs were on fire and her lungs were ready to burst with every breath, her eyes began to tear over. Her field of vision began to funnel, she could only focus on the door at the end of the hall now. She could only concentrate on reaching it in time to save herself.

Belvedere screamed out from downstairs and Frank called out his name in a panic. Ciara howled out and roared as Desmond made pained sounds. More heavy things hit the walls and floors of the mansion, then the wolf roared out again, this time much closer.

Vicki breathed in and out pumping her legs as hard as she could. The door at the end of the hall began closing, creaking shut as she approached. "No! Please!" She reached out to the door knob and the heavy oak door nearly slammed shut on her fingers.

She stood outside of the door, pounding on it and sobbing into the wood. She pressed herself against the door, sliding down to the floor in defeat. Her hand rested on the door knob, giving it one last halfhearted twist.

Great flashes of light came from the main hall of the mansion and the wolf bellowed. Belvedere cheered, yelling for Desmond. The entire mansion shook and Belvedere began screaming instead. Frank let out a shriek and there was the gnashing of teeth. Shadows danced on the walls of the Athenaeum. The wolf was going to win.

She was going to win and she was going to take her sweet time with Vicki, just as Zaldehyde had promised. Vicki sobbed into her hands, bumping her head against the door. She was going to die and her mother and father would have to live with the pain of it all. She wished that she could tell them one last time, everything that they needed to hear from her, anything that they wanted to hear.

Of course this was how it was going to end. Vicki wasn't nearly qualified enough to be the Housekeeper or anything else for that matter. She was useless at everything, but now at least Ciara Shuck would have a good meal. Wasn't that worth something? Maybe too her friends back home would be free of her burden and wouldn't it just be fitting that the girl who had ruined their 7th grade summer with dog snacks should end up as dog food herself?

"Please open!" Vicki cried out, twisting the door knob one last time. "Please!"

An unearthly howl shook the hallway and the wolf screamed out in a voice that gurgled somewhere in between the range of a truck engine and a grizzly bear. *"Where are you?!"* Glass shattered and wood splintered, a potted fern went sailing into the corner of the hall. *"You little bimbo!"* The walls shook and floor boards exploded under the massive power of those clawed feet. *"I'm going to wear your pretty little scalp like a hat!"*

Vicki held her mouth closed and scampered to her feet. Her legs trembled and they turned ice cold. Her entire body shook no matter how hard she tried staying still. She tried breathing through her nose to keep as quiet as possible but the panic swelled inside of her, she began breathing in loud huffs and sniffles.

"I want to hear you scream!" The wolf's shadow loomed at the other end of the hall, it grew and grew, the wolf searched everywhere for her prey. She sniffed the air loudly and cursed. *"I'll kill the fat one next! How dare you touch my nose!"*

Vicki cried out and whined under her breath, "I can't! I can't do this!"

"You stinking little brat! You smell like gingerbread and fear! I'm going to snap you in half!" The wolf dragged her claws along the walls, the dreadful scraping of nails on plaster made Vicki cover her ears. *"Come out here and scream for me!"* The wolf threw her head back and let loose with a piercing howl. *"I'll rip you to shreds!"*

The door behind Vicki began to rattle. She spun around and held the noisy door knob in place, it fought left and right clinking and clanking with every twist. She glanced down the hallway. The shadow of the wolf snapped her attention toward the sound. Vicki huffed and strained with the noisy handle until at last her bedroom door opened and she fell onto the hardwood floors beyond.

She fell to the floor and closed the door as quiet as a mouse locking it from her side. She caught her breath and turned to look for a good hiding spot, then she called out in surprise at the figure sitting on her bed. He scowled in her direction, dropping his monocle into his pocket. Vicki fell to the floor whimpering and clenching her fists together.

Eckhardt Charles stood from the bed looking down to his granddaughter with a stern expression. "Young lady, that will be quite enough of that!"

Chapter seventeen

Eckhardt grabbed Vicki by the wrist, pulling her to her feet. He straightened her posture and faced her back in the direction of the door. "Never before this day has any Housekeeper refused to do something so basic as open a door! Even the magic of the Athenaeum is powerless against you!"

Vicki turned back around staring up at the slightly translucent shade of her grandfather. "Grandpa!"

"Where is the girl that I know? The fearless little girl that sprained both of her wrists climbing trees? Where is that girl that went all the way to the peak of Mount Diablo alone?!"

Vicki put her hands to her mouth and barreled into her grandfather. She buried her head into his side, and his stern expression faltered. He reached a hand down to the top of her head and hugged her. She shivered and cried into the old man's coat wiping her eyes with the backs of her hands.

"I'm so scared here! I, I don't belong here!" Vicki cried out gripping onto his coat. "I messed everything up again, and that woman is going to get me! She's going to eat everyone!"

Eckhardt gave her head a few sympathetic pats. "Oh, my darling girl. Your words are twisted, so twisted against you, they work their power over you like old witchcraft." He knelt down in front of her, taking her by the shoulders. "That wolf is powerless against you in this place. She is the least of your worries. It's the beast inside of your head that you should fear."

Vicki shook her head and gave a shudder. "But she's, she's so big and she has claws and everything!"

"And yet she is powerless against you. She could not attack you in your home in Danville and she will not be able to attack you here in your home, in the Athenaeum." Eckhardt stood up and ushered Vicki forward to the bedroom door. "Open it."

"But I can't! She's right outside, Grandpa, she'll come in and get me!"

"Nonsense! You're the Housekeeper, nothing enters these doors unless you will it. None of the doors in this house should be closed to you, all of them will lead you to exactly where you need to be."

"But I'm not! Grandpa, I'm not the Housekeeper!" Vicki broke away from him gripping her hands together. "I can't do any of it! I'm not magic, and I'm not strong like you! I'm not smart enough to figure any of it out! Why did you choose me?"

Eckhardt tugged on his coat lapels, a look of pride on his face. "I didn't!"

Vicki wiped her tears away, mouth hanging open and eyebrows raised. "What?"

"I didn't select you, Vicki, not at all. You were to inherit the deed to my home in Manchester. It was always my plan that Magra should be considered for the role. I had the room prepared for her in the event of my passing." He looked down at Vicki and moved some stray hair away from her face. "Yet here you stand instead. I couldn't be more proud of you."

Vicki's lip quivered. "But, what?"

Eckhardt smiled and chuckled down at her. "I thought that it should go to Magra, surely she would be at home here. She possesses more than the required skills necessary to be awarded the title! Truly, she is the brightest witch in this family. Perhaps from all of Catemaco."

Vicki glanced around the room. The room *had* been sized for her magical cousin. The mirror, the bed, everything. How could her grandfather be proud of someone tampering with his last will and testament?

"But, Magra, wouldn't she give Aunt Zaldehyde her contract right away? She wants me to bring her the contract so she can rip it up!"

"Oh no, Magra is nothing like her mother. She is pure of heart, she would have done well here and stood up to your aunt. For her to have lost the inheritance to you, it warms my heart. You truly are remarkable." Eckhardt squeezed her shoulder. "And it isn't Zaldehyde who can destroy this contract, it is only you Vicki. You alone are worthy of holding such responsibility and power."

The door began to shudder and crack, the wolf snarled from the other side. She struck the door clawing it and howling. She continued beating on the door, rattling the door knob as she growled.

Eckhardt faced Vicki in the direction of the door. "Come Vicki, it's time. The Three Lords have sent me for this task and this task only. You wield such confounding power over yourself that not even the Athenaeum can help you! Come!" Eckhardt stepped closer to the door holding his hand out to her.

"But I'm not magic! I can't fight anything like werewolves and witches! I can't do magic, I can't!"

"You don't need it, Vicki! Wands and staves, all of it is just fluff and toys! The Athenaeum has no need for these things, she is strong enough for the both of you! She only needs a Housekeeper with particular quality!" The door shook, claws raked down the wood from the other side. "She needs one with courage and confidence! Character! Wands and spells are no substitute, you have what she needs! Come and see!"

"Grandpa, I don't have any of those things! Whoever put me in the will was wrong! I'm not brave or smart or anything!"

"Oh, you poor soul. You have become invisible, even to yourself. Come and see."

Eckhardt reached out and the door cracked open. The wolf had vanished, Vicki found herself looking at the mysterious locked room once more. The warm light of the room fell upon her and she relaxed her whole body. The floorboards beneath her moved like a wave propelling her forward to the glowing door. The glow enveloped her.

"You have to see the truth, Vicki. See it, and speak it."

The world around her changed, fog rolled in all around her and Vicki now stood looking at a moment of her life from long ago. Rachel sat in a dark place with only a school desk in front of her. School friends surrounded the girl, many of whom Vicki hadn't seen in more than a year. Vicki's best friend sat studiously at the desk absorbing some unheard lesson before giggling and turning in her seat to look back at a girl far behind her.

"God, what a little piggy," one of the school friends whispered about the new girl. Rachel whipped around in her seat, a small look of shame on her face. Another girl stood up from the crowd of desks, making her way to the lonely new girl in the back of the room. The world shifted around Vicki and her grandfather once more, the bright fog lifted from the floor and enveloped them both.

"See the truth!" Eckhardt's ghost opened the door further, the light spilled into Vicki's eyes bathing her face in colors. "See it now!"

The classroom disappeared. A tiny blonde girl with dark eyebrows sat wailing in the corner of a brightly decorated kindergarten room. She wept and sobbed facing the wall, taking great heaving breaths of panic. The young girl had thrown her crayons out in a temper tantrum, flinging them all to the floor, and now she was made to pick them up before she could join her classmates outside for playtime. The crayons kept falling out of her box no matter how hard she tried to keep the box steady in her hands. Vicki reached out for the girl but the fog enveloped them again and the world disappeared.

"Look!" Eckhardt smiled down at Vicki, he motioned to the ground beneath them as her eyes adjusted to the new world around them. "See what the Athenaeum has seen!"

They stood together in the backyard of the Voland household some six years back, watching on as history replayed before them. A much younger Vicki clung to her father. Vicki placed a hand over her mouth staring at the younger version of herself unsettled by the scene playing out. She gasped at the sight of a familiar colorful shoebox and gripped tightly to Eckhardt's coat.

The eight year old Vicki cried over the tiny shoebox in the ground. Her father knelt down and put his hand on her shoulder. The little eight year old girl was inconsolable. Mr. Voland handed a pink flower to her.

"Do you want to say something, Vicki?" Mr. Voland put a hand on the younger Vicki's shoulder.

"It isn't fair," the younger Vicki sobbed out. "Did I do something wrong? Is that why she didn't get better?"

"No sweetie, listen, sometimes it just isn't in our control. Sad things are always going to happen in life no matter what we try to do, you didn't do anything wrong." Mr. Voland gave her a big squeeze and he put her hand over the shoebox. "You did so much for her, she spent these last few days warm and fed, I know she appreciated everything that you did for her!"

"She never got to fly!" The younger Vicki sniffled.

"It's okay Vicki, maybe she just wasn't ready yet." Mr. Voland wiped a tear from the eight year old's eye.

The fog filled the room and the backyard disappeared from her sight. Vicki was back in her room at the mansion, teary eyed and standing at the mysterious door once more. Eckhardt threw open the door to the library, and the fireplace within exploded into pink flames. The room illuminated with a rainbow of colorful light, as the colors rained down on Vicki warming her face. The floorboards drove her closer and the light gave way to another moment from her life.

They watched from a distance as a happier version of Vicki proudly put her last box of gingerbread cookies on a fully loaded cart, straightening her sash and adjusting her beret as she smiled at her handiwork. The sun beat down on the scouts camp washing the wooded hillside underneath Mount Diablo with golden rays. Rachel came bounding up to her arms outstretched and smiling wide.

"Vicki, the scout mother just told us that we matched the San Joaquin valley! We're going to San Diego!" Rachel hopped up and down, both of them squealed with laughter and excitement. The two girls waved to a crowd of waiting scouts then pulled the cart to the parking lot together. They chatted and giggled as they walked on. Vicki stood back in the camp under a tree watching her younger more cheery self leave with Rachel.

Eckhardt joined her, dropping his monocle into his pocket and putting a hand on her shoulder. "This, Vicki, is the truth that you must see."

"I already know this, Grandpa, I see this like everyday." Vicki sat on the ground watching as the two girls skipped along, reciting a summer camp song. "I messed up, those are half dog treats. It's dog food and all the girls sold it to the customers, and we lost the San Diego trip because I wasn't paying attention to the boxes. They trusted me and I screwed everything up for everyone." She hugged her arms together swallowing down a lump in her throat. "And then Mom and Dad had to come clean up my mess. They always have to save me, like I'm still just a little baby. Mom wanted me to go back but I couldn't."

"Young lady, you have missed everything!" Eckhardt replaced his monocle and pointed out to the two girls. "What do you see there?"

Vicki looked up to her grandfather's stern gaze, then back out over to Rachel and her happier self. "The cookies, it's just me and Rachel and the cookies." Vicki sighed out. "Then I got mad at everyone who was mad at me."

The bright fog whipped around them and the world vanished in an instant. Vicki was suddenly sitting in her own room watching herself from the year before. The Vicki from the year before furiously tapped on her mobile phone protesting and huffing as she typed on the screen. She hid her face in her big fluffy pillow and muffled her scream into it. Eckhardt sighed, shaking his head.

"Utterly insignificant. Cookies and San Diego." He sat down on the bed with the prior summer's Vicki looking over her shoulder at the screen. "San Diego will be there for at least another one hundred and thirty years, those girls will have plenty of time to see it."

"They all worked really hard, Grandpa, we... they all did, they wanted to go real bad!" Vicki edged closer to the bed, watching as the other Vicki typed in responses and insults at the other scouts. "They would have gone too if some other girl had been put in charge instead of me."

"There was no one better suited for the job amongst your peers. Your leaders chose wisely, those gingerbread cookie boxes were the exact same color as the new dog biscuits! The other girls in that troop might have made the same error, if not worse!" He put his hands into his coat pockets. "Half of the girls in that troop can barely even spell their own name! Some of those girls are so dumb that they can't even breathe through their nose without taping their mouths shut! It's a wonder that they can read at all."

"Grandpa, that's not nice!... That's, that's... what I wrote, isn't it?"

Eckhardt stood up from the bed and walked over to the colorful closet opening the door of hand painted blue birds, motioning for Vicki to follow. "Mean spirited and in bad faith, and not even close to the worst of what you had to say about them. You all made mistakes in the days surrounding that event, everyone is allowed to make mistakes Vicki, especially your friends! Come this way!"

Vicki followed the ghost of her grandfather past the clothes and boxes, making it through the bright fog emptying out into another room. Vicki was shocked to see that they were now in her best friend's bedroom. Rachel sat on her own bed sniffling and holding her phone up to her face. She rocked back and forth on her bed, typing as fast as she could.

"Look at the truth, Vicki." Eckhardt gestured for her to sit on the bed next to Rachel.

The Rachel from one year prior typed in message after message but her pleas went ignored. The girl on the other end of the phone was more interested with defending herself against her fellow scouts. Rachel put a hand over her mouth and whimpered.

Don't listen to them, just ignore them! Don't feed into them! Jade and Kailee and everyone else aren't even mad at you, it's ok!

Rachel sent her message and flopped down on the bed. She hugged the phone to her chest then buried her face into her pillow, shrieking into it. The phone kept beeping with notifications and the girl on the bed sobbed out.

"I should have listened to her." Vicki put a hand out to Rachel's shoulder. "I, I was just so mad at them, I couldn't stop. I can't believe all of the stuff that I said. I was too mad to even look."

"You were mad at them? Is that why you began to ignore her?" Eckhardt came around to the side of the bed and extended his hand out to Vicki. "Her and only her? You had the time to answer every rotten comment about you from those other girls."

Vicki stood up from the bed. "I didn't, I wasn't talking to anyone! I kept getting attacked and no one was helping!..." The girl on the bed sobbed out looking down at her screen. She bit her lip and turned her phone off throwing her face back into her pillow and weeping into it. Vicki looked back at the girl on the bed. "I'm sorry Rachel."

The fog swirled around them again and Rachel vanished from sight. The world reformed out of the bright fog, Vicki and Eckhardt stood in the backyard of the Voland house once more. The little eight year old Vicki sniffled and wailed as she and her father stood over a tiny colorful box.

"I'm sorry little birdie," the tiny eight year old sobbed out, as she placed a flower on the shoebox. "I'm sorry!"

Vicki watched as her father pushed the soil over the box. He lifted the eight year old up into his arms. Eckhardt stood by her, hands behind his back. He watched on and glanced down at his granddaughter with a slight smile.

"You don't have anything to be sorry about Vicki, don't be so hard on yourself. This was going to happen whether or not you picked her up and brought her home." The two of them left the backyard and entered into the Voland house. "Sad things happen sometimes, that's part of life. Happy things will happen again too. They always do!"

Vicki's chest heaved and she swallowed down a lump in her throat. The world around them changed and they were transported to the scouts camp again. Rachel walked alongside the happier Vicki, the both of them lugging those cookies behind them. Eckhardt breathed out and ushered Vicki forward so that she could hear that conversation between the two girls one more time.

"Well, I kind of don't want to go if you don't go too, Vicki. I mean the other girls are fun and everything, but it would be boring without you." Rachel took her beret off, fanning her face from the heat of the spring day. "I'd rather just go to the zoo with you then. Is that weird?"

"No it's not weird," said the Vicki from the year prior, looking down at her phone's screen. "But I thought you really wanted to go see that band, how could it be boring?"

"Well, you're the one that gets everyone dancing and everything, we would all just be lumps in the hotel without you. I don't know how to get them moving."

The happier Vicki bumped her hip into Rachel. "Just do that, it's easy!" She laughed out as Rachel bumped back into her.

"It's not just that, you have like a magic booty or something!" The two girls started bumping into each other bursting into giggles as they sent each other flying.

"Just do it like this!" Vicki bumped into Rachel once more and the girl tumbled to the ground laughing. The world around them filled with bright fog and Vicki bit her lip as they were transported back to that kindergarten class.

"Just do it like this," said the other tiny girl, as she took the crying girl's box of crayons. She laid the box down helping to place the crayons back into it.

The little crying blonde girl with the dark eyebrows caught her breath and wiped her tears on her sleeves, still heaving and sniffling. "I can't do it!"

"You have to keep trying it, I'll try it too!" The other girl smiled wide and sat down next to the weeping kindergartener. The little girls both began putting the crayons into the box together.

"We did it!" The little girl wiped the last of her tears from her eyes. "We did it we did it!" She closed her box of crayons and hugged the girl that had come to help her. "I'm Rachel!"

The little helper hugged Rachel back. "I'm Vicki!"

The fog whipped around them and sent them back into the darkened classroom full of students. Rachel turned around with a look of shame on her face as her friends snickered and giggled at the new girl in the back of the room.

The bigger girl with the pink hair in the dark classroom ignored the pretty preppy girls in front of her, resisting the urge to run out of the classroom in tears. She tensed up as the smallest of the popular girls left her seat and came to sit closer to her. The chair legs scooted closer and closer until the girl was within whispering distance.

"I'm Vicki," the girl leaned over and whispered. "Omigod, I love that backpack, I have like all of TrayC's albums!"

The preppy girls in front of them snickered and the girl with the pink hair hid her face. Vicki brought her own backpack up to the desk showing it off to the new girl. She smiled back at Vicki's silly little holographic backpack decorated with the cutesy unicorns and multicolored sloths that their favorite singer had become known for.

Rachel got up from her seat at the front of the group and they all went quiet. She sat down on the other side of the girl with the pink hair. She grinned at Vicki and leaned over to greet the new girl.

"I'm Rachel."

Eckhardt stood proud looking down at his granddaughter as the classroom lit up around them. A few of the other preppy girls stood from their seats and came to greet the new girl too, as Vicki began to examine the new girl's bag. The new girl smiled brightly and her posture changed.

"She moved away again after that Christmas. I don't know whatever happened to her." Vicki faced her grandfather and she furrowed her brow. "I don't get it, why did you show me this?"

"Because she still remembers your name to this day. The kind little girl that got all of the other girls dancing." Eckhardt looked over to the group of girls. "Tell me Vicki, were you disappointed in Rachel when she was laughing at the girl before? Speak only the truth in this place."

Vicki frowned over at Rachel. "A little bit... She was laughing at her with the other girls, she stopped though! I mean I'm not always nice either... I've said mean things too. She's always gonna be my best friend though, no matter what."

The classroom disappeared. The world shifted around Vicki and Eckhardt, transporting them to a time and place only a few days prior. A sprawling wooded mountain park took form around them and Eckhardt motioned for Vicki to turn her attention to the nearby hillside.

Rachel walked along with four other girls from her troop, holding her basket of goodies as they climbed down the hillside. The girls chatted and complained about the injustice of their new homework assignments. Jade pressed into Rachel's shoulder as they came to a stop.

"Hey, listen, it's okay if she's not coming! We won't be mad but you're starting to make us all really sad watching you do this again and again!" Jade plopped down onto the ground with the checkered blanket. "People change, it happens!"

One of the other girls sat down and began spreading the sheet across the ground. "My brother works at Silver Oaks, he said that his boss would be happy to let us do our reading cart there! We can get it going by October," she said looking up at Rachel.

Rachel shook her head setting the basket down on the blanket. "I know, I know. I just don't want her to be alone all of the time, she's just having a rough spot. I-"

"Raaachel, how long are you gonna do this before you just accept defeat? You're like a glutton for punishment or something!" Jade opened the basket taking out a can of sparkling water. "She keeps turning us down for a reason, I don't even think she wants friends anymore. We all miss her too, but you have to let her be who she is now."

Rachel looked down at her feet, silently going about unpacking the luncheon. The other girls began chatting amongst themselves and she slipped away towards the pond. She wiped a singular tear from her eye, taking great care to keep it a secret from her fellow scouts.

A little blue bird with a bright orange chest landed in the tall grass just a few feet from the girl. Rachel looked down at the bird and her face fell into a deep sorrow, another tear ran down her cheek and she sopped it up with her sleeve. "Please come, just try! Please," she pleaded under her breath. She hid her face in her hands and let out a quiet sob. "God, just come back! Just try!"

The little blue bird sang out at Rachel. It took to the air flying into the heavenly azure sky far away towards the colorful peak of the mountain in the distance. The fog lifted and the park disappeared from sight.

Vicki stood in the light of the room once more, its fireplace crackled and cast dancing shadows across the warm walls. Eckhardt put his monocle into his pocket and smiled down at Vicki. Vicki wiped her tears with her hands.

"You have seen the truth at last."

"What truth? I still don't get it."

"The truth that you are worthy of such love. That you already possess it, and rightly so. You are worthy, Vicki, of everything! The Athenaeum has seen it too!"

Vicki furrowed her brow as the light from the room intensified. "But I'm, I haven't..."

"You haven't let your friends inside for a year now, and to even further detriment you have hid yourself behind every closed door that you can create for yourself!" Eckhardt slammed the door shut, and the glow from the room vanished; only the glowing keyhole still radiated a tiny bit of light. "No one has kept these doors locked but you, Vicki, it's you that must take ownership now! Open the door or all is lost!"

"But I don't know how!" Vicki wailed and reached up for her hat. She touched the top of her head and broke down into tears. "Grandpa, I don't know how to do any of this stuff! I can't! I don't even have the hat!"

"That silly thing is pointless! It hasn't worked since you put it on and you know it! Now speak the truth girl, why are all of these doors locked? What are you locking away from yourself?"

The door creaked and the frame shook. The distant howl of the wolf echoed through the room. "I'm not locking anything away! I'm just afraid!"

The door began to snap and splinter. Eckhardt placed his hands in his pockets glaring down at Vicki. "Speak the truth, or this place will become your tomb! Speak it! Hide behind that lie no longer, leave only the truth!"

The walls around the room buckled, the plaster began to crack and fall to the floor. "I am! I am telling the truth!" Vicki looked up to the door with teary eyes. She hopped up and down, whining as the room around her quaked. "Okay! Okay!"

The room shook and dust fell from the ceiling. Eckhardt replaced his monocle, standing at attention waiting for the young girl to speak. He watched as Vicki gripped her hair in her hands taking a long breath.

"Okay, it wasn't just that I was mad at the other girls!" The room quieted down and the rumbling ceased from all around the mansion. "I was afraid of losing all of my friends and it really happened... I was mean and I made everyone else hate me and then I was just empty! I just wanted to disappear! I wanted to be invisible and I thought I wanted to be alone!"

The mansion groaned and lights began to click on in succession down the hallways. Doors all around the Athenaeum creaked open, the windows cleared themselves of dust and cobwebs, light old timey music began playing over antiquated speakers all throughout the mansion. The Athenaeum began lighting up on the mountainside like a brand new theater on opening night.

"More Vicki! The whole truth! Get it out now, all of it!"

"I didn't want anyone to notice me or want to be my friend, I just wished that my other friends would go away too, so I didn't have to deal with feeling like this anymore! Like I'm not good enough for anything or anybody! I was scared that all of those other girls were right and that no one actually likes me, and I gave up and I quit! I just wanted to stay invisible and I didn't even want to try to feel better!"

"Why Vicki? Why didn't you want to feel better? Say it!"

"I... I was scared." The room shook and cracked along the doorway.

"Open this door! Stop hiding the truth, for the last time! Speak it now!" Eckhardt stomped his foot shaking Vicki by her shoulders.

"Because I hate myself!" The room went quiet.

Vicki fell to the floor and sobbed out. She wiped her nose on the back of her sleeve choking on her tears. "I hate myself for being so stupid and useless! Everyone always has to come rescue me and I'm weak! And I'm worthless! I can't ever do anything right! I just want to be invisible so no one finds out how I really am! So they don't see that I'm stupid and mean, so they can't hate me too!"

The door shimmered and creaked open. The fireplace roared on the other side, sparks of pink and blue came flying out of the doorway towards Vicki's feet. Eckhardt frowned down at her with a solemn look in his eyes.

Vicki stood to her feet and continued, "and I wish that I *could* come back to my friends, and I wish that I *could* tell everyone that I want to come back! But I won't let myself! Because I know, I know, I'll just fail again. I'll just let everyone down!" Vicki put her face into her hands and wept. "So I deserve to be alone! Because I'm a bad friend, I'm a bad person!"

The room filled with the dazzling pink and blue light of the fireplace engulfing Vicki and Eckhardt. The world around them began shifting rapidly to everywhere they had been until finally settling on the backyard of the Voland house. Birds chirped overhead and Vicki wiped the tears from her eyes as she watched her younger self pick flowers for her mother.

The little eight year old girl hopped and skipped through her backyard picking the colorful flowers near the base of the oak tree. She reached down for one of the pink flowers and gasped. She turned around cradling a tiny baby bird in her hands. It was weak and hurt.

Its wings hadn't quite come in yet and its feathers had only just developed. The little girl carefully placed the baby blue bird into her hands looking up into the tree high above. The bird nest swayed in the wind, other little birds peeped out as the winds tossed them around. The girl went running into the nearby garden leaving her bouquet of pink flowers behind.

"Mama look!" The little girl showed the baby blue bird off to her mother. "She's hurt! She fell down and she got hurt!"

"Oh no, poor little thing!" Vicki's mother reached down putting her hands underneath the bird carefully picking her up. "Oh Vicki, she's just a little thing, when they're this small it's hard for them to come back. I'm so sorry, I don't know if we can help her."

The little girl hopped up and down on her heels, tears gathering in her eyes and her lip beginning to quiver. "But Mama, her friends are waiting for her to come back! I can hear them in the nest! I can make her better, I know I can!"

Mrs. Voland gave a warm look to her daughter placing the bird back into her waiting hands. "If anyone can, Vicki, it's you."

Vicki cradled the weak blue bird in her hands and its large black eye opened. It raised its head up peeping at her. "It's okay! You're going to go home and live with your bird friends!" She held the bird close to her chest. "Look Mama, she's looking at me!"

"She sure is! You must look pretty big to her, don't you think?"

"Uh huh, someday she'll be bigger too!"

Vicki watched the eight year old go trotting along with her mother to the house. Eckhardt bent down picking up the pink flowers from the ground. He smiled down to her and held the little bouquet out. Vicki let out a sharp breath and took the flowers into her hands.

Eckhardt put his hand on her shoulder. "Twelve days, Vicki. For twelve days you kept that sick little baby bird alive and warm. Never once did you give up on her. Do you know how many living things are denied warmth for the extent of their living days? How could you call that girl useless, or bad? How could anyone hate that person?"

The world vanished and Vicki let the flowers fall back to the ground, the two of them now floated high above the Athenaeum looking down onto the lawn below. Old goblins gathered around in a circle laughing and chatting with each other. The residents of the mansion enjoyed a crisp autumn morning singing a tune from days long since past.

Eckhardt smiled motioning for Vicki to look upon the mansion. "Come and see what the Athenaeum holds dear. Not her treasure troves of magical scrolls or books from long lost eras, not even her own bricks and mortar. Even these contracts that the Three Lords have entrusted to her, they pale in comparison to her own love for these treasures. These little old forgotten things, these are the Athenaeum's only concern now." Eckhardt smiled down at the goblins and other creatures of the mansion then crossed his arms. "She is like them, you see, old and forgotten. Once she was the greatest library in all of Ätherside, full of joy and well cared for. Now they all need some tending to, some warmth, in these last sunny days."

"But Grandpa what if I do fail again? What if I keep messing up, even if I try my best?"

Eckhardt pointed down to the goblins below. Desmond, Frank, and Belvedere moved through the crowd handing out hot ciders and ugly little cakes. "There is no *if*, young lady, you must *always* do your best! Even when you know that you are destined to fail, you run at it and you give it your best! And when you fail, and when you fall, you let your allies catch you!" Eckhardt waved his hand through the air and the world began to shift around them again. "You are only ever truly a failure when you choose to stay down! You can only stay down if you won't let others help to pick you back up to your feet, when you choose to stay alone!"

The world swirled around them and they were back in the Voland household. The little eight year old girl sat in her room with the blue bird worrying for her new tiny friend. She held back her tears as she gripped the little colorful shoebox that had become the bird's makeshift hospital bed and motioned for the other girl to join her. The other taller girl stood by the box and edged closer, a weak peep came from the box as she approached.

"I don't think it looks so good." The eight year old Rachel leaned over and looked into the box. "When my cat died he looked like that." She frowned and looked over to the other little girl.

"She's sick, I'm trying to make her better." The eight year old Vicki sighed and gripped her hands together.

"But what if she can't get better? What if she dies?"

The younger Vicki put a small bit of cotton down around the baby blue bird to keep it warm. "She might get better if I keep trying! We have to keep trying it. Her friends are waiting for her to come back!"

Rachel sat down next to her, leaning on her shoulder. She began to pull apart some cotton balls fashioning it into a small blanket. "Okay, we will." Rachel's words became distant and she vanished in a haze from the younger Vicki's side. A locked door now stood where the other girl had been.

Vicki went running over to where Rachel had been, searching around with her hands. "Rachel!" She yanked on the door to no avail. The younger Vicki closed up her shoebox and wept alone. The world lifted from her sight and she fell to her knees. "I didn't mean to shut you out! I'm still here!"

A fresh breeze blew through the mansion from within the halls, the doors to the entrance flung open and the ruins of the fountain out back exploded with fresh water. The Athenaeum shook as old broken rooms straightened out and uneven foundations righted themselves. A blue bird came flying in from the nighttime sky. It flew all the way up into Vicki's room through the newly opened colorful window landing on the petrified griffin's head, singing a happy little bird song as it fluttered its wings. The stone surrounding the griffin began to crumble.

Eckhardt dropped his monocle down smiling warmly at Vicki. He took her by the shoulders lifting her up to her feet. "Finally, here is the girl that was never afraid to open those doors." He patted her arms turning her around to the door. "Not afraid of little red men, nor big bad wolves, or even of the people that will always love her."

The door opened for Vicki. The warmth of the fireplace drew her inward, she stepped over the threshold without even really noticing that she was moving at all, nor did she take notice that her pigtail had vanished or that the ring upon her finger now glowed in golden light. She only felt the presence of something familiar and joyous as she crossed into the room. The writing desk sprang to life before her tear filled eyes, the quill jumped up onto a scroll that laid out on the shining wooden desk top.

The letters written out by the pen leaned heavily to the right, scribbled by the magic of the Athenaeum. The silver shimmering ink sparked with a strange electricity settling into the newly minted scroll. The Athenaeum forged its new contract.

Vicki Voland

Housekeeper

Assignment and Novation

Vicki picked up the shining silver capped scroll. Stamped at the bottom of the scroll where her signature was expected glowed the standard of the three symbols that she had encountered before. The drop, the moon, and the bolt. Vicki looked back to her grandfather cradling the scroll close to her chest.

"Grandpa, this is the same writing from your will! Who just wrote this?"

Eckhardt stuck his chest out and straightened the collar of his coat. He turned to the fireplace looking up to the painting over the mantle. "The Three Lords could come to no decision on a replacement. In such cases, where the welfare of the Athenaeum is concerned, they defer to the wisdom of the Athenaeum herself. It seems that there is simply no one better for the position."

Vicki stepped closer to the fireplace letting her eyes adjust to the light. Up above the mantle hung a watercolor painting of Mount Diablo. Its striking pink and blue brush strokes cascaded off from the canvas creating a stream of colors above her head. Vicki's watercolor signature radiated out from the corner of the painting with its rainbow beams glowing out into the air.

She brought a hand up to her mouth marveling at the painting that she had created for her grandfather not so long ago. A special energy flowed from that painting and Vicki recognized it immediately. This was the azure sky of Mount Diablo, blowing out that serene heavenly breeze into every corner of the mansion, the same breeze that she loved to feel upon her skin as she walked around her hometown. A breeze and a sky that she had captured some time ago, painting it onto a canvas as she stood in the wooded park along with her fellow scouts.

"It's her favorite one. Every time that I tried to move it back to my quarters she'd move it back in here, plucked it right out of my cabinet. She is powerful, this house. The one who tampered with my will, Vicki, *is the Athenaeum*." Eckhardt inhaled deeply relishing the mountain air. He checked his ancient pocket watch and replaced it back into his old coat. "She has seen into you, seen what I have always known to be true deep down. You demonstrate all that she needs. If anyone can keep this house in order, if anyone can help, it's you."

"The Athenaeum chose me? It... She, she chose me over Magra?"

"She chose wisely. Don't be afraid of failing her, Victoria. Look at all of the trouble that she went through to bring you here. The Athenaeum has total trust in you. Trust her back and she will be your keeper too." Eckhardt gave a hard squeeze to her shoulder. "At last she is in those good hands that she yearned for. Your doors are opened again, the Housekeeper is here. Well then my dear, it is time."

Vicki spun around to look up at him. "No don't go yet! I- there's still some time left isn't there? I don't want you to go yet!" She ran over to him and wrapped her arms around him. "Please stay!"

Eckhardt gave her a gentle hug, then leaned in and lifted her from the floor. "Give your mother my love, won't you? And sorry about this pig business, the Athenaeum threw that one in on her own." He squeezed her as hard as he ever had in life. "I walk away from this place with the greatest joy. My most remarkable granddaughter, it's time for you to come back to all those friends of yours."

"I know!" She released her grip around his shoulders. "I know! I will." Her lip quivered and she held back her tears.

"Now then, Housekeeper, the only way back is through that wolf. She's big and strong, and quite clever. She's standing in your way and it's just you and this old house against her, now what are you going to do about it?" Eckhardt straightened his posture and stood looking down at the girl. Vicki turned away from him letting out one last heavy breath. She took her first few steps away from him then started into a full sprint out into the hallway.

"That's a good girl." Eckhardt polished his monocle on his coat collar and smiled. He began fading into peace and nothingness once more. "Steel, her words are steel."

Chapter eighteen

Jerry charged head first at Ciara Shuck. She caught him by the horns with her huge claws flinging him far back into the hall with ease. Belvedere came running up behind the wolf smashing a large cast iron skillet over her back, screaming out and wearing an old cauldron over his head like a helmet. The wolf spun around growling at the little mustachioed man. He raised his skillet high into the air again giving a battle cry.

Ciara grabbed the skillet out of his hand throwing it into the wall. Her great razored hand gripped him by the neck yanking him to her. Her slobbering mouth opened wide and she brought her other clawed hand up to his nose.

"I'm going to eat your face after I rip that little whelp to pieces!" She dragged her index claw across Belvedere's mustache. He screamed as his long bristly hairs fell down to the ground. Ciara laughed. "Now that's a close shave!"

Frank's hands wrapped around the wolf's neck forcing her to drop the screaming cook to the ground. Ciara tore at the cables around her spinning to face the stitchwork girl. Frank stood her ground, she pulled the wolf towards her with all of her might.

"Lady, you got a real problem with other people's hair, you know that?" Frank yanked her cables towards the floor but the wolf resisted. Ciara slashed at the cables that connected the arms to Frank's shoulders finally cutting one of them away. Frank cried out losing her grip on the wolf's neck.

Desmond bolted around the werewolf outpacing those green eyes with ease, he climbed atop her back smashing her face repeatedly with his walking stick. "Bad dog! Bad, bad, bad!" He let loose with a flurry of strikes to her back and quick as lightning hopped in front of her continuing the assault. He jabbed his stick into her ribs sending the wolf backward howling in frustration.

"You hypocrite! You'd eat her too if you could! You disgusting little bat, I'll break your teeth!" The wolf pounced and Desmond aimed his stick end at her. A bright pink flare went shooting out of the cane but Ciara was too quick. She swiped the flare away in mid air sending it crashing through the nearby window. Glass shattered all around them. She landed on top of the already bruised and beaten vampire.

Desmond held the stick up in front of him blocking the huge gnashing fangs of the wolf. She bit into the cane and pinned him to the floor shaking her head violently to rip the cane out of his hands. The cane finally snapped under her massive bite and she wrestled the two halves away from him.

Ciara held the splintered cane high above her head slamming it downward towards Desmond's chest. He caught it with both hands straining to keep the stake out of his heart. He began screaming as the wolf pushed down with her full weight using both hands to drive the stake down. Frank limped over wrapping her good arm around the wolf's neck pulling as hard as she could. Belvedere stumbled forward and grabbed the wolf's tail yanking it back with a pained yell.

Ciara paid no attention to the little annoyances. The stake came closer and closer to the vampire's chest, his arms shook with exertion. He screamed as the tip of the stake hit the button on his shirt.

The broken window in the main hall rattled, glass came floating up from the ground outside and the shards fit themselves together again. The window repaired itself, the lights of the mansion glared brilliantly throughout the hallways, and pleasant old timey big band music began to play in the air. The wolf stopped her assault to look around at the changes taking place around her.

The floorboards all went up and down like a tidal wave shaking dust and debris from themselves as they slapped back down into place. The walls shook and the mansion began to contort into a less wayward lean. A fresh breeze came from the hallways and door after door opened on every floor. Little goblins came out and leaned against the railings to get a better view of the action down below. A cyclops leaned over searching with his one great eye looking all around.

"What's going on, what did I miss?"

"That big ugly chihuahua is attacking the nurse!"

The goblins started booing and jeering from their places all around the mansion. Ciara roared at them and continued her attack on Desmond. The wolf glared down at him smiling with her horrific white fangs.

"Hey!" The wolf ignored the voice from the spiral staircase. "Hey, you big dumb lopsided mutt!" Vicki threw one of her pink running shoes squarely into the ear of the werewolf.

Ciara whipped her head around to face the girl standing at the stairs. She stood to her feet throwing Frank and Belvedere away from her with ease. She kicked Desmond with her powerful leg sending him through the air up over the railings into the second floor balcony. Ciara discarded the stake and growled at Vicki.

"There you are! I can't wait to pick you out of my teeth!"

Vicki slipped her other sneaker off and bolted the rest of the way down the steps. "Shut it!" She marched up to the wolf with her shoe in one hand and her contract in the other pointing out to the front door. "I'm done with your dumb test, the house wants me here and that's it! Get out! You're not gonna hurt me or my friends anymore! Leave!" She stomped her foot on the floor sending the floorboards up around her, making the wolf recoil just a small bit. The mansion lit up all around them.

Ciara opened her mouth into that razor sharp smile raising a clawed hand above her head. "My, what a big mouth you have!" She howled out with laughter and lunged at Vicki.

"Stop!" Vicki threw her other shoe at the wolf, it sailed past the wolf's head and Ciara laughed at the small morsel in front of her.

A floorboard flew up in between Ciara Shuck and Vicki. It slammed itself into the wolf's nose with such force that she whined and whimpered in pain. Ciara stumbled backwards holding her muzzle and sniffling as she gingerly touched the end of her nose. Another floorboard smacked her in the back of her head and the wolf cried out. She spun around swiping at the air with her claws. She growled and turned back to Vicki.

Vicki stood defiant in front of the wolf. She placed her hands on her hips and stared back at Ciara Shuck. "I'm telling you one last time!" She pointed to the front door again. "Get out!"

Frank helped Belvedere up to his feet and she yelled out. "You better listen to her, furball! We don't wantcha jumping on the furniture anymore! Take it outside!"

Desmond shot up from the railing of the second floor adjusting his collar, pretending that he was not at all shaken with his near stake experience. "Lady, I think you outstayed your welcome." He rolled his sleeves back down to his wrists and leaned over the railing together with the residents. "I don't want to see her have to paddle a puppy, but I'll go whip up a bowl of popcorn right now if that's what's going down!" He started making popping sounds with his lips.

The wolf scoffed and lunged at Vicki once more, getting down on all fours charging up at her from the floor. A loud record scratch came over the old speaker systems of the Athenaeum. The floor boards betrayed Ciara again, this time they flew upward and formed a wall in front of the defiant girl catching the wolf's claws in their wooden bodies. The floorboards slapped back down into place trapping Ciara to the floor, her claws firmly stuck down below.

Old rock and roll music began blaring over the speakers, *Keep A-Knockin'* blasted so loudly into the wolf's ears that she winced in pain. The boards behind her began slapping her rear end at high speed and the wolf yelped out struggling to get free of the wood. The floorboards finally relented, throwing the wolf into the air with a force so great that she nearly hit the roof of the Athenaeum.

Ciara fell through the air howling and waving her legs around hoping to land on her feet. She screamed just before she hit the floor below shutting her eyes tight. The music came to an abrupt halt throughout the mansion, Ciara's scream echoed through the halls. The wolf landed safely in a bed sheet spread out into the air around her. She opened her eyes looking around confused as to who her savior might be. Floating towels gathered all around her and she grumbled as they began to twist themselves up into long thin whips.

The towels began whipping themselves all over Ciara's body as the sheet bounced her up and down in the air like a trampoline. The towels snapped and cracked, the wolf howled out in pain and fear as the laundry hit her again and again. The sheet wrapped itself tightly around the wolf's arms bouncing her back to the floor at Vicki's feet.

"Leave!" Vicki commanded. She pointed to the doors again and they swung open wide. The wolf hobbled to her feet and snorted at her. Vicki reached out grabbing the wolf by her ear dragging her to the doors of the Athenaeum and pushing her to the main entrance. "You get out of my house, and don't come back here again."

The wolf stumbled and growled. She stared at the goblin assessor, who sat in the corner on his bench, his stone tablet still at the ready. He put his chalk down to the tablet and began to write, ignoring the wolf's hateful gaze. Ciara spun around one last time to Vicki. Her claw swiped out from underneath the sheet, nearly catching the girl's shirt.

Ravenous ivy came exploding into the Athenaeum from the front door entrance. It wrapped itself around Ciara's arms, legs, and neck. The speakers slowly whirred to life again. *See you later alligator* played on as the residents of the Athenaeum began to whistle and wave at the wolf. The ivy tightened and the wolf whimpered as it began dragging her out to the doors, Ciara clawed the floor as she was pulled away and the sheet around her arms retreated back into the mansion. The ivy stood her up in the doorway turning her to face the outside as the goblins began singing along to the old music.

"Don't just sit there! Help me," Ciara cried out as she wriggled. She glowered at Zaldehyde. The towering witch simply returned an unsympathetic cold stare. A loud mooing echoed through the mansion and the beating of hooves grew closer and closer behind Ciara. The wolf turned her head at the commotion just in time to see the red cow charging head first to the doors.

"I'll get the door, boss!" Jerry slammed his horns into the wolf. One of his horns gored into the wolf's hindquarter and she howled as she went careening through the air. The Athenaeum played one last note to match the wolf's cry before returning to silence.

The wolf landed at Zaldehyde's feet, rolling along the ground and coming to a skid at the coffin shaped briefcase. Ciara's hair pulled back into her pores hissing and wiggling like wounded snakes. Her muscles shrank and her body returned to normal, showing the bruises and welts she had suffered from her ill fated battle. She curled up naked on the ground hugging her abdomen weeping and heaving as the wolf completely vanished from her.

Vicki stood in the doorway with Jerry, soon joined by Desmond and the others. The Athenaeum glowed behind them, casting its light outside onto the lawn. Zaldehyde stood from the coffin up to her full height, wasting no time in retrieving her wand from her colorful dress. The origami spell book landed upon Zaldehyde's shoulder ruffling its pages as she moved toward the house.

"House magic. How cute." Zaldehyde held her hand down to Vicki beckoning her forward. "Give me that scroll. We'll tear it up together and you can return home from this horrible little place."

Vicki stepped back into the doorway clutching her contract close to her chest. "No!" She stared at the witch and at the coffin by her feet. "I'm not giving it to you! I'm... I'm supposed to be here!"

Zaldehyde squeezed her fist so hard that her arm shook. "Listen to me, child, destroy that stupid contract or you risk war with me. Do you understand what I'm capable of? Do you know that I live in both worlds? I will make your life a living hell, here and there!" She waved her black femur bone in the air and the coffin behind her opened. "Leave this place behind! Don't be a fool! It's worthless to you, these vile creatures are nothing! Nothing!"

"They're my friends!" Vicki shouted stepping forward. Desmond held her by the shoulder stopping her from leaving the safety of the mansion. "And this house is not worthless, this is everyone's home, and she has a name!"

"You petulant little cur, I'll rip your life apart if I have to! I'm ready to do just that!" A little red hand poked out from the coffin gripping its side. Vicki gasped and stumbled backwards. Zaldehyde hissed at her. "Just rip up that contract and we can be done with this! We can be done before any of this has to start!"

"No!" Vicki trembled gripping the contract tight. Another little red hand poked out from the coffin. Vicki stepped forward again right at the threshold of the Athenaeum. "No, I'm not afraid of you! You're just a bully and you're sick! You're just a bully!" The red hands flew back into the coffin disappearing into the darkness within.

Zaldehyde gnashed her teeth together, stomping her foot into the ground. The entire building shook with her power. The moon disappeared behind the darkness that Zaldehyde commanded from all around her and what little light had glimmered in her eyes now vanished. Those two fierce black voids stared down at Vicki and her friends.

"I'll show you fear such as you have never known, little child. There are no words in your language to describe the things that I can do to you! Every cold chill that you will ever know from this day forward, it will have my name carved into it, I will cut my name into you so deeply that your blood will be my signature!" Zaldehyde sneered at the little girl in the doorway. "You're protected in that house but you're nothing without it. One day, I'll huff, and I'll puff."

Desmond and Frank both stood in front of Vicki shielding her from the witch's gaze. Belvedere placed a hand on her shoulder and Frank brought Vicki's head into her arm. Vicki clutched onto her scroll. Shimmering light sparked out of its silver cap.

Zaldehyde screamed out, **"AND I'LL BLOW YOUR HOUSE DOWN!"** The mansion shook and rattled, the residents were thrown around as Vicki braced herself against the others. Zaldehyde took in a deep breath clenching her fists as she leaned forward shouting as loud as she could. "You're nothing special outside of that house! **YOU'RE NOTHING!**"

The words echoed through the halls and they shattered windows. They gained in momentum and power, blasting through the mansion shaking the entire foundation of the house. Vicki held her ears as the words bounced around and reverberated in her chest. Plaster began to fall from the ceiling and she cried out. She ran out of the door screaming drawing those words back outside with her.

Desmond chased after her. "Vicki, no! Don't go out there!"

Frank went limping out onto the lawn to stop the girl as well. "Get back in here, she's crazy! She'll kill you!"

Vicki went running off the front porch to face Zaldehyde. The thundering words crashed into her and sent her to the ground, she stumbled back to her feet and continued out to the lawn. The witch towered over Vicki laughing down at her.

"**YOU'RE WORTHLESS!**" The words came out of Zaldehyde's mouth like a train rumbling out of a dark tunnel. Vicki held her ears, the words shook the ground around her. "**WORTHLESS!**"

"No I'm not!" Vicki shouted back. "I'm not worthless!" The words knocked her down to the ground and threw the others back into the house. They pressed down harder and harder into her body until she screamed out from the pressure.

They gained power like a thunderstorm increasing in intensity as the cyclone of words spun around the girl on the ground. They crushed her with their weight holding her down into place. The words drowned out every other sound in the world silencing the words and screams of her friends in the house.

Visions of the previous summer bounced around in Vicki's mind, the words of the other girls in her scouts troop cut into her even now and Vicki could feel the disappointment of all of her friends. They all hated her, every single one of them couldn't stand her, especially Rachel. Of course no one wanted her around anymore, not after everything that she had said and done. She truly was *worthless*.

Zaldehyde's words crushed Vicki against the ground battering her as they crashed down upon her again and again. Even Vicki's own mother could hardly stand to look at her now and it was little surprise after the great cookie fiasco. At the very least her mother wouldn't be completely shocked that Vicki had failed her yet again. Zaldehyde cackled at the struggling little thing squirming before her.

Vicki writhed around on the lawn gasping for air as Zaldehyde's words continued slamming into her. The words squeezed her chest so tightly that she began seeing stars at the sides of her vision sending her into a dizzy spell. Those stars danced around forming clear images of disappointed faces all around her. Rachel and Jade, her entire scouts troop turning their backs to her, cold shame ripped at Vicki's stomach.

Worthless! The word slithered into Vicki's ears drowning out even her own choking breaths. **Worthless, worthless, nothing!** Deafening silence filled her soul save for the final word crashing through her head. **Nothing!**

She gasped and she choked to no avail, only oppressive crushing force filled her lungs. The stars took over the night and she tried sucking in one last gulp of air before the whirlwind of words came smashing back down into her for their final assault. As clear as a bell and as distant as home, a familiar voice whispered from behind the thundering cyclone in her head.

"Vicki, I don't think you're any of that stuff, you shouldn't let it get into your head like that!" Vicki's chest heaved, drawing in a heavy breath. Fresh mountain air filled her lungs and she screamed out covering her ears.

"I'm not worthless!" Vicki struggled to her knees, fighting against the crushing power of Zaldehyde's lies and refusing to stay down. "I'm not worthless and I'm not a nothing!"

Then came a song from the sky, distant and quiet at first, it was familiar and strangely serene in the face of the thundering words that surrounded Vicki. The song became sweeter growing louder and louder as the singing came closer to the ground. A single blue feather fell onto her face as Vicki fought against the screaming whirlwind of words around her.

The griffin dropped from the sky sailing down to Vicki with her massive wings outstretched. She had grown considerably larger, her wingspan reaching at least twelve feet and her great talons gripping the lawn with unwavering strength. Those tiny bunny legs had become fearsome and lean, they could give a powerful kick to any beast and send it flying. The griffin looked down at Vicki with her big dark eyes and nuzzled her sharp beak into the girl's shoulder. Vicki grabbed out for the griffin's wing steadying herself against the blue feathers.

Zaldehyde's words withered and faltered, the griffin's song repelled the thundering sound. The ground stopped shaking and Vicki hugged the griffin's neck tight. The griffin fixed her eyes on the tall witch, ears perked and ready, her blue feathers shining in the returning light of the moon.

Zaldehyde narrowed her eyes at the two of them and she took in another deep breath. **"YOU'RE WEAK!"** She slammed her foot into the ground bracing herself. **"YOU'LL DIE!"**

The griffin reared up on her hind legs stretching her wings out wide. She opened her beak letting loose with a piercing sound, a high pitched call that sent Zaldehyde's words flying straight back into her mouth. Zaldehyde screamed, covering her ears gagging on the words that she had cast into the air. She choked and rattled falling to her knee. The origami spell book retreated into the night sky abandoning the witch to her fate.

The gargantuan witch glared at Vicki, opening her mouth to speak at the girl wheezing and gripping her throat. She stood up fuming at the defiant girl and her friends. She coughed and rasped in a few breaths. Rage coursed throughout the witch's body, she trembled and all color left her pale blue face. She spat forth a black cloud from her mouth, her lungs rattling with labored breath.

Zaldehyde lifted her wand into the air and she, along with Ciara Shuck and the coffin, vanished in a great cloud of white fog, fleeing in a peal of thunder.

Vicki held onto the griffin sinking to the ground heaving out great breaths of relief and exhaustion. The griffin knelt down to Vicki, gently placing her beak on the girl's shoulder. She lifted her upward and let Vicki rest upon her wings, then carefully carried her back towards the mansion.

The Athenaeum's lights burst into brilliant colors as the girl entered the threshold again. Frank and Desmond both helped her down from the large feathery wings. Frank smiled giving Vicki a tight hug with her one good hand.

The goblin assessor marked off his stone tablet and stood up from his bench. "Pass."

Little cheers erupted from the railings all around the main hall. The goblins, ghosts, and ghouls all called out from up above. They threw little bits of paper and shimmering cranberries down at Vicki. The butter-obsessed old man whistled with his fingers and Mrs. Klobbreak applauded as loudly as she could.

Mrs. Klobbreak leaned over to the butter-obsessed old man. "That's the girl that Eckhardt was always telling us about!" She turned to the near sighted Cyclops beside her. "That's Vicki! That's his granddaughter!"

The goblin assessor broke the tablet in two as the seven o' clock gong sounded throughout the Athenaeum. The Housekeeper was home. Vicki smiled and hugged the stitchwork girl back as hard as she could.

Desmond squeezed Vicki's shoulder. "That's the real stuff."

Chapter nineteen

Max leaned back and forth, staring at the griffin as he followed her movements from the bed. She called out in song then rested her head between her talons. Her blue wings caught the green sunlight and reflected a brilliant azure onto the ceiling of Vicki's mansion bedroom.

"That is so cool."

Vicki came shuffling into the room carrying a box stuffed full of colorful bedding. "You can pet her! She won't bite. Mercedes is just the best bird ever!" Vicki stroked the griffin's ears and scratched her beak.

"Mercedes?" Max gave a cautious pet to the griffin's wings. "Where'd you get that name?"

Vicki ruffled the feathers on the griffin's neck, turning to meet her parents at the bedroom door. "I'm sure I saw it on a library book before, it even had a griffin just like her on the cover. She likes it!"

Mrs. Voland entered her daughter's new part time bedroom, cringing at the walls. "Honey, no, you shouldn't have Ganesh right up against a poster of your band like that."

Vicki stared at her new arrangement on the walls. Her favorite Korean boy band stood in a semicircle sending steamy looks down into the hearts and souls of their fans. Ganesh looked on from his tapestry, casting a look of disbelief off to the side. The little pewter Buddha sat in the corner surrounded by a bright pink feather boa tied securely around the statue. The ancient painting of the tentacle-faced elder god had been adorned with puffy shark stickers around its frame.

Vicki turned back to her mother and grinned. "I think it looks good!"

Mr. Voland entered into the room and set his box of papers and painting supplies down. He did not seem to particularly care for Mercedes, as the griffin paid extra attention to his rather thick eyebrows. Vicki thought that Mercedes saw them as two wiggling caterpillars on his face.

"That kid out there with the white hair is a real treat," Mr Voland said as he gripped the sides of his head. He put his hands on his hips looking around the room, smiling to himself. "This has been one strange week, hasn't it?"

"It's only gonna get stranger," Vicki said with a grin. The four of them exited for the main hall of the mansion, leaving Mercedes to another one of her naps. She cuddled up to Vicki's little red patchwork blanket and chortled as they left the Housekeeper's room.

Goblins stopped to greet the family as they passed by. The Athenaeum was alive with sight and sound. A mummy resident careened down the hall pulling large white rats out of his chest cavity and complaining about the heart burn that they caused. A nearsighted cyclops bumped into the mummy and the poor old bandaged man fell to pieces. The pieces began jeering at the clumsy cyclops as the Volands stepped over the crumbled complainer.

The main hall buzzed with electricity. An army of white rats rode a steady train of folded towels and sheets through the air. They all floated down towards the laundry, proudly displaying themselves for the Housekeeper's approval. One of the rats stopped to wipe a bit of mummy dust off from Vicki's shoes. She gave the rat a smile and a salute, it rejoined its comrades in linens and continued onward. Belvedere waved to the family from behind the cart that he pushed along, which was piled high with boxes of mood food.

"Good morning Housekeeper!" Belvedere sang out, proudly wearing his half mustache. The mood foods all lifted their lids and waved goodbye to Vicki, making little bubbling noises as they went by.

Vicki waved back blowing the mood foods a little kiss. The mood foods swooned back into their boxes, forming hearts and smiles as they fell. She ran over to Belvedere wrapping him in a quick hug.

"Are you going to be super offended if I pack my own lunches when I come back?" Vicki asked, being careful not to squeeze his bruised ribs too hard.

"Not at all. Snack packs are welcomed! Just don't bring any of that filthy peanut butter into this house!"

"You've got it!" Vicki nabbed one of the mood food boxes from the cart and dashed away.

The Voland family stepped outside onto the lawn of the great mansion, moving out among the circles of goblins that sat singing Halloween carols. Mrs. Klobbreak tugged on Vicki's shirt as they passed by and they both gave each other a happy grin. Vicki handed the little blob of food to the elderly goblin with a wink. Jerry carried one last moving box away from a waiting hearse, carefully making his way around the small and frail residents.

"Okay boss, where's this one go then?" Jerry rattled the box full of clothes and shoes.

"Up by the dresser." Vicki passed by him with a smile. She spun around on her heels with a look of panic on her face. "And don't open it!"

"Wasn't gonna!"

"And Jerry, I took a head count this morning of all the residents," Vicki said with a chipper tone. She put her hand on her hip motioning for him to come close. "So you better not go munching on any of the little goblins while I'm gone." She narrowed her eyes at him then giggled. She reached up to give him a few pets between his eyes.

The big red cow went bolting away, mooing all the way back into the Athenaeum. The Voland family reached the large black hearse at the main drive where they all stopped to greet the vampire and the stitchwork girl. The two of them stood together, waiting to say their goodbyes to Vicki. Mr. And Mrs. Voland took their places in the back of the hearse leaving the door open for Max.

"Grandpa was right, Vicki. This place picked you for a good reason. There's no doubt about it," said Max as he stared out over the mansion and the mountainside.

Vicki gasped and reached into her pockets. She held Max's black wooden ring in her hand. "I had a crazy thing happen with a door in there and I think it kinda recharged this thing! Test it out, try and make me lie about something!"

Max took the ring giving it an appraising look. "Alright. Vicki, are you the greatest sushi chef in the world?"

"Of course!" The ring glowed a dark purple and they both smiled. Vicki bounced up and down whispering to Max, "do you like oinking and splashing in the mud?"

"You bet!" The ring glowed again and Max chuckled. He took a deep breath. "I'm proud of you, Vicki." The ring remained black, he put it into his pocket.

Vicki's face grew a little warm and she hid her smile. "Ew, you don't have to say it so loud!" The ring glowed in Max's pocket and she shoved him into the open door.

"Omigod, I don't need to ride all the way home with this!" A purple glow came from within the hearse and she shut the door.

Desmond removed his cap, flashing his toothy grin at her. "She'll be in good hands til you get back. I don't think tall, pale, and loathsome will be making an appearance any time soon. You go get you some of that sweet sweet vacation!"

Vicki raised an eyebrow. "Well, what about you? Haven't you been on the clock since like the nineteen hundreds? Maybe you could go on vacation too... or like maybe I don't know, go back home for a little bit..."

Desmond held up his hand placing his cap back on his head. "Ain't nowhere else I want to be, this is it!"

"Are you sure?" Vicki pursed her lips together. "This is where you want to be?"

"Sweet corn, you were right. *This* is home." He spun his walking stick around in his hand and gave her a little flourish of his fingers. "Doesn't hurt that I get paid overtime too."

Jerry poked his head out from the great doors of the Athenaeum and shouted, "Dez, the goblins are having a go at flushing each other down the bogs again!"

Desmond smiled at Vicki and threw his head back in laughter. "I love my job!" He vanished in a blur, streaking into the mansion.

Frank put her arm around Vicki looking off towards the Athenaeum. "You never said your brother was such a cutie. What happened, was he adopted into your family or something?"

Vicki laughed, pretending to be insulted. "I don't think he'd be into you, he likes classy girls. Girls with a pulse."

"A pulse, huh? You wanna see how many beats I give ya per minute?" Frank waved her fist in front of Vicki's face. "You better come back soon, you're the only one around here that can clean the toilets without touching them."

Vicki leaned into Frank's side. "I'm gonna miss you too," she said elbowing her in the ribs. "Oh, this thing!" Vicki grabbed at one of the cables pulling it upward, tightening the stitchwork around the girl's shoulders.

Frank felt at the stitching, giving her a grin as she headed back towards the Athenaeum. Hans Bohnberg peeked up from the driver's seat of the hearse and looked out over the mountainside. He tapped his skeletal fingers against the roof of the car, getting Vicki's attention.

"October isn't very far off, you'll be back soon enough. Your friend is right, the Athenaeum is in good hands while you're away." The trees around the main drive all rustled in a chilly breeze and the skeleton lawyer brought his suit coat closer to his bones. "It all begins in earnest next time, the hard work of it. I know this may sound silly, in light of what your aunt put you through this last weekend, but are you ready for the responsibility of it? Are you going to be able to handle it if things become a bit hard?"

Vicki looked back from the hearse one last time before joining her family for the ride back to Earthside. "I'm where I'm supposed to be... and..." She looked out over the mansion to her friends and to the residents. "I have people to fall on if it gets too tough." She grinned and settled in for the ride home.

Mrs. Voland opened the car door for her daughter, letting her out into a crowd of girls in front of the school. She helped Vicki out of the car taking her large backpack and bagged lunch. "You could stay home one more day if you still need to rest."

"No, I'm okay! I got a lot of sleep yesterday and I've been kind of sleeping like the whole summer anyways. Are you sure that they can come and do their book thing?" Vicki took her lunch and swung her backpack over her shoulder.

"Of course! They're going to have to coordinate it with the troop leaders, but I think it's going to be fine to do. Are you going to go with them, are you allowed to?"

Vicki bounced on her heels, clutching the little brown bag in her hands. "Uh huh, it's a scouts thing, but that's okay. I kind of want to anyways, you know? To help."

Mrs. Voland smiled down at Vicki placing a hand to the side of her face. "If anybody can it's you. You have plenty of experience now, don't you?"

Vicki gave her mother a long hug. "Thank you!" She ran off to the crowds of other students, standing out among them with her brightly colored shoes and holographic backpack. She waved at her mother then bolted into the school.

She ran through the crowds of students, galloping past the classrooms and hallways. She finally reached the cafeteria and searched around. She hopped up and down trying to see over the taller kids and grumbled at the height of her classmates. Vicki climbed atop a nearby drinking fountain. A group of kids laughed at her and she shot them a quick smile back. She found the girl with the dark eyebrows and hopped off of the fountain, sprinting full speed to the table, she hoped she could reach her before the first class bell rang.

Rachel sat at the table surrounded by the other girls in her scouts troop. She set aside her yogurt sticking her tongue out in disgust. She searched over her tray of school breakfast and sighed, reaching out to grab her milk. She fumbled the milk carton as she was bounced into by a much adored and dearly missed smaller girl.

"My mom says yes!" Vicki scooted into the other girl's side crowding into her space. "But you need to have the troop leader call her for stuff first."

Rachel's face lit up and she smiled. "She did?"

Vicki leaned into Rachel's side and gave her a quick nod. "Uh huh, and I can help sometimes!" Vicki pulled back, peeking into her lunch bag and trying not to look too desperate. "Uhm, if you still want me to I mean."

"Yeah, duh! That's like the best part of it!" Rachel nudged her in the ribs. "You're looking way different today, Vicki, I love it!"

Vicki smiled and pulled out two cookies from her lunch bag. She placed one in the hands of Rachel. "I am way different," she sang out. She kicked her feet back and forth and bit into her cookie. "I can help a bunch too, but I'm starting like an internship thing at another retirement community on the weekends. It's not my mom's place, we thought that maybe that wouldn't be fair, you know? Because necromancy is bad."

Rachel grinned and bit into her cookie too. "Do you mean nepotism?"

"That too, they're both bad."

"Well, maybe I can come and visit your place sometime! That's really cool, Vicki, it's like you're the grown up out of all of us now!" The first bell rang out and the girls all got up from the table. "I bet you can handle the stress better than I could."

Vicki looked down at Rachel's feet, admiring her new sneakers. She froze in place nearly dropping her lunch bag. "Yeah, I can handle anything." She looked back up into Rachel's eyes giving her a concerned grin.

"What's wrong?

"Oh nothing! It's just that the place I'm helping out at, the people are kind of weird that's all. Some of them look pretty scary, I think they might have medical things and stuff like that..."

"It's okay Vicki, if I can't visit that's okay, I wouldn't want to get you in trouble or anything! I hate being scared anyways, I can never hide it."

"Me either, I guess." Vicki looked back down at her friend's legs, furrowing her brow before following the girl to class. "You can come visit me at the place though no matter how weird or scary it is! They might be okay with you hanging out too. We'll never know until we try, and I don't mind getting into a *little* trouble!"

Rachel turned to face Vicki. "Oh, I guess that's true. Maybe I'll check it out sometime then if you think I'd be welcomed."

Vicki followed behind her best friend and smiled. "I'm sure you will!" She caught up to the taller girl with the dark eyebrows and the tufts of black hair sticking out from her shoes. Rachel's legs were just a little too long and skinny for the rest of her body, and her teeth seemed just a little too sharp when she smiled, but Vicki didn't mind any of it. She bumped her hip into the girl and giggled. "We just might have to keep you on a short leash!" Nothing was going to stand in her way, even if there was a wolf in there.

www.ingramcontent.com/pod-product-compliance
Lightning Source LLC
Chambersburg PA
CBHW030426120726
47903CB00003B/824